DIABLO GOLD

ALSO BY WAYNE D DUNDEE

DIABLO GOLD

BRASKA
BOOK TWO

WAYNE D DUNDEE

WOLFPACK
PUBLISHING
— EST 2013 —

Diablo Gold
Paperback Edition
Copyright © 2025 by Wayne D. Dundee

Wolfpack Publishing
1707 E. Diana Street
Tampa, FL 33610

www.wolfpackpublishing.com

Paperback ISBN 979-8-89567-067-5
Ebook ISBN 979-8-89567-301-0
LCCN 2025938186

DIABLO GOLD

DIABLO GOLD

1

All Braska wanted now was to have a good breakfast somewhere and then go to his hotel room for a few hours of restful sleep. True, he was already seated on the edge of a roomy bed where he'd just spent most of the night. The bed, however, happened to be in a room belonging to a delightful gal named Maizie O'Dell, a soiled dove who worked out of the saloon downstairs. And when Maizie's services were engaged for the night in a manner such as Braska had done, she took considerable pride in seeing to it that the activity involved was frequent and memorable but hardly restful.

Hence, Braska was feeling pleasantly satisfied but also thoroughly spent. With Maizie snoring peacefully in the swirl of blankets behind him, he had already quietly dressed and pulled on his boots and was taking time for a smoke before making his departure. Remaining to try and get some sleep beside Maizie, he'd decided, was too risky—she might wake up and think that making another memory was called for. Not that

that would have been the worst experience to endure, but Jesus, enough was enough. Besides, he was hungry as hell.

"Maizie! Goddammit, open up!" The harsh, demanding voice and the pounding of a heavy fist on the room's flimsy door made a simultaneous, jarring disruption to the quiet morning.

Braska reached to stab out his cigarette in the night-stand ashtray, and as he drew his hand back, he let it come to rest lightly on the grips of the Colt holstered at his hip.

The man on the other side of the door hollered again. "Come on, Maizie gal! I'm headin' out soon on a long run, and I need me a session with your sweet self to tide me over. I been waitin' all stinkin' night!"

Maizie's face lifted out of the covers, and she pushed back a spill of tousled, bleached hair. "Huh? Wha..."

Over his shoulder, Braska said dryly, "Seems you've got a mighty eager admirer on the other side of the door."

As if on cue, the door rattled under some more furious pounding. "Doggone it, gal, open up. I need to see you bad—real bad!"

"Who is that?" asked Maizie, now wide-eyed and looking a little frightened.

Braska stood up. "Only one way to find out, I reckon. I don't think he's gonna go away otherwise."

He went to the door, threw back the bolt, and yanked it open. The man on the other side came stag-gering in, out of the narrow hallway. He might have been partly thrown off balance by the door opening so suddenly, but it didn't take long to see his balance was also affected by something else. His bleary eyes and the reek of whiskey emanating from him made it plain he was more than a little drunk.

Those bleary eyes locked on Maizie. "Darlin'," he slurred plaintively. "Why'd you keep your poor old Chucky waitin' so long?"

From off to one side, where *Chucky* hadn't taken any notice, Braska said, "Because she was already busy, Hobbs. And still is."

Chuck Hobbs turned his head slowly, and the bleariness in his eyes took on an annoyed glint. "You," he muttered. "You're that new fella, ain't you...Lansky, or something like that?"

"Make it Braska," came the response. "And I been workin' for Herbert & Haines for three months now, if you want to call that new. Long enough, at any rate, to know that this mornin's Harrietville run is due to be pullin' out about now and you're scheduled to be the shotgunner on it."

Hobbs's lips peeled back in a sneer. "So what's it to you, one way or 'tother? If you're so goddamn smart, then what you *ought* to know is that when I'm in town, Maizie is my girl and I don't head out on no run without first gettin' me some of her sweet sugar. Yet you been the one hoggin' her attention all stinkin' night!"

"You don't own me, Chuck Hobbs," snapped Maizie.

"Shut up! I've sure as hell shoved enough money your way to damn well have the right of layin' claim if I say so!"

Hobbs was the kind of big, solid brute who, even drunk, could be a handful if he turned belligerent. Recognizing this, Braska planted his feet and braced himself before saying, "That ain't hardly how it works, bub. If you hadn't already wore out your welcome before, I think you just did now. So beat it. Smartest thing you can do is go report for your job and hope Ol' Man Haines don't can your drunk ass on the spot."

"You go to hell. I'll beat it when I'm good and ready," snarled Hobbs. "And as far as Haines cannin' me, he ain't got the balls—I'm the best shotgun guard he's got or ever had."

Braska knew what it would trigger, but he couldn't resist. Sometimes, you run into the kind of blowhard you just *got* to puncture some of the air out of. Smiling a wolf's smile, he said, "Best until I came along maybe... same when it comes to samplin' Maizie's sugar."

As expected, Hobbs instantly exploded. He hurled himself at Braska with an enraged roar, head lowered like a charging bull, arms windmilling, balled fists swinging wildly.

Braska blocked two ridiculously sloppy punches, twisting away in a partial pivot as he did so, allowing Hobbs to rush past and ram full force into the wall. As the fool, half stunned, bounced off from the impact, Braska twisted back around and threw a shoulder block into him, driving him through the open door and out into the hall.

From the bed, Maizie let out a single shriek and then was quiet.

Like a hunter going after an animal he's wounded, Braska shoved out of the room and went after Hobbs. The second-floor hallway of the Whistle Wetter Saloon was a short, narrow passageway serving only two rooms on either side. To Braska's right as he exited Maizie's room, the corridor ended at a wall with a tall, rectangular window that, had it not been boarded over, would have looked down on an alley running between the saloon and the next building. To the left, it led to a boxlike balcony surrounded by a low railing with an opening for stairs leading down to the first-floor barroom.

Hobbs was off center to the left of the doorway, trying to get balanced and turned around in time to meet Braska's follow-up. He did so with a slashing back-hand that came faster than expected when Braska advanced on him. It came at a hurried, poorly aimed upward angle, though, striking a skimming blow right at Braska's hairline. It had enough impact to snap his head back, but not much else. In fact, the hard, thick bone of Braska's forehead may have done more damage to Hobbs's knuckles than the other way around.

His momentum carrying him through the unex-pected punch, Braska bulled in and drilled a left hook into Hobbs's ribs, hammering him back against the hallway wall. He tried to pin him there long enough to get in another hook, a quick right, but Hobbs dropped his elbow in time to block it. Shoving off the wall, Hobbs threw his powerful arms around Braska's middle, trying to tie him up in a clinch. He also tried a head butt, but Braska twisted his face away and took the impact of it on the side of his neck.

Still locked together, the two combatants staggered farther toward the balcony, bouncing off one wall and then the other, their stomping, kicking feet clattering on the bare wood floor of the hall loud enough to sound like a herd of cattle was loose in the building.

Finally, Braska jerked an arm loose and immedi-ately used it to whip around with the elbow, crashing it to the side of Hobbs's face. Without hesitation, he drew back and did it again. This was enough to cause Hobbs to drop his powerful arms and stagger back a step—but not before pumping his knee high, aiming for Braska's groin as a parting shot. A turned hip blocked that, though, and the failed attempt only threw Hobbs all the more off balance.

This led him to make an even more desperate attempt—a grab for the gun riding on his hip. Braska reacted with a piston-like kick that drove his boot heel into the wrist of Hobbs's gun hand before the .44 could clear leather. But not before Hobbs's fumbling, stabbing finger inadvertently triggered a round that blasted a hole in the floor, missing his own foot by only a fraction of an inch. That, compounded by how the shot roared and reverberated so shockingly loud in the cramped hall, seemed to stun Hobbs and freeze him into a moment of total immobility.

This gave Braska his best opening yet, and he took full advantage of it. Uncorking a whistling roundhouse right, he tagged Hobbs on the hinge of his jaw, left side of the face, and spun him around like a top. The sound of the punch landing was like two wooden blocks clapped sharply together. Braska not only heard it, but felt it run all up through his arm and knew it marked the end of the fight, that Hobbs was going to go down and not get back up.

What he *didn't* know or expect, however, was that —before Hobbs went down—his staggering spin would carry him out to the middle of the balcony, where he would make a final lurching turn ahead of pitching outward to crash through the railing and down onto a saloon gaming table that collapsed and went flat under the impact.

Maizie ran past Braska, wrapped haphazardly in only a bed sheet. He followed her, and together, from the edge of the balcony through a gaping hole in the railing, they looked down on the form of Hobbs lying spread eagle atop the collapsed table.

"My God, you killed him!" gasped Maizie.

"No, he ain't killed," Braska assured her. "But it's a cinch he ain't in no shape to be gettin' back up askin' for sugar or makin' no stagecoach runs...leastways not any time soon."

What was more, he told himself with a weary, sinking feeling as he heard the approach of excitedly jabbering voices drawn by the sound of the gun-shot and related din of battle, he had a strong hunch the same was likely true when it came to him getting that big breakfast or the restful sleep he'd been counting on.

2

"Don't look 'round and make no big deal out of it," Braska said in a calm, matter-of-fact tone, addressing the man swaying and bouncing beside him in the driver's box of the stagecoach, "but we've picked up some company on the trail behind us. Four riders about five hundred yards back. Don't seem to be drawin' no closer, ain't laggin' no farther back."

At his right shoulder, deftly working the reins of the six-up team pulling the coach, Jake Muelhausen replied, "Whatya figure they're up to?"

"Your guess is as good as mine. How much further to Barkley's?"

"'Bout five miles. And nothing between here and there but flat, open country. Meanin' no canyons or pinch points where they could block us off. If they're lookin' to hit us, they're gonna have to swarm us to get it done—and they'd better make a move pretty quick if that's what they got in mind."

"We ain't carryin' a strongbox that'd attract any undue attention. What about passengers? Any of 'em got the look of enough wealth to maybe have caught the eye of some polecats lookin' to separate 'em from it?"

"You saw 'em get aboard same as me."

Braska shook his head. "No, I didn't. I got shanghaied into makin' this run at the last minute—after your regular boy Hobbs turned up unfit for duty back in Leaning Rock. Remember? The old man collared me to replace him and the passengers were already loaded when I climbed up in the box."

"Yeah, that's right," allowed Muelhaussen. He cut a sidelong glance over at Braska. "You got a real casual way of sayin' how Hobbs *turned up unfit*, you know that? Without mentionin' how you made him that way."

"*Helped* make him that way," Braska corrected. "The busted jaw was on me. The rest, the cracked ribs and dislocated shoulder, was his own doin' for gettin' the notion to take a nose dive off that balcony. Matter of fact, I could argue the whole works was his doin' for the way he barged in on me and Miss Maizie in the first place."

Mulhaussen twisted his mouth wryly. "Yeah, that sums up Hobbs pretty good. He developed what you might call a bad habit of bargin' in wherever and whenever it suited him. He got away with it mostly because he has a pretty rough layer of bark on him—and also due to old man Haines cuttin' him extra slack on account of him and his shotgun turnin' back half a dozen holdup attempts on Herbert & Haines coaches."

"He might be handy with a shotgun, but it sure didn't appear to carry over when it came to usin' a handgun. Damn near blew off his own foot in that hallway."

"That don't surprise me none," chuffed Mulhaussen. "Why he bothered carryin' a holster gun never made sense nohow. Seen him practicin' with his two or three times out back of the horse barn and it was downright pitiful to watch. Took him a half hour to drag it out and then he couldn't hit nothing with it after he did."

Braska had no response for that.

Mulhaussen gave it a beat, then said, "You know, once Hobbs heals up, he'll most likely hold a grudge against you over what happened. Comes to that and he takes a mind to try and square things, I wouldn't count on him comin' at you straight on. Especially since you beat him the first time."

"Thanks for the warnin', but I already had him figured for that type." Braska gave an indifferent shrug. "Don't expect it'll come to any such, though. I don't figure I'll still be around by the time he's done healin'."

"Why's that?" Mulhaussen wanted to know. "You ain't gonna turn tail, are you? Would'nt've figured that of you."

"I'm thinkin' it ain't gonna be up to me. You didn't see how mad Ol' Man Haines was when he saw how bad I busted up his fair-haired boy. Not to mention how much he had to pay in damages to the saloon owner to keep him from filin' charges that would've got the both of us tossed in the hoosegow. Even then, I don't know that he would've bothered keepin' me out if he hadn't been desperate for somebody to ride this already delayed run with you. That's why, as soon as he can get himself *un*-desperate, I got a hunch I'll get told to hit the trail, and I'll no longer have a job."

Mulhaussen scowled. "I suppose that *might* be the case. Ain't unheard of for the boss to be a stubborn, ornery cuss sometimes. But it'd be a plumb damn shame if he treated you that way."

"Don't worry about it," Braska told him. "I'm a driftin' man, already been at this shotgun guard job longer'n most I take on. Time was comin' near to where I'd've been movin' on anyhow."

"If you say so," Mulhaussen allowed reluctantly. "But ask me, I'd call it better news to hear that prickly damn Hobbs was the one movin' on. Yeah, it made a body feel safe havin' him ridin' 'gun alongside you, but his surly damn temperament—especially if he was hung over, which was gettin' more and more frequent—was surefire no treat to spend time with."

"Well, how about let's quit spendin' time talkin' about him then," said Braska. "How about instead gettin' back to the question of any of our passengers maybe bein' an attraction for those hombres back behind."

"Okay. The short answer is that none of 'em looked to me like anything representing much of a payday. Just ordinary folks. An older gent and his niece—or maybe it's granddaughter, I forget which. A couple drummers, one pushin' ladies shoes and 'tother fancy stationary for letter writin' and such. And finally, a fella on his way to the funeral of some distant kin. Any of that sound like outlaw bait to you?"

"Not particularly. But then, looks can be deceivin'. Reckon all we can do is wait and see...and be ready in case something pops."

Muelhaussen made a sour face. "Yeah, and that's the worst part. Now that I know those hombres are back there, I got an itch between my shoulder blades like I used to have when I was soldierin' in Injun country.

Most of the time nothing happened, but you always knew the bloody devils was somewhere out there. Sometimes I think it's better to flat be surprised and find yourself in the middle of trouble rather than be all knotted up thinkin' something *might* happen. I swear, I hate packin' 'round that kind of...of...what's the word I'm lookin' for?"

"Anticipation? Anxiety?" Braska suggested.

"Yeah, one of them. Hell, both of 'em. The rest of the way to Barkley's is gonna seem a site longer than it oughta, I know that much."

"I feel for you, but if you don't mind, I'd just as soon suffer a little anxiety without anything happenin'. I already had to miss my breakfast back at Leaning Rock. Call me selfish, but I'd like to at least grab a meal at Barkley's before havin' to deal with another round of trouble."

"You never heard me say I *wanted* a piece of trouble, did you?"

"No, and you ain't hearin' me say I'm ready to buy that those fellas back there are on their way to church choir practice. But, wherever they're headed, it don't seem their interest is in us. Elsewise—like you said a minute ago—they ought to've made their move by now."

"So maybe they got some kind of business at Barkley's. All well and good, except it puts us right back to havin' to wait and see."

They rolled on in silence for a ways, sun hammering down on their shoulders and backs and yellowish dust swirling up in their faces as the coach rumbled over the winding ribbon of the stage trail slicing through the rugged, pale brown Arizona landscape.

Balancing the double-barreled coach gun across his thighs, Braska dug out the makings and built himself a smoke. Not quite thirty-two years of age, he stood a bit over six feet tall on a frame packing lean, flat musculature that propelled him with catlike grace. His face was ruddy and rectangularish in shape, marked by flinty eyes, a somewhat hawkish nose, and a thin-lipped mouth often held in a tight, grim-looking line yet fully capable of twisting into a quick, rakish grin if the mood struck him. In short, a face apt to be called neither handsome nor homely but one folks, nonetheless, tended to remember.

With war service, a sacrificial prison hitch, and family entanglements all behind him, Braska was currently two years into finally living a lifelong dream of roaming the western frontier—being *a driftin' man*, as he'd told Mulhaussen—unbound by anything except where his whims and the wind might take him. Born to a cattleman who established a modestly successful ranch, the Bar S, just south of the Nebraska panhandle, Braska had known from boyhood that sticking with the family business wasn't for him, and not once he was old enough to strike out on his own. The war intervening and taking the life of his father had left him feeling obligated to the ranch longer than intended. Complicating and prolonging that even further was a series of travails driven by the aim to keep his younger brother Link out of trouble in order for him to eventually take over. But, in the end, it all went down as a futile effort. Braska's mother passed away in the midst of it, and Link died tragically at the close. The Bar S fell into the hands of others and was renamed, erasing his father's dream and years of hard work. A niece via

Link's failed marriage was Braska's only surviving family.

So, with his own dream to wander left intact, though scarred and delayed, Braska had struck out to fulfill it. His drifting so far had taken him across Colorado, a brief juke up into Wyoming, then down through Utah and to the point of Nevada, then cutting back to his present locale here in the middle of Arizona. Though his lifestyle of mostly living off the land and sleeping under the stars kept expenses minimal, he still preferred to dress up his staple of wild game with adders such as biscuits, beans, bacon, a few canned goods and the like. Not to mention now and then visiting saloons in various towns he came to for a cold beer, a shot of redeye, and occasional dalliances with others of the same sisterhood Maizie belonged to. All of which required layouts of cash, and that meant taking on occasional short-term work to maintain a level of ready funds. He'd been telling the truth when he said that this job riding shotgun for the Herbert & Haines Stage Line that he'd been at for close to three months now was the longest he'd stayed at any one hire. The work was interesting, the pay was decent, and up to now, it had suited him not to be in any rush to move on. With the heat of the kind of punishing summer this region was known for building fast, however, he'd been musing lately—well ahead of possibly being hurried along by what had transpired between him and Hobbs —that the time to do so was drawing nearer. His wallet had gotten sufficiently fattened so that any time he took the notion, he could afford to go comfortably on the drift again for quite a spell—and do it someplace where getting baked daily under a merciless sun wasn't part of the deal.

As if reading his thoughts, Mulhaussen now spoke beside him, saying, "Another two or three weeks, the midday temperature hereabouts'll get so dang hot you won't hardly have to strike a match to light yourself a quirley."

"Feels mighty close to that already," replied Braska, exhaling a plume of smoke.

Mulhaussen cackled. "Shucks, you ain't seen nothing yet." He was a wiry, leathery-skinned runt of fifty or so, bred and born to the desert so thereby long since adapted to its harsh extremes. On the one hand, Braska couldn't help but admire that kind of ruggedness, and on the other, it still didn't make him any more inclined to stick around and endure the same when he didn't have to. Nope, he decided, it wouldn't be long before he'd be riding on out of this furnace.

In the meantime, the stage trail continued to set their course through today's piece of it. Making periodic twists, often for no discernible reason, it at one point dipped down into a long, shallow stretch of loose sand that caused the pulling team to work extra hard over the closing miles before they'd be switched out and earn a deserved rest. Then, when the trail finally rose out of the sand and became solider ground once again, Barkley's Way Station could be seen in the dust-hazed distance.

"Ah," exclaimed Mulhaussen, savoring the sight, "now comes the trade-off that makes this ass-bustin', kidney-jarrin', dust-eatin' work bearable, even without you bein' extra starved on account of missin' breakfast.

One taste of Moon Eyes's warm biscuits washed down by a pitcher of cool butter-milk will soothe everything from your tonsils to your toenails!" Then, to announce their approach and help assure that the fare he'd just described would be ready and waiting, Mulhaussen signaled the station by raising a dented old bugle to his lips and blowing a long, loud, squawkingly off-key blast.

Moon Eyes was the Ute wife of Simon Barkley, the barrel-chested former mountain man who ran the station. Braska had made this run a handful of previous times, making him well aware that Mulhaussen's praise for Moon Eyes's cooking was hardly an exaggeration. It was far superior to anything served at any of the other way stations he'd encountered, and on this visit in particular, he meant to put away a heap of it.

As Mulhaussen swung off the trail and into the broad, hard-packed front yard of the station, Barkley's rangy teenaged son and the whip-lean vaquero hired on to help handle changing out teams and tend stock during the intervals were already on their way out of the corral area, leading six fresh pullers. The jehu obligingly pointed his current team in close to intercept them and then braked the coach to a reasonably gentle, slightly rocking halt directly before the front doors of the station's main building.

"Arrivin' at Barkley's Station, folks! Be about a half hour stop for switchin' to a fresh team and such. Be a good chance to get out, stretch your legs, and grab some coffee or other refreshment. And, as a personal recommendation, a chance at the best vittles your gonna find anywhere on the run!"

Mulhaussen gave this spiel as he was climbing

down from his side of the driver's box, the side closest to the station. Once on the ground, he went to the coach door, opened it and began assisting passengers out through the cramped opening.

Braska ascended silently on his side. Hungry as he was, there were other things also on his mind that caused him to tarry a bit as the others began filing inside. Thinking of the riders coming along farther back on the trail, he brought the coach gun down with him. Also, once on the ground, just for good measure, he thumbed the keeper thong off the Colt holstered on his right hip. After taking a second to twist some kinks out of his back and shoulders, he walked to the rear of the coach and scanned back to check the progress of the oncoming horsemen. He hadn't said anything to Mulhaussen, but over the last mile or so, after they'd left the stretch of loose sand and were closing on the station, the riders appeared to have lagged off to a little greater distance than before. Not a lot, just enough to be noticeable and to seem curious.

Curious. That was the word that summed up the whole business with those riders. Whoever they were and whatever they were up to seemed just plain curious. Braska couldn't quite work up a sense that they posed a threat—yet at the same time, there remained something unsettling about them.

Well, it wouldn't be much longer, he told himself, before he ought to be able to get some kind of better read off the bunch. They were coming down the trail now, and in just a matter of minutes, they'd be turning into the station yard.

But then, as Braska watched their approach while

putting on an outward show of disinterest by leaning casually against the coach's rear boot and digging out the makings for a fresh smoke, the horsemen did something even more curious...they stayed on the trail and rode right on by!

3

"I'LL BE DOGGONE. THEY JUST KEPT A-RIDIN'."
After ushering the passengers into the station,
Mulhaussen had also come around to the rear of the
coach and was now standing next to Braska.

"They sure did," Braska agreed, putting the
makings back in his pocket without finishing the build
of a cigarette.

"That's almighty curious, wouldn't you say?"

A corner of Braska's mouth quirked up slightly.
"Yeah, I'd say that's exactly the word for it."

"What's goin' on? Who was them fellas just rode
by?" These questions rumbled from the massive chest
of towering Simon Barkley, who'd exited the station and
was striding toward the two coachmen. At six-foot-six,
even with his right leg permanently stiffened due to
once being hooked by a buffalo horn, his strides were
still nearly half again as long as an average man. He had
a full beard, iron gray in color, that fanned out thick
across his chest and the same-colored thatch of hair atop
his head was worn long and tied into a ponytail

reaching down between his shoulder blades. His attire of buckskins and moccasins, though his mountain man days were well behind him, made his appearance more that of a trapper showing up for a Rocky Mountain rendezvous than the proprietor of a stagecoach way station in the middle of Arizona Territory.

"Who them jaspers was, is a more and more puzzlin' thing," Mulhaussen said in response to the big man. "They showed up behind us a while back and just sorta hung off about a quarter mile. At first we thought they might be trouble, but when they never came no closer or never did nothing, we then figured they must be on their way here. You didn't recognize 'em?"

"I didn't get that good a look, just steppin' out the door like I was. But nothing about what I did see looked familiar." Barkley cut his eyes to Braska. "How about you? You was closest when they went by."

"Didn't matter, wasn't none of 'em anybody I ever saw before. But whoever they are," Braska stated, "they're a hard lookin' bunch. Grim faces, plenty trail worn—men and horses alike. And the men all heavily armed."

"Almost sounds like a pack of desperadoes," said Mulhaussen. "But that don't make no sense, not ridin' the open trail and allowin' themselves to be so plainly seen."

Barkley scowled. "Yeah, this ain't the most hospitable country. Man needs a good reason for ridin' it. And I never seen *nobody* who came this way and didn't stop at least long enough to water their animal."

"Curiouser and curiouser," muttered Braska.

"What's that?"

"Nothing. Never mind." Braska made a dismissive

gesture. "But what's further down this trail—any close-by towns of any size?"

"Not 'til you get to Harrietville, where our run ends. That's about sixty miles," said Mulhaussen. "Otherwise the closest of any size, and you'd have to swing considerable to the east, would be Hadley or Peeples Creek. But you're talkin' another eighty, ninety miles to reach either of them. And nothing more in between 'cept our overnight stop at Floater's Station."

"How about any ranches down the trail that might be lookin' for such men as I described?"

"You mean gun toughs to fight some kind of range squabble?" Barkley wagged his head. "Ain't nothing like that goin' on anywhere near that I'm aware of. Most of the ranches out this way are shirttail outfits too busy fightin' to scratch out a livin' to have any time left for fightin' each other."

Braska shrugged. "I've seen men squabble over some mighty piddly matters."

"I can't argue that," Barkley allowed. "But if they're gunnies for hire like you make 'em sound, I gotta figure they must be headed for one of the bigger operations farther to the south and east."

"Yeah, you get down closer to the border, the cattlemen through there got Mexican bandits raidin' 'em on a regular basis," said Mulhaussen. Then he added, "Hell, as far as that goes, they also got revolutions poppin' up south of the border practically every other week. There's always a market for American pistoleros to go down and fight in them, too."

"Reckon it must be something like that." Barkley dragged his thick fingers through his beard. "Still kinda odd, though, that whoever them riders was they didn't at least stop long enough to water their horses."

"Well, that suits me just fine," announced Mulhaussen. "Because it also means they didn't decide to stop, unexpected-like, and put a dent in Moon Eyes's vittles that might've crowded out a regular customer like me."

"You know Moon Eyes always has plenty of food on hand," Barkley told him.

"Uh-huh. And what else I know," the jehu argued, "is an old saying about there bein' a first time for everything. I don't ever want to be on the wrong side of the first time Moon Eyes might run low on grub. So I ain't wastin' no more time standin' out here frettin' about then riders—I'm goin' in to eat!"

So saying, he turned and headed into the station. Braska and Barkley quickly fell in step behind him.

Inside, the thick adobe walls of the station provided a welcome coolness to the brutal heat without. In addition, the interior air was filled with the tantalizing aromas of Moon Eyes's much-praised cooking.

The public room of the establishment was a spacious area with a long wooden table at its center, bracketed by attached bench seating. The kitchen and private rooms for the family were off to one side. On the other side was a large stone fireplace and a pair of smaller, round-topped tables with chairs for non-stage-coach travelers who perhaps wished for some privacy or to tarry a bit longer. There was also a short plank bar from which Barkley served beer and a limited variety of liquor if requested.

At the far end of the room were two curtained cubicles, one for ladies and one for gents, where guests could wash off some accumulated trail dust if they chose. Braska and Mulhaussen made for the appropriate one of these, their passengers apparently having already availed themselves before taking seats at the table. On his way past the kitchen, Mulhaussen called in to Moon Eyes: "I'll have a heapin' plate of my usual, darlin', just as soon as I get scrubbed up so's you can gaze on my clean-cut handsomeness for a change, instead of that ugly ol' buffalo you're married to."

Moon Eyes—a sawed-off little plumpkin nearly a full foot shorter than her husband, with a round body also clad in buckskins and a round face framed by silky black hair worn in two long braids trailing down over her generous bosom—smiled and waved a spatula in response.

When they were finished washing up, Braska and Mulhaussen came back out through the curtains and headed to join their passengers at the long table. That was when Braska, who up until then had never gotten a good look at their human cargo, received his second big surprise of the day. It came in the form of the man sitting next to quite a lovely young lady—the pair Mulhaussen had described as an elderly gent and his niece or granddaughter, he hadn't been able to remember which. The relationship between the two was of no consequence to Braska, at least not initially. What mattered was his recognition of the man. And *where* he had last seen him.

In the same instant that Braska's eyes locked on Ira Tate—or whatever he might currently be calling himself —Tate's gaze also fell on him. While Braska stayed stone-faced, playing it safe because he was unsure if they should acknowledge knowing one another due to the circumstances surrounding how that came to be, Tate's mug immediately broke into a wide grin, and he threw all caution to the wind.

"Braska! Braska fella, can that really be you? I'll be dipped in molasses and rolled in cracker crumbs!"

Tate rose from the table and advanced on Braska with an outstretched hand. He was average in height and build, early fifties, wearing his years pretty well, especially considering how he'd spent a recent chunk of them. The hair at his temples and through his neatly trimmed sideburns had more white in it than Braska remembered. But his color was good, and he'd put on some needed pounds to offset his old gauntness. His attire of trousers and a light jacket was of decent quality, nice boots not too badly worn or scuffed, and no gun belt around his waist.

The two men gripped hands and pumped their arms back and forth. "By gol, it's good to see you again," declared Tate. "But out here in the middle of blazin' hot nowhere—who would've thought, eh? What the heck brings you down this way?"

"I should be askin' you that," countered Braska. "I'm a workin' stiff ridin' shotgun for the Herbert & Haines Stage Line. You're the gentleman of leisure sittin' back and gettin' yourself hauled around."

Something ever so briefly skittered in and out of the friendly gleam in Tate's eyes. He said, "I'm hardly a man of leisure...leastways not yet." Then, holding Braska's hand an extra beat while Mulhaussen moved on to where Moon Eyes was putting down a plate for him at the table, Tate leaned a little closer and added in a low voice, "We need a chance to talk privately as soon as possible. Be well worth your time to hear what I've got to say."

Braska was at once suspicious but equally as fast intrigued. "After we grab a bite, there oughta be a few minutes before the stage rolls again," he responded.

They then went on to their own places at the table.

After he'd shoveled in a couple spoonfuls of venison stew and taken a big bite of biscuit, Mulhaussen addressed the others, saying, "Though it seems Mr. Tate is already acquainted with my shotgun guard, seein's how Braska climbed on after everybody was already in the coach and so got introduced to none of the rest if you, I reckon that oughta get took care of now."

From there, he proceeded around the table, naming off the other passengers and allowing Braska to exchange acknowledgments with each. There was skinny, jittery Tibbs, the ladies' shoe salesman; corpulent, sweaty Baker, the stationary drummer; and stocky, ruddy-faced Kettleman, the Leaning Rock businessman on his way to attend a funeral in Harrietville. Then, last but not least, there was the young woman traveling with Tate who turned out to be no kin at all but rather the niece of an old friend being escorted by Tate to conduct some family business in Harrietville. Her name was Miriella Clemente, and she spoke with a faint Spanish accent. It wouldn't have mattered, though, if she'd made clucking noises like a chicken—her delicate, almond-eyed beauty was such that all the men present would have hung on her every word regardless.

It was obvious that a camaraderie of sorts had developed among the passengers during their ride so far, and thus an amount of easy, friendly talk was being continued during the meal. Only Kettleman, befitting a person in mourning, was somewhat reserved. Same for Braska to a large extent, though for different reasons. But reluctance by anybody else to speak up was more than offset by Mulhaussen, who ate and jabbered with equal gusto.

Part of Braska's quietness was due to him wondering what it was Tate wanted to talk to him about. What was he up to that might be *well worth your time* if Braska heard him out? Then there was the matter of the girl. Her name, Clemente, nagged at Braska as something that ought to be familiar, but he couldn't quite place it. Clemente. Where had he...then, abruptly, he remembered. And just as abruptly, he formed an almost certain hunch that the girl was some part of what Tate wanted to talk to him about.

Right about then, he also became aware of Mulhaussen asking the question Braska had feared somebody might get around to. "How about it, Mr. Tate? How is it that a respectable-lookin' gent like yourself, travelin' in the company of a refined young beauty, ever had cause at some point to cross paths with a rascal like my partner Braska?"

Looking like he too had been wondering if the question would arise and was therefore prepared for it, Tate replied as cool as if butter wouldn't melt in his mouth. "An unfortunate fact of life, friend Mulhaussen—one I bet you and most of the men around our table can appreciate—is that somewhere in his misspent past, most young fellas ran with a rascal or two. Braska was one of mine, and I suspect he probably considers me one of his. But we both came out of it reasonably unscathed and are now the sensible, mature specimens you see before you today." He paused to grin slyly. "And to say too much more might strain the boundaries of some statute of limitations somewhere."

What amounted to a slick, slightly teasing non-answer was met with a few wry chuckles and a knowing wink or two, and seemed enough to satisfy Mulhaussen and everybody else. Then, they all went back to eating and conversing about other matters.

4

After he'd cleaned his plate twice and had a slice of pie for dessert, Braska excused himself to step outside and have a smoke. That was his signal to Tate to come out and join him if he wanted to have his private talk.

Exiting the building, Braska saw that the new team was all hitched up and waiting. Over in the corral, the six horses just switched out were getting rubdowns and being watered and grained before being left to enjoy a well-earned rest until called into duty once again.

At a corner of the station, Braska found a slice of shade thrown by the roof overhang. There, he dug out his makings and built a cigarette. He'd just lighted up and taken his first drag when Tate came out and walked over to where he was. Pulling a long nine cigar out from an inner pocket of his jacket, he held it up and said, "Bum a light off you?"

Braska snapped another lucifer to life and held it for him. Puffing a cloud of smoke, Tate said, "Thanks. If it gets much hotter, you'd think a fella could damn near only have to wave a cigar or cigarette in the air to get it lighted. Jesus."

"Mulhaussen, the coach driver, claims when full summer sets in and it gets really hot, you actually have a chance for that," Braska told him.

"When it gets *really* hot? What does he call this?"

"Just warmin' up for the real thing, I guess."

"Jesus," Tate said again.

Braska eyed him under a cocked brow. "Speakin' of dealin' with the heat, I got to hand it to you for the way you dealt inside with the question about where we knew each other from. You handled it mighty smooth by spewin' a mouthful of nothing yet makin' it sound good enough to satisfy 'em."

Tate grinned around the cigar jutting out between his teeth. "That was genius at work, old friend. If you can't dazzle 'em with facts, snow 'em under with enough blather to make 'em think you must have said something acceptable."

"Then maybe you just did some of the same to me," Braska said when he was done, "because I ain't sure I followed it, but I still gotta admit it still sounded pretty shrewd."

Tate shrugged. "Okay. If not genius, it can live with shrewd."

"So this business you're so anxious to talk about in private...there shrewdness involved in it too?"

"Likely be some called for before it's done. But right now it's more about luck. The kind of once-in-a-lifetime stroke of good luck—no, hell, make that once in a *hundred* lifetimes—that has me standing on the brink of a fortune!" Tate's eyes glinted with a sudden surge of excitement. "And it's a fortune plenty big enough to be shared. That's where you can come in. I knew it the minute I saw you step out through the curtains of that wash-up area inside. Crossing paths with you again can only mean another piece of good luck for me. And some for you, too."

Braska exhaled some smoke. "Let me tell you right now that if you ain't talkin' something strictly on the up-and-up, then don't waste your breath sayin' no more. I'd like a crack at a fortune same as anybody, but not bad enough to risk goin' back behind the walls for it."

"That's the beauty of this fortune I'm talking about. Nobody's got no legal claim to it except whoever can lay their hands on it."

"Sounds like you're playin' around with words again."

"Look. Have you ever heard of the *Diablo Lobos*— the Devil Wolves?" When Braska shook his head, Tate continued, "No, coming from up north that probably ain't surprising. But twenty or so years back, all down south of here and along the border, the Lobos cut a hell-raising swath that nobody failed to take notice of. They were renegades, disillusioned soldiers left over from the Mex-American War. Anglos and Mexicans alike, led by a half -reed hombre called Enselmo *Ed* Wolfe. Their beef was that the war they'd fought and bled and seen comrades die for was all a big waste that left too much dissatisfaction when it was done. The Tejanos, like Wolfe, wanted Texas to remain an independent republic, not join the union as another state, and the Mexicans who threw in with him were sore that they not only never got what they went to war over in the first place—that being the border between countries to be marked by the Nueces River not the Rio Grande—but they also lost California and Oregon out of the deal.

"So Wolfe took this bitter, pissed-off rabble and turned it into one hellacious big gang. Damn near a small army, numbering over fifty men at their peak. He convinced 'em that while things were still in disarray in the wake of their war and the U.S. side was fussing over slavery and the looming threat of secession and a new war—one between existing states—brewing in the east, there'd be the chance for a determined, battle hard force of men to carve out a slice of the borderlands and make it their own."

Braska grunted. "Sounds like some more recent die-hard Southern fanatics who refused to accept how the Civil War ended when it finally did come—and took similar stabs at resurrectin' the Confederacy."

"Maybe Wolfe set the pattern for 'em. And even though he failed in the end, he sure made plenty of folks—all the way back to Washington—turn their heads and take notice of him."

"If this tale your spinnin' is about a failure, how does it wind up leavin' a fortune for you to be standin' on the brink of?" Braska wanted to know.

"Because the high number of raids that Wolfe and the Diablo Lobos made at the peak of their rampaging netted an amazing amount of wealth in relatively short order—before they were ultimately betrayed then trapped and wiped out in their stronghold up in the Sante Veyos Mountains."

"So what you're talkin' about is stolen money."

"Stolen, yes. But not money."

"I like the sound of this less and less, and I sure as

hell don't like gettin' it dished out in riddles," Braska growled irritably. "Start makin' sense or we can forget this whole thing. Mulhaussen's gonna pretty quick be bringin' out the others and wantin' to get rollin' again."

"Okay, okay. The fortune I'm talking about is in ancient artifacts and relics—most of it made of gold, some silver and precious gems—dating back to the time of the conquistadors. In other words, booty such invaders originally pillaged from the Aztecs or whoever down in South America. But instead of shipping *all* of what they acquired back to the homeland, like they were supposed to, some of those old pirates obviously pilfered off certain items for themselves. Over time, who can say how or why after so many decades"—here Tate gave an elaborate shrug—"these valuable pieces got passed around, probably to descendants and what not, and many of them ended up in the private collections of wealthy estate holders and big land owners all up through Mexico and along the border. Historic booty they had no legal claim to except by the right of raw possession."

"So in the process of hittin' the rich estates and big rancherias on either side of the border," said Braska, beginning to get the picture, "Wolfe and his Lobos started also uncoverin' some of those private collections."

Tate nodded. "That's right. The main purpose of their raids, of course, was always for money and supplies. The stashes of ancient treasure falling into their hands was an unexpected bonus."

"But when their stronghold in the Sante Veyos got wiped out—by the Army, I'm guessin'—didn't all that treasure get confiscated as part of it?"

Tate's mouth curved into a sly smile. "That would've been the case if Wolfe had kept the relics at the stronghold. But the *breed* always claimed to have a strain of conquistador blood in him, and apparently, some of their pirate tendencies came along with it. Whatever his reasons, he made the decision to sort out the treasure pieces from the rest of what their raids yielded and store them in a separate place, a place known only to him and a select detail of trusted men who accompanied him on periodic trips to keep adding to this secret stash. In the fighting that broke out when the Army made their strike on the stronghold, Wolfe and the men of his treasure-hiding detail were all killed —all save one, that is."

"Ignacio Clemente," said Braska.

Tate's eyebrows lifted. "How did you figure that?"

"For starters, I matched it to the name of the girl you're travelin' with," Braska told him. "I recalled Clemente as also bein' the name of the little Mex fella who was part of our cell block back at Hellstone. I never paid much attention to him because he hardly spoke any English, and like most of the others in our block, I didn't—and still don't—know Spanish. But you do. You and him bein' kinda chummy because you were the only one who knew what he was sayin' is something else I recall."

"Damn right," Tate confirmed. "At first I felt kinda sorry for the little runt because nobody else *could* understand him and so, like you just said, mostly ignored him. So I let him know I was an exception. For a long time, that was about it. I wouldn't say we were exactly chummy, we just talked together once in a while.

"But then, not long after you got your release, Ignacio took sick and never really came out of it. You know how the medical staff at Hellstone was. Before long, as he got steadily sicker and weaker and it became clear he wasn't gonna last a whole lot longer, he started opening up to me. Telling me about the Diablo Lobos, how he'd been part of them...and finally, about the secret treasure stash." Tate paused and set his jaw tight for a moment. Then he continued, "That was a year ago and just short of seven months before I got my own release. Since then I've been following up on the things Ignacio told me and well, it's brought me to this point."

"And the girl is part of it?"

"Yeah. A big part. Some of what Ignacio told me, see, was a message for his brother Benalito. Sort of pieces to a puzzle that Benalito would know other pieces to. But it turns out the brother is deceased. Luckily, his daughter—Miriella—has a rough idea of what his contribution might've been. Together, we're aiming to fill out the puzzle in hopes it will end up taking us to the treasure."

Braska dropped the remains of his cigarette onto the dirt and ground it underfoot. Then, eyeing Tate, he said, "That's a helluva yarn, amigo, and I guess I oughta be flattered you trust me enough to spill as much as you have. But why is that? What makes you figure you can trust me and what is it you think I can add that'd be of any help?"

Tate's answer was delayed by the appearance of Mulhaussen and the other stage passengers emerging from the station. Glancing over their way, Mulhaussen called, "Time to load up and get rollin' again, fellas."

"Shit," said Tate under his breath. Then, continuing to meet Braska's gaze and keeping his voice lowered, he added, "We'll have to take this up again later, at the next stop. In the meantime, think about what I've told you and what you have the chance to share in if things pan out."

5

WITH MIDDAY COME AND GONE, THE STAGE ROLLED away from Barkley's in the already brutal but still climbing heat of the afternoon. It wouldn't peak for another two to three hours, diminishing only as the sun descended in a cloudless copper sky until the same baked air gradually took on a startling chill under the moon and stars. By then the passengers would be bedded down for their overnight stay at Floater's Way Station before completing the run to Harrietville the following day.

Kicked up by the churning wheels and pounding hooves, a cloud of brownish-yellow dust immediately wrapped around the coach and clung stubbornly even as it continued in motion. Leather curtains, freshly oiled by the team switchers at each stop, were secured in rolled bundles above the coach's side windows on the outside—available to be unfurled and dropped down to serve passengers as a buffer against dust or inclement weather. But, in cases like today, it would also mean blocking out any stray breeze that might cut through and bring a whiff of fresh air. So at least for the time being, the occupants agreed to leave the curtains unused. Feeling oppressed by the heat and also lulled somewhat by the kind of torpor that often comes after a meal, said passengers collectively adopted poses of just sitting drowsily still and quiet and letting the miles fall away.

Up in the driver's box, Mulhaussen, who'd been so gregarious and talkative back at the station, now also settled into his own quieter phase except for the commands he barked to his new pullers. This was partly due to him concentrating on getting the feel of the new team while at the same time allowing them to get accustomed to his voice and his touch on the reins. Since all involved—man and animals alike—were veterans at their respective tasks, however, it would only take a short time for a kind of harmony to be reached.

As for Braska, he was glad Mulhaussen wasn't still in a talkative mood. What he'd just heard from Ira Tate had given him plenty to think about and so, while he was rolling that around inside his head, the last thing he needed was somebody else trying to make conversation right beside him.

Conquistadors...a fortune in gold and silver artifacts dating back to some ancient civilization...outlaw raiders aiming to carve out a new country suited strictly to themselves...Jesus, what a yarn. In his years on the drift, Braska had tried his hand at a number of different things and contemplated a few others. But any thought of prospecting or fortune hunting had never entered into it. Yet now his thoughts were locked on that singular track, racing down it full tilt, with a pile of already-dug gold and silver potentially waiting at the finish line.

Not that he didn't still leave room for some consideration of Ira Tate as well. Tate had seemed quick to trust him, at least to a certain extent. But that didn't make it smart for Braska to reciprocate too eagerly. After all, he hadn't laid eyes on the man in over two years and only knew him at all from the time they'd spent together in prison. Braska was in Hellstone for six years, Tate was part of his cell block for only the last two or so.

Some men form close bonds during incarceration, others stay as cold and detached as the stone walls containing them. Braska's attitude had leaned more toward the latter, though he did build guarded friendships with a handful of those regularly about him. Tate became part of the handful. He was affable and intelligent, cut from considerably different cloth than many of the surly hardcase types common to the setting. Even his crime had been nonviolent in nature. Embezzlement, Braska recalled, having been caught siphoning off large quantities of money from the bank where he worked. Thinking back on it now, Braska reckoned that must explain why he wasn't presently going around heeled—he apparently just wasn't the gun-packing type.

His less violent nature, in fact, was what had led to Braska forming a friendship with him in the first place. When word spread, after Tate had been in Hellstone for a while, that his past was not only that of a hated banker but his crime was theft committed via some paperwork shuffling rather than standing behind a gun like a *real man*, some toughs out in the prison's common yard thought it would be fun to rough the *nance* up some. To his credit, while he may not have been a gunny or a typical hardcase on the outside, when cornered Tate proved neither to be a powder puff easily willing to serve as a punching bag. He was a powder puff who punched back, and was managing to do a pretty effective job of it.

That's when Braska waded in and stood back to back with him. He'd tried to hold off, not get involved, but the five-to-one odds were more than he could stomach. Plus, by that point, Tate had already begun showing some kindness to little Ignacio back in the cell block, and Braska had taken note of the decency in that. It made Tate all the more deserving of a decent break in return. So, even though Braska's participation still left the odds lop-sided at first, it wasn't long before the toughs started dropping, one by one, and staying down. Once their numbers advantage was gone, those who could still stand dragged off the ones who couldn't in a wordless declaration of having had quite enough fun.

Reflecting further on the incident as the stage continued to roll and lurch along, Braska decided it might be the primary explanation for why Tate had been so quick to feel he could still trust him, even after the intervening years. Not the most solid or careful reasoning perhaps, but not entirely loco either. And speaking of acting loco, Braska told himself, it was all well and good for him to practice his usual caution, but at the same time, he needed *not* to be loco when the chance at a fortune could be dangling before him.

With Barkley's falling steadily farther behind them, the surrounding landscape began taking on some different features. The terrain remained relatively flat, revealing clumps of sage and bramble bush scattered more frequently across the carpet of drab brown. Rock outcrops also started thrusting up here and there, the trail winding close in and out of several. They were mostly brief, jagged-topped stretches reaching no higher than six or eight feet and then tapering off and disappearing after only a couple dozen yards. Though a few contained larger, grotesque shapes and some tall, weathered cones once in a while, for the most part they made Braska think of rows of broken stone teeth.

After the new team had been at work for a couple of hours and had carried them roughly a dozen miles, there suddenly came a loud pounding from inside the coach. Accompanying this, the voice of one of the passengers—Tate, it sounded like—hollered, "Driver, you need to stop! We've got a desperately sick man back here!"

"Hurry up before he heaves all over everything and everybody," called another voice. "Get on that brake, man!"

Scowling and letting out a string of curses, Mulhaussen hauled back on his reins and started slowing the horses. They balked and staggered raggedly for a moment, confused by the abrupt reversal from what they were usually hollered at to do, but then fell into step once again and ceased pulling. When the time was right, Mulhaussen cranked on the brake and brought everything to a creaking, rocking full halt.

Braska immediately jumped down and went around to the side of the coach. The door popped open just ahead of him getting to it, and Tate emerged, coming out backward in a barely controlled tumble. He was reaching inside even as his feet hit the ground.

Braska could see he had his hands under the arms of the stocky man, Kettleman, and was trying to pull him out, too.

Spotting Braska out the corner of his eye, a red-faced Tate grunted, "Give me a hand—this hombre ain't no lightweight!"

Braska leaned his shotgun against the wheel, shoved the door open as wide as it would go, then wedged himself in as best he could to get a partial grip on Kettleman. Together, he and Tate dragged the man out of the coach and tried to lay him on the ground. But he was groaning and thrashing about too violently to remain still.

Thrusting up onto his knees, doubled forward with his arms wrapped over his stomach, Kettleman bellowed, "That goddamn Indian squaw poisoned me! My guts are on fire!"

Tate put a hand on his shoulder. "Try to take it easy. I don't know what's wrong with you, but we all ate the same food as you so it don't seem—"

"Whatever it is, it's ripping apart my insides!" wailed Kettleman, continuing to hug his stomach and toss his head from side to side.

Mulhaussen came around the rear of the coach, his face gripped by a mix of puzzlement and concern for the poor wretch.

"Somebody give me a canteen," Braska said to those still in the coach.

When Miriella handed him one, he began unscrewing the cap and took a step closer to Kettleman, saying, "Here, fella, maybe this'll—"

He never got the rest of the words out. Suddenly, shockingly, Kettleman straightened up out of his hunched-over position. One of the arms that had been hugging his stomach swung out wide and in its fist was a Colt .45 he'd yanked from his waistband. Leaning forward and down with the canteen, Braska's head made a perfectly obliging target. The barrel of the .45 crashed against it, just above his ear, making a sickening iron-on-flesh-and-bone thud.

Braska's knees instantly buckled, and he felt screaming pain shoot down through his neck and shoulders. He'd been knocked out before and knew what was coming next. And it did. His last half second of conscious thought was an awareness of the hot, gritty surface of the trail rushing up to slam against the side of his face opposite from where the gun barrel had struck. Then the pain and everything else went away, and there was nothing but blackness.

6

"THAT'S ENOUGH, HOLD OFF POURIN' ANY MORE...I think he's startin' to come out of it."

The voice sounded murky, far away. Yet Braska somehow knew it really wasn't. It sounded familiar, too, but he couldn't place it. When he opened his mouth to question the source, he inadvertently sucked some water down his throat, and it sent him into a mild bout of choking and coughing.

"Where's that hanky?" said a different voice. "Wipe his face off, for God's sake, before we end up drowning him."

When Braska felt a hand pressing a cloth down on his face, he instinctively resisted. He knocked the hand away. Then he dragged his own bare hand down over his face, skimming away the excess moisture. In the process of this, his thumb passed over his right temple and sent a bolt of pain shooting all through his head and down his neck. He remembered then. All of it. Everything, that is, up until he'd lost consciousness.

Knowing it was going to hurt, Braska slowly forced

his eyes open. He was right, the bright afternoon sunlight brought fresh stabs of pain. Fighting through that and blinking away the blurriness, he was able to focus on the three faces hovering over him. Two of them belonged to the drummers, Tibbs and Baker, the third was the leathery, frowning mug of Mulhaussen.

"Jesus," Braska groaned. "The scenery sure didn't improve any while I was takin' my gun barrel nap."

"You're lucky to be able to soak in any scenery at all after that wallop you got from Kettleman," Mulhaussen responded, his voice the familiar one Braska hadn't been able to place in his initial grogginess.

"Kettleman!" Braska echoed the name in an angry snarl. He pushed up on his elbows and saw he was still lying on the ground, partially propped against one of the coach wheels, his face and shirtfront soaked from being splashed by canteen water to revive him. He twisted his head from side to side, sweeping his gaze to look past the three men bunched directly in front of him. "Where is that sucker-punchin' bastard anyway?"

"Long gone, I'm afraid," answered Mulhaussen, his mouth twisting sourly. "You ain't gonna believe this, but that lowdown snake was all the while in cahoots with those horsemen who passed us by earlier. His sick act was a setup to get me to stop the stage so the other four could come boilin' out of the rocks and swarm us just as soon as you and your shotgun was took outta the picture."

"Swarm us for what?" Braska wanted to know. "I thought we decided before that we wasn't carryin' anything valuable enough to..." He let the words trail off and swept his gaze anew. Signs of a bitter realization started to show in his eyes. "Where's Tate and the girl?"

"They're gone too," came the answer. "They was hauled off over something they know between 'em—about the location of some kinda buried treasure or maybe just a stash of stolen loot, the talk we overheard wasn't exactly clear. Anyway, whatever it is, it's the thing of value that Blevins and his bunch were after."

"Blevins?"

"That would be Red Dog Blevins," explained Baker, the stationary salesman. "He's a notorious outlaw who normally operates down in west Texas. From all the *Wanted* posters I've seen on my sales route down through there, I was able to recognize him when he and the others came out of the rocks."

Mulhaussen spat. "I'd've never known him by sight, but I sure enough've heard the name. Like the man said, in the past he's always stayed down Texas way. But wherever he's at, all reports say he's one mean hombre."

"That's certainly true. From reports *I've* heard," said Baker, "it's a wonder he rode away and left any of us alive in his wake."

Braska's gaze tracked to the front of the coach where there was no sign of the pulling team. Empty harnessing gear lay scattered on the ground. "Red Dog may have left us alive," he grated, "but it appears he otherwise didn't leave us in particularly good shape."

"He didn't for a fact," agreed Mulhaussen. "After strippon' away all our guns and weapons, his men scattered the horses to hell and gone. Not only that, they then slashed the reins and other gear to ribbons so as to make sure that, even if any of the nags came back around, we wouldn't have nothing to harness 'em back up with. I expect I could rig up something regardless, if given the chance. But that won't happen—those horses won't come back here, they'll look for the closest water."

"Barkley's?"

"Most likely. Eventually, for sure. But if they sniff out a creek or water seep of some kind closer by, that could cause 'em to stray off for a while."

"So where does that leave us?" asked Tibbs, the twitchy, nervous little shoe salesman.

"I been thinkin' on that, and the way I see it," replied Mulhaussen, rubbing his jaw, "we ain't got but three or four choices. We can sit here and hope for somebody to come by—which ain't very likely seein's how this road is so little traveled except for the stage run, and I know for a fact there ain't another of our line scheduled to come through until day after tomorrow. *Might* be a roamin' cowboy from a ranch somewhere, but that ain't anything can be counted on, and I don't know if there's even any ranches anywhere halfway close.

"A second option is to wait for somebody from Floater's to come lookin' after we're too late showin' up for our scheduled stop. But we ain't due there for another four hours or so, then add another couple before they'd get overly worried it might be something serious. Temporary breakdowns and delays of one sort or other ain't exactly unheard of. Be full dark by the time they decided to send somebody to check, then it'd depends who was on hand before whoever got tasked would head out right away or wait for daylight."

"But we're quite a bit closer to Barkley's, right? What if some of our horses *did* start showing up there?" asked Baker as he mopped sweat from his face with an already-soaked handkerchief.

"Could be our quickest hope," Mulhaussen allowed. "But it'd still depend on if and how soon any horses came 'round. Once any did, though—dark or not —you can bet Simon'd come checkin' right away."

"Then the only other option," said Braska, "is headin' out walkin' back to Barkley's."

"Under the right circumstances, that might be considered the surest way." Mulhaussen paused, his eyebrows pinching together as he cut a sidelong glance over at Baker and Tibbs. "But it wouldn't be no easy hike for anybody makin' it. Twelve miles'd take six, seven hours of steady goin'. The way's mostly flat, as we all saw. But walkin' through dust and sand drags heavy on a man's feet, regardless. And though the sun's startin' to ease up some, it's still gonna be plenty hot for quite a spell yet."

Baker scowled in the midst of wiping more sweat from his fleshy, beet-red face. "You might as well go ahead and say it out plain. You don't think me and Tibbs could make it."

"Oh, you could make it. Eventually. But doin' it'd beat the livin' hell outta you." Mulhaussen's face pulled into a long frown. "And I ain't sayin' it'd be much different for me. I could take the sun okay, yeah, I already been baked thorough by that devil. But that don't mean sittin' on my ass in a stagecoach driver's box has made these bony-kneed old pins of mine ready for a long trek on shank's mare. Not by a damn sight."

"Which leaves me," stated Braska.

Mulhaussen gave him a look. "Maybe, maybe not. Don't sell yourself as bein' too high and mighty neither, junior. You're packin' around a cracked skull, remember? You don't even know yet if you can stand up on your own."

As if that was a challenge gauntlet thrown down, Braska promptly rose to meet it. First, he pushed to a straight-up sitting position. Then, reaching back with his right hand to get some leverage by gripping one of the wheel spokes, he pushed the rest of the way until he was standing. It took some teeth gritting, and once accomplished, he teetered a bit. But he'd by damn made it, and with no help either.

Glaring at Mulhaussen, he said, "There. It may take a couple minutes to get my sea legs under me, but I'm standin'. And I'll be able to *keep* standin'—and walkin'—for as long as I need to." He paused to pat the chest pockets of his shirt, which had gotten soaked from the dousing to revive him. His mouth twisted wryly. "I appreciate all the work you fellas put into bringin' me back around. I purely do. But I sure wish you wouldn't've drowned all my makin's in the process. Was I able to light up a quirley right about now and drag in a couple lungfuls of smoke, it'd sure help fetch me along."

Mulhaussen wagged his head. "You stubborn mule. Ain't you got some extra makin's up in the box?"

"In my possibles sack under the seat, yeah."

"I'll go get it for you," offered Tibbs.

As the spindly little man started away, Mulhaussen called after him. "Under the seat on my side you'll find a bottle of rye whiskey—that I keep on hand strictly for medicinal purposes and emergencies such like this. Bring it along, too. I expect a belt or two wouldn't hurt any of us, and might especially help Braska with his healing."

A handful of minutes later, Braska had a cigarette

going and the other three were passing around the bottle of rye. "It occurs to me," Mulhaussen said somewhat abruptly after taking a swig, "that if that bunch of owlhoots hail out of Texas, then they must've either moved up this way recently or at least one among 'em has some past familiarity with these parts."

"What makes you say that?" asked Baker.

"The way they staged this ambush. Seems plain to me that they knew this trail and how it would lead in among this string of close rock formations. That gave the four riders who passed us by earlier the chance to lay in wait and then move along parallel with us, keepin' out of sight, until their inside man got the coach stopped with his phony act so's they could jump in and finish gettin' the drop on us."

Baker frowned. "Rather elaborate, wouldn't you say? The Blevins gang I heard about robbed plenty of stagecoaches by simply riding them down and shooting them out without any resistance. I'm not complaining that they *didn't* do that in our case, mind you, I'm merely saying..."#

"But the difference here," said Tibbs, "is that on those other occasions they were after a strongbox or payroll of some kind. Right? This time they were after people and the information they possess. Meaning that riding in with guns blazing would have carried the risk of Tate or Miss Clemente catching a bullet—a chance the gang could hardly afford to take."

"That makes sense," allowed Mulhaussen. "And as far as them leavin' us alive behind 'em, they wasn't takin' much risk there neither. Considerin' the situation they left us in, we sure as hell ain't no threat to siccin' any kind of posse after 'em—not for a whole day or more just to let anybody else know."

"Could be. But I aim to do my damnedest to cut it down thinner than that," grated Braska. "Tate and the girl are important to 'em only as long as they've got information the gang wants. Once that's pried out of 'em and verified—and you can bet goin' after it ain't gonna be no pleasant experience—they'll have no further use. 'Cept maybe the girl. They may keep her alive for a while, for reasons I'll leave to your imagination."

"That poor child!" Tibbs murmured in a harsh whisper.

"That's why I mean to head out and not waste no more time about it." Braska flipped away the remains of his cigarette and motioned for the bottle of rye. After he'd taken a long pull, he handed it back to Mulhaussen, inquiring, "Where's the canteen you fellas used to douse me back awake?"

When it was held out to him, he shook it and found it still over half full.

"That's the one from the driver's box," said Mulhaussen. He looked at Tibbs. "How about the two from the coach?"

The little drummer checked and reported back, "One's full, the other close to three-quarters."

"I'll make do with this one, you keep those," Braska said.

"You should take the full one," Tibbs argued.

Braska shook his head. "I'll make do. There's only one of me, but three of you. Listen to Jake, he'll take care of you. I'll be back as soon as I can with Barkley and some help."

Mulhaussen stepped up to him. "I still think you're rushin' it, considerin' that wallop to the head you took. Yet I also know it's useless arguin' with the mule stubbornness inside that same head." He reached out and gave Braska a clap on the shoulder. "Godspeed to ya, lad."

Braska grinned crookedly. "Thanks, Jake. While you're at it, hold out some good thoughts for my old pal Tate and that girl, too."

7

To THOSE WHO KNEW OF THE PLACE, IT HAD OVER time, been called by different names. Some knew it by no name at all, just counted on it as being a reliable source for water in a parched land where water was crucial to survival. These days, it was most commonly called Jackrabbit Tanks. There was some disagreement over whether this came about due to the pre-ponderance of such critters to be found in the area, or if the jumble of weather-scoured rocks within which the water lay looked sort of like a crouching long-ear when viewed from a distance. In any case, all that really mattered was the water to be found there.

Cotton Wilkes sighed wearily as he leaned back against the smooth face of a boulder cast in a strip of cooling shade on a ledge six feet above the lower of Jackrabbit's two tanks. Wilkes was a wiry-muscled man of fifty, an even six feet in height, with sun-squinted eyes and a thick mane of butter-yellow hair. His bristly, unshaven jawline and the normally well-trimmed goatee that surrounded his mouth now looking tangled and unruly, combined with his sweaty, dust-caked clothing to paint the picture of someone who's been riding a long, hard trail. In a faintly husked voice, he said to the man next to him, "Ordinarily, I might question the wisdom of halting here for the night when we got two, three hours of good light left to cover more distance. But I'm so damn tired and fried by the day's sun, I welcome the hell outta not forging on no more 'til tomorrow."

Squatting beside him, Jeff Gint grunted. "That's the whole idea. Stop for a good, long rest here, saturate ourselves with water, then hit it hard again tomorrow across this empty, baked-over hellscape of a land. I thought we rode some hot, dusty, dry trails down in Texas—but shit, that was a breeze compared to what Red Dog has drug us through up here. Him and that high-handed damn Kettleman."

Gint was a big, blocky man. Well over six feet tall, thick-torsoed, broad across the shoulders and chest, with long, powerful arms ending in frying pan-sized hands. His face was hard and chiseled, featuring narrow, menacing eyes and a lantern jaw that sported whiskers resembling the hackles on a razorback.

Wilkes lifted his freshly filled canteen and took a big gulp. "Yeah, it ain't been easy going since we got up in this neck of the woods, that's for sure. And with those mountains Kettleman has us headed for being another two days away, I don't expect it's gonna be much more pleasant until we reach 'em. I just hope he knows more water holes in between, like he says he does."

"Like Kettleman says, like Kettleman says," mimicked Gint. "Don't it rankle you none to have him callin' the shots so much of the time? It does me. I been ridin' behind Red Dog for three years and change, and it's suited me just fine. Now this Kettleman shows up and all of a sudden it feels like Dog is followin' his lead as much or more than makin' his own decisions. I'm havin' trouble feelin' comfortable with that."

"As long as the decisions that get made are good ones and especially if they mean a powerful big haul like this current thing is supposed to gain us, then what difference does it make? Kettleman was Dog's commanding officer back in the war, remember—I reckon it only makes sense for Dog to still treat him with a touch more respect than he'd show anybody else."

"Well, he wasn't *my* commandin' officer," Gint argued. "So he'd better not try orderin' me around direct. I got one boss, and it ain't him."

"Have it your way." Wilkes shrugged. "But even you gotta admit Kettleman set up that stage holdup pretty damn slick."

"Big deal. How many stages did we rob down in Texas without his help? Twenty? A couple dozen? And we rode away from each one of 'em with money to show. What's more, we rode away not leavin' no live witnesses behind us. Tell me that's something Dog wouldn't've done this time around, too, if Kettleman hadn't talked him out of it."

"Maybe, maybe not." Wilkes's expression scrunched with annoyance. "Again, what difference does it make? Like Kettleman pointed out, the way we left that bunch stranded back there in the middle of nowhere, it's gonna take days before they can get a posse or any such called together. And all those times we cut down witnesses, what good did it really do? We still ended up with our mugs plastered on *Wanted* posters from Hell to breakfast. Those men back there didn't know us from your Aunt Gertie's pet cat—why leave a calling card sure to stir an extra batch of attention our way?"

Gint made a face of his own. "Boy, you're sure swallowin' big spoonfuls of Kettleman's medicine too, ain't you? Next thing, you'll be salutin' and callin' him Major."

"Stuff it, Gint."

"All right, all right. Just let me point out one more thing to show how your slick planner don't cover all the bases every time. Not havin' mounts ready for neither the major nor these two captives we took on—why didn't somebody have that thought of in advance? And I'll even include Dog in on sharin' that."

"Well, since I ain't or don't pretend to be no slick planner myself," Wilkes was quick to respond, "I'd only be making a guess to say it was a matter of time. When we missed our chance to nab those two before they left Leaning Rock and had to resort to the backup plan of catching up with 'em on the trail, we barely had time to ride our asses off in order to get ahead of that stagecoach and make it to the ambush spot. I don't see where that left any chance to stop and catch a breath, let alone round up any spare mounts."

Gint's mouth pulled down at the corners like he'd bitten into something bitter-tasting. "Okay, I gotta admit that holds water. I reckon if we'd had the time, we would've tried for some fresh mounts for the whole lot of us."

"Well, it'll still work out. McLaffert's dropped back to that ranch we saw signs of earlier, to scrounge the lacking nags. He moves like a ghost and has a way with horses like nobody's business."

"Hell, combine that with his appetite for shoveling grub into that stringy frame of his," said Gint, "and I ain't got much doubt he'll have 'em back in time for supper."

"Speakin' of which, before long, we'd better start gathering up some creosote and whatever else we can find to fuel a fire for said supper. Dog said we could kick back and rest some, but then working up a meal would fall to us."

"You'd think havin' that gal on hand," said Gint, his gaze straying to another shaded spot on the far side of the pool where Blevins and Kettleman were huddled in low, intense conversation with Tate and Miriella Clemente, "would make her the logical one to handle cookin' chores."

"Maybe in time. Right now I figure Dog and Kettleman see her best used for coughing up more information on where to find that buried treasure."

"Yeah, I reckon I agree with that...for now." Gint paused, his mouth slowly spreading into a lewd, knowing smile. "But, sooner or later, any gal who looks as good as her rates bein' put to one very special use."

"I can't argue with the notion," said Wilkes almost wistfully. "But was I you, I wouldn't get my hopes up to high."

Gint laughed nastily. "You ain't me, pard. And when I look at her, it ain't just my hopes that keeps gettin' up high."

———

Dogeron Red Dog Blevins was growing steadily more irritated. "Lemme get this straight," he growled. "You expect us to believe that the dying information you got from the old greaser in prison was nothing more than some kind of verbal clue—some *puzzle piece*—that had to be fitted with something his brother knew and only then would the pieces add up to where the Diablo treasure can be found? Is that it? But there's no kind of map that can be drawn from those pieces?"

Ira Tate winced under Blevins's fierce glare. "Yes, that's what I'm telling you. It's the truth!"

Blevins lashed out and backhanded Tate hard across the mouth. "Liar! You didn't round up the girl and come all this way without some kind of aim, some clear indication of where to find what you're after."

"Red," said Frank Kettleman in a low, firm tone. "There may come a time when such tactics are required, but I don't think we're necessarily there yet."

Tall, stockily built, Kettleman had an oddly narrow face perched on a thick neck. Matching streaks of gray painted his hair at each temple and a precisely trimmed pencil mustache separated the space between the tip of his long nose and a thin-lipped slash of mouth. But it was the deep timbre in his voice and his piercing, ice-blue eyes that gave him an overall commanding presence.

By contrast, Blevins, also stocky of build, an inch short of six feet, had a broad, fleshy face set on hardly any neck at all. His features were coarsened and deeply seamed by exposure to the elements, a once fair complexion dusted lightly by freckles now reddened and ruddy to the point of blurring out any trace of the freckles. He, too, had blue eyes, though washed out and pale, no facial hair, and a wide, thick-lipped mouth. The sense of command he put forth came from an aura of pure menace. And yet, in the presence of Kettleman and the few cautionary words he'd spoken, the outlaw leader seemed to ease back almost meekly.

Continuing in his calm, rich voice, the former Confederate army officer said, "When it comes to buried treasure—and trust me, I've done a fair amount of study on this—something about it seems almost invariably to make those with true knowledge of its whereabouts resort to elaborate schemes and measures to keep the location secret. Something as common and simple as a map put to paper is very rare. Pirates, conquistadors, even certain orders of priests who amassed great wealth in the form of raw gold ore and pagan adornments from the native tribes whose *salvation* they were overseeing...all, at one time or other, hid sometimes vast quantities of this acquired booty in well-concealed places with nothing but very intricate clues leading back to it."

"But why did the ones who hid it leave it in the first place—and why not go back for it themselves?" Blevins wanted to know.

"Most often, the larger quantities got left behind due to an initial lack of means to transport it. As to why the original depositors never returned"—here Kettleman gave an elaborate shrug—"who can say? Any number of things could have intervened. War, disease, rebellion, betrayal...it was usually only a small handful of individuals who knew the exact location, remember, so—as was the case with Ed Wolfe and his chosen few—

a sudden misfortune could eliminate everyone in the know."

Wiping a trickle of blood from the corner of his mouth where Blevins had struck him, Tate frowned at Kettleman and wondered how it was he seemed to know so much about the Diablo Gold.

As if reading his thoughts, Kettleman smiled thinly and said, "Don't look so surprised, Mr. Tate. Your friend Ignacio Clemente may have been a rare surviving member of the Diablo Lobos, but that hardly made him the only one who knew their story. Furthermore, neither were *you* the only one attached to your prison cell block who spoke and understood Spanish. I believe the name Walter Fritz is familiar to you?"

Tate grimaced at the mention of the name. Yeah, he wasn't likely to forget Fritz—head of the guard crew assigned to the Hellstone cell block occupied by Tate, Ignacio, Braska, and the rest. One tough, hardnosed pack of bulls with Fritz setting the tone.

"I see by the expression on your face that recognition is clear," Kettleman continued. "Like Red here, Fritz served with me in the late war. During that tumultuous time, an iron bond was forged among several men in our company. One that, even though our paths may have diverged in the years following, remains strong and lasting and is understood to be there if ever needed to be called upon. That bond and Fritz's recollection of my long-standing interest in the Diablo Lobos and their lost treasure was what led him to contact me after he overheard—and understood, unbeknownst to either of you—the things Ignacio was imparting to you as he lay dying.

"This, then, knowing you would be bound to make

a try for the treasure as soon as you got the chance, led me to have a team of men ready and waiting to begin shadowing your every move upon your release. Unfortunately, they got over-eager after you made contact with Senorita Clemente in lieu of her dead father, Ignacio's brother, and it became clear she knew enough to abruptly set the two of you preparing to strike out based on the information you'd pieced together."

"So that clumsy attempt to waylay us back in Prescott—that was your doing?" asked Tate through clenched teeth.

"Regretably, yes. Though not by my direct command, I assure you." The muscles at the hinges of Kettleman's jaw bulged visibly. "Still, a combination of over-eagerness by my admission, and clumsiness by your assessment—amounted to unacceptable incompetence in total. Though, I'll admit, also a few clever moves on your part as well."

Tate made a sour face. "Unfortunately, judging by our present circumstances, you obviously weren't willing to let it go at that."

With a smug look, Blevins was the one to respond. "Damn right the major didn't let it go," he said. "He shit-canned that first team of stumble-bums and called in his trusted old lieutenant and the firepower of the crew I have at my disposal to get the job done right."

"The job will be done," Kettleman reminded him, "when the Diablo treasure is uncovered and in our hands."

"Just a matter of time," Blevins said confidently.

Kettleman returned his attention to Tate. "As in all things, I dislike leaving a matter unfinished. So let me complete explaining about my long fascination with not *just* the treasure, but the whole Diablo Lobos story...the abiding interest Walt Fritz remembered me showing and talking about and what made him contact me when he overheard Ignacio's mention of it. As a young man, you see, I, too fought in the Mexican-American War and came away somewhat disillusioned and bitter at its close. For a brief time, I even toyed with the idea of joining the force Wolfe was putting together. But the injustices being suffered by the South and the cause that would eventually become the Confederacy drew me instead."

"You don't seem very good at picking winners," Tate muttered.

That instantly earned him another backhand to the mouth, delivered this time by Kettleman.

"Stop hitting him!" protested Miriella. "You just finished saying that kind of thing was not necessary."

"To be precise," Kettleman replied, his voice totally calm once again, "what I said was that the time for such hadn't necessarily been reached. But then your friend's mouth—partly in an attempt to appear bold and unafraid in front of you, I suspect—managed to reach it. But only momentarily, I hope, if he shows the sense to keep a civil tongue and not be in a hurry to test my patience."

"And you'd be advised to keep the same thing in mind for yourself, senorita," added a scowling Blevins.

Miriella glared coldly in response, Tate merely hung his head. Nothing more was said for several beats.

Until Kettleman spoke again. "Very well. Let me explain how we're going to proceed for the next couple of days. In a little while, our comrade Kelce McLaffert will be returning with mounts for myself and you two.

In the morning then, we will start out—off trail, cross country via a series of water holes that I know of from previous travel through the area—on a two-day trek to the Sante Veyos Mountains, where the Lobos once had their stronghold. I have been there twice in the past.

"I'm well aware that the treasure we're seeking was purposely hidden somewhere apart from the stronghold. But it's always seemed logical for me to believe that Wolfe wouldn't have wanted this other location to be excessively far away. The Sante Veyos are quite a small mountain chain to begin with, very barren and rugged, with two or three other even smaller, equally rugged offshoots close by. I've always suspected that one of those others is where Wolfe decided to cache his collection of artifacts and relics." Here, Kettleman paused for a moment, closely eyeing both Tate and Miriella before continuing. "And the fact that the two of you were on your way to Harrietville, an obvious point from which to take better-known trails branching toward the Sante Veyos and those smaller offshoots, tells me that whatever indicators you're following mirror my speculations."

Finding his voice again, Tate said, "If you have it all figured out, then what do you need us for?"

"Did you not hear the word *speculation*?" Kettleman responded. "While I feel the things I've laid out are reasonably accurate, I, at the same time, recognize they still need some refinement. I'm counting on you and Miss Clemente to provide that with the puzzle pieces you're able to add."

"And if we divulge them to you, do you expect us to be foolish enough to believe you'd then turn us loose and let us live?"

Kettleman once again smiled that thin, cold smile. "If our end goal was *not* to let you live, then what you'd be wise to consider was how you would rather die. We could make your deaths quick and relatively painless. Or, if you leave us no choice but to resort to other tactics—the ones I've so far indicated a willingness to put off—then your deaths could be preceded by a great deal of agony."

"And I have men in my crew," said Blevins, "who are real good at dishin' out that kind of thing."

"If you kill us and what we have told you is false or inaccurate, then what?" challenged Miriella. "You get no second chances at questioning a corpse!"

"Like we'd be stupid enough to kill you before we verified what you spilled," Blevins snorted disdainfully.

Kettleman sighed. His gaze cut back and forth between Tate and Miriella. "All of this, if you once again hark back to my *precise* wording, stems from me addressing the question of *if* we had a goal to no longer let you live once you provided information leading to the treasure. And it's true that the two of you have no worth beyond holding such information. But consider something more: If you *did* provide same and it proved out, neither would you have any worth as a threat or potential problem of any consequence for us afterward. You'd have no legal recourse, no legitimate counterclaim, nor even any evidence to bring forth if you tried." The former Confederate major paused once again and this time the smile he produced was more a mocking sneer. "And let's face it, Tate...despite the clever maneuvering you pulled off that one time in Prescott, the notion of you returning as some hell-bent avenger out for payback is hardly an image to strike fear in the hearts of men like us."

Blevins guffawed loudly at that last part.

Tate ignored him and focused on Kettleman. "So we're right back to expecting us to believe that if we play nice and cooperate in helping find the treasure, there's a chance you might let us live. That it?"

"Let's call it a possibility. But resistance or a lack of cooperation or any attempted trickery...those are pretty much a guarantee of something far less pleasant." Kettleman held out his hand, palm down, and moved it in a sideways slashing motion. "Enough talk. Think about what's already been discussed. Think hard. You have from now until we reach the Sante Veyos to come up with the right decision."

8

THE WALK BACK TOWARD BARKLEY'S WAS HARDER going than Braska had counted on. More accurately put, harder than his stubbornness to accept his diminished condition had allowed him to consider.

But, as Mulhaussen pointed out, that same stubbornness kept him plodding on regardless. At a slower pace than he wanted, true, but still—except for the times his legs took on a degree of sponginess that forced him to stop and drop back on his haunches for a while—steadily forward. The throbbing in his head was a constant that he refused to let play any part in slowing him more.

He reckoned about four hours had passed. The sun was gone now, a pinkish gold smear just above the western horizon marking where it had disappeared. The air was growing markedly cooler. His shirt was still wet from old body sweat, though, and his face was covered with patches of salt crust from dried perspiration.

In four hours he normally would have expected to

cover seven, close to eight, miles. But, much as he hated to admit it, he knew his broken pace on this occasion had brought him considerably short of that. Probably closer to only six. Barely halfway. Damn, that was a depressing thought!

Trying to cheer himself up, he thought: *But once you hit halfway, means you're then headed through and out!*

Pig shit. What difference did that make? Didn't mean what was left was going to be any easier. And if the cooling air caused his already strained legs to start cramping, it might even get worse.

But there was nothing to be gained by bellyaching about what was or fretting over what might be. The only thing for certain, Braska knew, was that he simply had to keep going, keep plodding forward. That's all there was to it. He'd assigned himself this task, and he had to see it through...

As it had been in the daytime, with not even a breath of air stirring, the surrounding terrain in every direction seemed still and silent. Living things of the non-plant variety knew in this environment that to move carelessly risked drawing the attention of a possible predator. And so, though movement among the living did take place, it was kept to a minimum and done so cautiously that none but the keenest eyes and ears were able to perceive it.

Braska, though a seasoned veteran of many outdoor settings, was not yet attuned enough to this one to be able to pick up on very many of the small, subtle movements occurring about him. He did hear a couple of distant coyote yowls and the victory screech of a hawk diving down out of the high currents and seizing a too-slow jack out of the scrub growth. Otherwise, his ears were filled only with sounds he himself was creating— the puff of his labored breathing, the determined, irregular *plop, plop* of his footfalls.

Until, very faintly at first, then gradually louder, then even more gradually taking on recognizable features...there came the clopping sound of horses' hooves accompanied by the creak and jingle of harness rigging and the groan of wagon wheels.

And then, lifting his face with his heart soaring and his eyes straining to see through the descending gloom of dusk, Braska was able to make out the approaching shapes fitted to those sounds. It was a buckboard drawn by a two-horse team, animals and rig aswirl in the trail dust they were kicking up that showed milky white in the faded light. And smack in the center of it all—sitting high and wide on the driver's seat of the buckboard, his massive silhouette leaving no room for doubt—was none other than Simon Barkley!

———

"AFTER THOSE OWLHOOTS CUT 'EM LOOSE AND scattered 'em, your pullin' team must not've done much roamin' before they aimed themselves back toward our place. First there was one, then the others began straggglin' in not long after. All within about a half hour or so. A-course, we didn't wait for the whole works to show up before we started scramblin' and makin' preparations to come for a look-see. It was plain that something had gone bad wrong...and now that we're clear on what it was, seems to me the next order of business needs to be gettin' those pullers hitched back up to this here coach so's you fellas can return to rollin' and spread word of what happened to the first law dogs you're able to reach."

Thus spoke Simon Barkley as he sat within the flickering glow of a campfire that crackled and popped on trail's edge near the stranded stagecoach. Seated close around him were Mulhaussen, Baker, Tibbs, and Braska. Standing still and silent out on the edge of the throbbing light was Barkley's tall, copper-skinned, lithely muscled teenage son who went by the name of Arrow.

The campfire had already been burning brightly when the buckboard, complete with its recently acquired hitchhiker, came rolling up. The reception by those who'd remained with the coach was as welcoming as Braska's had been out on the trail. And when Barkley and Arrow began unloading some of the provisions they'd brought—blankets, ground coffee, biscuits and a pot of stew from Moon Eyes's kitchen—it became even more enthusiastic.

Now, hunched around the fire with blankets draped over their shoulders against the night chill and cups of fresh-brewed coffee and bowls of reheated stew distributed among them, all were reviewing and discussing how best to regroup and proceed from what had befallen the ill-fated stage run. Mulhaussen and his remaining two passengers were in favor of a suggestion made by Barkley. That being to take them back to his place where they could get cleaned up and rested a bit before returning in the morning with their horses and replacement rigging so the team could be re-hitched and they'd be able to continue belatedly on their way.

A dissenting voice to this, speaking strictly for

himself, was that of Braska. It happened that the
Barkleys had responded in a manner meant to cover as
wide a range of contingencies as they could think of—
and had done a darn thorough job. The buckboard
addressed most of it. For one thing, occupying its seat
rather than forking a horse better suited Simon's game
leg, for another, it allowed a greater variety of provisions
to be loaded up and brought along, and third, antici-
pating there'd be bodies to retrieve—hopefully all still
alive, but recognizing there might be wounded or dead
as well—the hauling bed would further serve that
purpose.

But then, just to be sure, somebody had thought to
also tie on a couple of saddle horses. And it was the
inclusion of these—making one of them available to him
as a mount—that prompted Braska to once again want
to strike out apart from the others.

"Look," he said, "there's no denyin' it's important
for the coach to get up and runnin' again. And Simon's
plan for how best to go about it is not only sound but
mighty generous, considerin' all the more he'll be
pitchin' in to help make it happen. The trouble is,
even if every step of it goes smooth, you're still lookin'
at another two, maybe three days before reachin'
Harrietville where the closest law of any kind can be
found. That'd be at least four days from when the
gang hit where we sit. So, say they throw together a
posse in Harrietville. What chance in hell are they
gonna have for cuttin' sign of Blevins's bunch after
that long? And in the same amount of time, how much
ground will the gang have covered...and how much
abuse might Tate and the girl have suffered in the
process?"

"But what other choice is there?" Barkely wanted to know.

Braska inclined his head. "These mounts you thought to bring along."

Barkley's bushy eyebrows lifted. "Yeah. I see what you're thinkin'—somebody could jump on one of them, ride out hard and make it to notify the law in Harrietville a whole lot quicker."

"Uh-huh. Reckon that'd be an okay use for one of 'em."

Now Barkley's brows pulled down into a frown. "The way you say that...you got something particular else in mind for the second horse?"

"You damn betcha he does." This response came not from Braska, but rather from Mulhaussen. Everybody glanced his way even though the old jehu kept his own gaze locked on his shotgun guard. Continuing, he said, "I can see the wild-ass glint in his eyes and I recognize it plain. This crazy fool wants one of those horses for himself—so's he can go direct after Red Dog's gang on his own!"

"That's exactly right," Braska wasted no time admitting. "So how about it, Simon? I got money in my pocket. I'm willin' to do whatever it takes—beg, borrow, or buy—to put one of those animals under me. That'd naturally include the Winchester rifle in its saddle boot. I'll offer to buy the rifle off the second horse, too, since those polecats stripped me clean of my own weapons. Hell, I might even consider that bow and handful of arrows I see tucked behind the saddle of the Appaloosa —except I'd probably risk pokin' my own eye out. What do you say?"

"I say I wouldn't feel at all comfortable participatin' in helpin' a body commit suicide," came the answer.

"You're sellin' me awful short without ever givin' me a chance, wouldn't you say?" Braska grated.

"One lone man goin' against that pack of blood-thirsty cutthroats—you call that havin' a chance?"

"I call it a helluva lot better chance than Tate and the girl will have if left very long in the hands of those curs. Every minute of every day that passes takes 'em closer to becomin' buzzard meat—and for the girl, that might be something she prays for before they're done with her."

"Damn you! Don't you think that's something me and the rest have thought about too?" roared Barkley. "But that don't change the sorry damn reality of things or make it smart to recklessly throw away more lives after ones already lost. This ain't the first I've heard of Red Dog Blevins, word reachin' clear up here from down Texas way about the butchery they done in addition to just robberies and such. It's a miracle him and his crew left anybody alive here in the first place. Chasin' after 'em and beggin'—"

"The only thing I'm beggin' for is a goddamn horse!" Braska cut him off. "I ain't stupid enough or reckless enough to be lookin' to throw my life away. I ain't aimin' to try and face down that whole bunch. But if I can catch 'em by surprise—and let's face it, the only reason they *did* leave anybody alive was on account of calculatin' there'd be no chance of pursuit for days— then that'd give me an edge. A damn slim one, yeah. But enough of one, maybe, to yank away those captives. *That's* what I'm hopin' to accomplish!"

Barkley's glare bored into him. Grudgingly, he said,

"By damn, I gotta allow as to how something like that *might* work. Seen similar things done a time or two back in my mountain man days—gettin' captives freed from Injuns."

"And when it comes to anybody who'd measure up for such like, I'd count Braska among 'em," spoke up Mulhaussen. But then, his brow puckering with doubt he couldn't hold in check, he added, "Only that'd be without takin' into consideration the cracked skull he's still carryin' around."

"Now, blast it, don't start in on that again!" Braska protested.

"You can't just ignore it, pard," Mulhaussen snapped back. "You said yourself that hike you set out on a little bit ago had you wore near to a frazzle before Simon and his boy showed up."

"A good horse would make all the difference," Braska insisted. "And both of these that the Barkleys brought with'em look to be of fine stock."

"They are. The best," said Barkley. "The Appaloosa gelding belongs to my son, though there's no way he'd part with him—*or* the bow and arrows. But the bay filly has desert mustang blood in her and will stay with the best."

"You'll sell her to me then?" Braska asked.

A battle of indecision played across the big man's face. Until, finally, he said, "No. I don't want to end up with blood money on my hands...so I'll loan her to you in the cockeyed belief that you just might be tough enough and stubborn enough and lucky enough to pull off what you're settin' out to do. And honest enough to bring her back if all that pans out."

"I'll do my best not to let either her or you down," Braska said earnestly.

Barkley nodded. "How soon you figure to head out?"

"Figure I'll wait for the moon and stars to be up full, see how much light they provide. I won't lie, I could use the couple hours' rest until then."

"You a good enough tracker to follow sign by night?"

Braska twisted his mouth some. "Can't claim it's my strongest suit, since it was never a skill I had call to hone particularly sharp. But I get by. And I figure the tracks I'll be locked on will be fresh and clear enough in this sandy ground to help me out. Plus, I got a pretty good idea where they're headed."

"Oh? Where's that?"

"The Sante Veyos Mountains."

"What makes you think so?"

"Something Tate mentioned to me back at the station," Braska said. Then, knowing he had to say more but not wanting to give too much away, he added, "I thought he was talkin' about him and the girl takin' a stab at doin' some prospecting there. But based on what Jake and the others heard the stage robbers say about hidden treasure or buried loot or whatever, I guess that's what he was hintin' at."

"But he *did* say the Sante Veyos, eh?"

"Uh-huh. And as the crow flies, based on some maps I remember seein' back at stagecoach headquarters, they lay south and a bit west from here. Right?"

"Uh-huh. About a two-day ride. And the country underneath where that crow would be flyin'—did your maps show that it's almighty empty and harsh the whole way?"

"In other words, about like what we're standin' in the middle of now."

Mulhaussen chuffed. "You could say that...if you was leanin' heavy on the charitable side."

"The biggest thing would be water," Barkley said sternly. "You ain't gonna be rigged to start out packin' much extra. So that'd make two days of crossin' that mean stretch some mighty tough goin' less'n you knew where to find water along the way."

"If Red Dog's crew is headin' across, then don't it figure they must know? And if I'm followin' them, then I'll reach the same as they do."

"*If* they know. Them bein' fresh outta Texas, how could they for sure?"

"The way they set up the ambush of our stage, we figured somebody among 'em must know this area pretty good," Mulhaussen told him.

"Maybe, maybe not. Even then, what if Braska should lose their trail—where would that leave him?" Barkley's face pulled into a deep frown. "I gotta admit, I'm startin' to crawfish some in my thinkin' that this might be a workable notion after all."

"Then I should go with Mr. Braska, Father."

The words came softly, almost gently, yet were enough to cause the face of each man at the fire to snap around. They found themselves staring at Arrow, Barkley's son, who had spoken from where he remained standing on the periphery of the campfire's light.

"What makes you say this, my son?" Barkley wanted to know.

Arrow took a step forward. "Because I know the

land and how to find water. What is more—and I don't mean to boast, but as you are well aware, Father—I can ride and track and hunt as good or better than any man in the territory. My assistance to Mr. Braska could be of benefit to this thing he seeks to do."

Before Barkley could reply, Braska said, "Whoa. Hold on a minute. I appreciate the offer, kid, I really mean that. But this thing I seek to do, as you put it, carries the risk of buttin' up against more trouble than just the worry of goin' thirsty. I'm willin' to heap that on myself, but I ain't keen for draggin' nobody else—especially not no young lad like you—into it with me."

"My son is eighteen years of age," Barkley stated. "Was he still with his mother's tribe, he'd've by now had to endure several grueling and dangerous tests to earn his passage into manhood. I have taught him the same skills he would've needed for those tests, and I assure you he'd be up to passin' 'em. What's more, durin' the years after I first quit the mountains and scouted for the Army out of Fort Collins, Colorado, Moon Eyes and me made sure he attended the school there where he breezed through learnin' to read, write, and speak English with the best of 'em. The kind of teachin' I *couldn't* provide. He was given an Indian name at birth, but his mother and I grew to call him Arrow because, at everything put before him, he hit the mark as straight and true and strong as the finest shaft. Any man havin' Arrow at his side for any task should consider himself damned fortunate."

Braska looked taken aback. "You sound like you're *encouragin'* me to bring him along."

"That's between you and him. If you take anything I said to mean I'm anxious to see my son enter into this undertakin' of yours, then you're a fool. At the same time, I'd suggest you not be even more of one and too quickly dismiss something that might help keep you alive." Barkley's eyes took on a shrewd cast. "Tell me... what were *you* doin' at eighteen?"

Braska grimaced before answering. "I lied about my age at seventeen in order to join the ranks of the Union army so I could go fight in the war."

The old mountain man merely gave a faint nod. "I'll say no more then."

9

"MR. BRASKA...THE MOON IS UP, AND THE LIGHT IS good. I tracked the sign of the outlaws out a quarter of a mile or so. If you wish to get started, I think we can continue following them without much difficulty."

Braska shoved his blanket down and lifted himself up on one elbow. He was instantly awake and just as instantly aware that the throbbing in his head seemed to be absent for the first time since its meeting with a gun barrel. He took that as a good sign. Equally encouraging were the words spoken by Arrow as he stood expectantly over where Braska had spread his blankets.

Braska sat up and looked around. "The others get off okay?"

"Yes. Some time ago. They said you needed all the rest you could get so did not want to disturb you. I am to pass along, once again, their wishes for us to have good luck."

"Yeah, we'll take all of that we can get," said Braska.

Arrow pointed. "I left the pot with some hot coffee in it on the edge of the coals. Otherwise, I went ahead and saddled and packed the horses for leaving as soon as you are ready."

"Sounds like you've been busy. I appreciate it." Braska stood up. Though the pain in his head may have subsided, the leftover aches in his feet and legs, courtesy of his recent hike, caused him to move with a measure of stiffness not to be appreciated.

He went to the coffee pot and poured some steaming mud into the cup Arrow had also left out. As he raised the cup and blew some cooling breaths across the contents before taking a drink, his gaze swept his surrounding, all awash in silver-blue illumination from a fat slice of moon and an accompanying spray of stars. The scene, with everyone else gone on their way back to Barkley's and the empty coach sitting abandoned in the middle of the trail, had an eeriness to it. Yet, considering the hour, the brightness and clarity was at the same time exhilarating—especially for the purpose of the task at hand.

After venturing a sip of the brew, Braska said, "You say you followed the tracks of the gang out for a ways?"

"Yes. Four horses, headed south-southwest as you expected. Two of them left deep prints, signaling they were carrying double. A pair of heavy men each. A third also left deeper marks, only not so much—a rider and the girl. Just one of the horses carried but a single rider."

This caused Braska to pooch his lips thoughtfully. "Say now. That don't put those hombres in quite as bright a light as we were thinkin' based on how slick they ambushed the coach, does it? Not havin' enough horses to go around for a getaway out across hard country don't hardly stack up as slick plannin' all the way through."

"Riding double will not only slow them down," said Arrow, "but as the heat of day builds, it will wear out their animals that much faster. All to our advantage, no?"

"You bet to our advantage. Leastways as far as catchin' up with 'em." Braska twisted his mouth wryly. "But that ain't apt to make things any easier once we do."

Arrow had no response for that.

"Tell me. Off in the direction they're headed"— Braska gestured with the cup in his hand— "is there any place they might be able to pick up the horses they're lacking?"

"There are some scattered ranches and homesteads. I'm not familiar enough with them, though, to know if there are any with spare horses they'd be willing to sell."

Braska scowled. "Just remember, the bunch we're settin' out after ain't exactly known to give much of a damn what other folks *want* to part with." He drained his coffee down to the dregs, then flung what was left in the bottom of the cup out into the night. "Come on. Best we get to it—for the reasons we already know, plus for the sake of some poor unsuspectin' bastard who might get trampled in between before we can get to 'em."

———

FROM WHERE SHE LAY BOUND IN THE SHADOWY darkness amid the boulders surrounding Jackrabbit

Tanks, Miriella Clemente spoke softly. "Senor Tate... Ira...are you awake?"

"Unfortunately, yes," came the cautiously whispered response. "These are hardly circumstances suited to a restful night's sleep."

"I know what you mean. I'm freezing, and this slab of rock they left us lying on is certainly no help."

"Freezing one minute, baking your brains out the next...nothing about this land, this godforsaken leftover corner of Hell is fit for..." Tate let his bitter lamentation trail off to nothing.

After he'd been quiet for a beat, Miriella whispered again. "I've been listening carefully for some time now, and I believe the others are sound asleep. I think it's safe for us to talk quietly. Day will be breaking soon, however, and I heard the major, the one we knew as Kettleman, state he wants to get an early start."

"Major!" Tate spat. "Major over what? Nothing but rabble!"

Miriella's tone took on an abrupt sternness. "If we are to have any chance at all, then we had better collect ourselves and try to come up with some kind of plan rather than merely bemoan our fate and accept it as hopeless. If you are not willing to work toward that end, then say so now and I will know I am on my own!"

Tate went quiet again. Until, his whisper less raspy than before, he said, "Jesus, gal...you're right. I'm sorry. I'm the one who dragged you into this, and now that things have taken a bad turn all I've been doing is slinking belly down and whining like a whipped pup."

"You didn't drag me into anything I wasn't willing to be part of."

"Thanks for saying so. Which just strengthens, like

you also said, how we're in this together and needing to stick with that in order to try and counter the bad turn. I won't forget again."

"I won't let you."

They both went suddenly quiet as there came a burst of snorting and slumber-deep groans and the brief thrashing of a heavy body from over where the bedrolls of the gang members were spread. After a few moments, everything settled back to the regular pattern of snores.

Then Tate whispered, "Seems like, while I was lost feeling sorry for myself, you went ahead and put in some thought about the fix we're in. You come up with anything that might help change it?"

"Nothing very concrete. But the added horses that man McLaffert returned with may offer some opportunities."

"How so?"

"It means that when we ride out again, this time we —along with Kettleman—will be on our own mounts. Still with our hands bound, no doubt, and with our horse likely tethered to that of one of the gang members. Nevertheless—"

"Nevertheless," Tate finished, seeing where she was headed, "it would give us a hell of a lot more freedom than we had earlier today when we were each practically strapped to the back of one of those curs."

"More freedom right at the start—and the possibility of even more if one of us managed to break loose from our tether."

"Whoa. What do you mean *one of us*? I thought we just got done settling how we were gonna always stick together."

"That means sticking together as far as looking out for one another, but not necessarily being directly at each other's side. Don't you see," said Miriella, "even if only one of us was able to escape, it could still benefit the other. Number one, it would split up the gang and force some of them to break away and give chase. That would give the remaining captive a better chance to make good his or her own escape. And if the first one got away clean, they'd have the chance to find help that could be brought back for a rescue."

It took a minute for Tate to respond. "Sounds to me like a lot of *ifs* and *maybes* in there. Starting with the *big if* of getting any chance to slip a tether in the first place. You can bet that Kettleman and Red Dog both will lay down some mighty strict orders to whoever's on the other end...still, it's *something*. A possibility. More than we had before...I gotta tell you, though, I don't know if I'd have it in me to ride away and leave you the way you're suggesting, no matter how much of a chance I got."

"If the opportunity presents itself, you *must* be willing to seize it!"

Miriella responded so intently that her voice rose higher in volume than she meant for it to. This caused her and Tate to once again go dead silent, listening to make sure none of their nearby captors had been aroused.

Once they were satisfied there was no sign of disturbance, Miriella spoke again. "Even if only one of us escapes," she insisted, "it is a victory over these evil men. And if it in some way ruins their ability to find the treasure they are so desperate for, all the better."

"The treasure," Tate chuffed softly. "Funny how—

speaking for myself at least—it no longer seems so all-consumingly important. Not compared to staying alive and getting away from these devils."

"Yes. Life should be viewed as the greatest fortune of all...in most instances," Miriella said.

Tate didn't respond right away, finding the phrasing a bit curious.

Before he had time to wonder about it for very long, Miriella added, "I want a promise from you, Senor. Over and above what we've already settled about you making a break if you get the chance."

In the dark, Tate frowned. "I didn't know that much was fully settled. And I'm not sure I feel any more at ease with how this is headed...but go on."

Miriella paused—choosing her words carefully, Tate sensed—then proceeded. "When I was a little girl, after my mother died suddenly, my father wanted to get away from everybody, from every reminder of her. He set out to pursue his dream of prospecting in remote mountains. At first, that included an attempt to leave me behind with relatives. But I begged so hard to go with him that he finally relented. The years that followed, though very lean and rugged at times, made for some of the best memories of my life. At one point, his brother Ignacio came and stayed and worked with my father for several months. It was during that time that they discovered the cave with the strange carvings and paintings on its walls—the one Uncle Ignacio mentioned in the message he sent with you from prison. At the time, however, my uncle proved to lack sufficient patience for the long, hard hours and uncertain yield that is prospecting. So he took what meager earnings his digging did produce and moved on. That was well before my father finally struck the substantial vein that allowed us to leave the mountains and for him to live out his declining years fairly comfortably back in Prescott."

Tate listened patiently, not sure where this was headed or how it was going to arrive at getting some sort of promise out of him.

"The matter of life and death," Miriella continued, "took on some very stark definitions during those prospecting years. First, of course, was the planning and stocking of adequate provisions. Then, there was the constant challenge of surviving the elements. But more than any of that, at least to the imaginative mind of a young girl, was the Indian threat."

"Indians?" Tate echoed.

"Apaches. Back in those days, they were still very much on the loose and always on the warpath. They would strike out on the flats—ranches and homesteads, freight haulers, sometimes even small settlements—then flee to hide up in the mountains when soldiers arrived to give chase."

"And your father took you into those same mountains, knowing that was where savages might be showing up?"

"It was where there was the best chance to find gold," Miriella answered, plainly seeing that as reasonable justification.

Tate refrained from further comment.

"My father was very skilled at sensing when the Apaches were anywhere near and at keeping our dig undiscovered by them," Miriella continued. "Yet he also knew there remained a chance he might be caught off guard. For this reason, he instilled in me some very grim truths. He explained how, if the Apaches captured him alive, they would torture him for an agonizingly long time before allowing him to die. If they captured me, I would either be taken back to the tribe where I would become a constantly abused and mistreated slave for as long as I could endure...or be immediately ravaged by my captors until they tired of taking turns with me and cut my throat."

"Jesus," Tate hissed, "those are some awful hard things to be telling a little girl!"

"They were important things for me to know and comprehend," Miriella countered. "It was what made the countermeasures we might have to take, understandable and bearable."

"What countermeasures?" Tate went ahead and asked the question but he already had a sickening feeling he knew what the answer was going to be.

Miriella confirmed this, saying, "To kill ourselves rather than fall into the hands of the Apaches. My father said he would do us both if that's what it came to. In the event he was unable to carry that out, it would fall to me. He had his own gun and he gave me a two-shot derringer that I carried with me all during our time in the mountains. We made a promise we would do everything in our power not to let the other or ourselves be taken alive."

"Jesus," Tate said in a hoarse whisper.

"That's the promise I want from you now, Senor," Miriella urged him. "I can't say for you, but when it comes to what this pack of filth will have in store for me when they decide the time is right, I don't see them being any better—maybe even worse—than those Apaches. If nothing happens to intervene between now and such a dreadful fate, if I'm unable to avert it on my own by doing something like maybe throwing myself from a high cliff, promise me you'll try to find a way to help me, to spare me. Cave in my skull with a rock if that's what it takes!"

Tate was unable to make the promise she so badly wanted to hear. All he could do was once again rasp out, "Jesus!"

10

"THEY SPENT THE NIGHT HERE, THEN BROKE CAMP and rode out early," said Arrow.

"How long?"

"Close to four hours ago."

Standing on the rim of Jackrabbit Tanks's lower pool with a dripping, freshly filled canteen in one hand, Braska frowned off toward the southwest. "Damn. I was hopin' our travelin' through part of the night would've narrowed the gap on 'em more than that. But with three of their horses carryin' double, their goin' is still bound to be slower than ours as the day's heat climbs. We'll have to settle for gainin' on 'em then."

"That would be true...except for a change that has occurred," Arrow replied.

Braska looked at him. "And that is?"

"The sign shows that one member of the gang left camp, angling back toward the east, and returned with three additional horses. All seven of those we pursue are now mounted individually."

"How the hell could that've happened?" Braska

demanded. "Where would they know to find extra horses out here in the middle of nowhere?"

"Without following the tracks of the one who went off," Arrow said, his tone surprisingly calm, "I can only guess. But the most likely answer is that the animals came from one of those ranches I told you are scattered widely hereabouts. Traveling in the day time, it could be the gang caught sight of one of them while we, passing in the dark of the moon, never noticed."

"And where there's a ranch," Braska mused, scowling, "it's only logical to reckon you'll find some horses—whether or not, like we already discussed when it comes to cutthroats like we're chasin', the rancher is lookin' to part with any or not."

Arrow adopted a scowl of his own. "Meaning the rancher involved may not have been left in very good shape as a result...do you think we should backtrack to where those three horses came from and find out?"

Braska thumbed back the brim of his hat and dragged the palm of his free hand down over his face. "Shit. That's a lousy choice to be faced with. Much as I don't want to lose any more ground to the bunch out ahead of us and the captives we know for sure they're draggin' with 'em, the thought of ridin' off and leavin' behind some poor bastard who might be layin' wounded or bad hurt don't hardly set easy neither."

"There's always a chance the horses were rounded up and taken quietly. Maybe the rancher isn't even aware yet they are missing," said Arrow. Then he added, "On the other hand, it could be the rancher was alerted and tried to interfere and the horse thief killed him. In that case, we would lose time going back and be too late to do any good regardless."

d some smoke rolling, they were
m to begin making out a few
three in number, all wearing wide-
ll sitting their saddles with the kind
nly comes from hours spent in one.
t surprisingly made them wranglers
ranch.

urprising, however, was the gradual
the centermost of the trio appeared to
ong, strawberry blonde hair flowing out
high-crowned Stetson, classic oval of a
y rounded shoulders...no, this definitely
ordinary ranch hand.

traightened up a little and hung his quirley
er of his mouth as the three checked down
rew rein a half dozen yards short of where he
waited for the dust cloud they carried with
roll past, then drawled amiably, "Mornin',

was the girl who responded, her tone crisp, her
r arrogant, almost haughty. "Who are you, and
business have you in these parts?" At no more
twenty-one or -two, she was in that transitioning
e between being called merely *cute* or *pretty* and
oming described as *beautiful*. Not even faded Levis
d a common checkered blouse could subdue that.
ler striking cobalt eyes, cupid's bow mouth, and the
high, firm breasts filling out that blouse were too much
woman.

Whether or not her arrogance came strictly from a
self-awareness of the effect her kind of beauty could
have, particularly on men, or if there was something
more in addition to that, Braska didn't know. But no

"M.

hi

appro
hunch
about tho

"Mayb
Arrow. "Dor
at ease?"

"You just
jabbed a thumb ov
drop back. Lose you
hurry to come out u
tions clear."

In a matter of secon
had ghosted out of sight.

Braska moved over to w
to a thorny bush a few feet
hung his canteen from her sadd
himself close to the booted Winc
from her shoulder. He gave the rifle
sure it was seated loose enough for an
that, he wished he had his Colt stra
waist—the one the damn outlaws had str

The riders coming out of the east w
nearer, though still just a knot of indisti
wrapped in the dust cloud their mounts were
up. Unhurriedly, Braska took the makings f
pocket and fashioned a cigarette as he watched
approach.

90

By the time he ha
close enough for hi
features. They were
brimmed hats and a
of easy grace that
This likely and n
from some nearby
What was
realization that
be a female. L
from under a
face, smooth
was not your
Braska
from a cor
and then
stood. H
them to
folks."
It
mann
what
than
sta
be
a

matter, he didn't like it worth a damn and was in no mood to pretend otherwise.

Taking the cigarette from his mouth, he said, "For starters, who I am is somebody who don't much cotton to gettin' barked at and made demands of. As to my business here, any fool oughta be able to figure it's on account of the water. Beyond that, it's my own."

This got a reaction out of more than just the girl. The hackles instantly raised on the men to either side of her and the hombre on her left, a burly number with mean, close-set eyes and a whisker-blued lantern jaw, didn't waste any time voicing his displeasure. "Here now, bub! That ain't no way to talk to any lady—and damn sure not the daughter of Ranse Brighton. You'd best be beggin' your pardon and doin' it mighty quick!"

In a low, flinty voice, Braska replied, "And what you'd best do, *bub*, is get yourself real comfortable waitin' for that to happen...'cause it's gonna take a long time before it does."

Lantern Jaw looked eagerly over at the girl. "How about it, Miss Tayla? All right I get down and teach some manners to this mouthy saddle tramp?"

A gleam of fierce excitement was quick to form in those lovely cobalt eyes of the young woman now identified as Tayla Brighton. "I think," she said coolly, "that would be a lesson well deserved. Go ahead, Fletch. But leave him in decent enough shape to still be able to give some answers about the Weldmans and those missing horses."

"You want some help?" asked the second wrangler, a middle-aged, average-sized number with a handlebar mustache.

"Naw, Burt, you just sit tight," Fletch told him with

a smug grin. Then added, "Less'n I need some help scrapin' him up after I'm done."

And so, just like that, Braska had a fight on his hands.

Fletch swung down from the saddle and came forward, his smug grin stretching wider and his balled fists held up high and ready. "You could have apologized the easy way, you dumb ass," he snarled. "But I'm kinda glad you didn't. This way I get to *knock* one out of you."

Braska said nothing. He studied the big talker's balance, how he carried himself, trying to judge if he actually knew anything about fighting or if he was just another bunkhouse roughneck. First impression was that he was somewhere in between.

Braska momentarily considered reaching for the Winchester, but dismissed the notion. This didn't have the feel of something likely to escalate into gunplay. At least not yet. And if it took a turn in that direction, he knew he could count on Arrow being ready to intervene. So, as long as the second wrangler, Burt, didn't try to horn in, Braska was okay with some one-on-one action. In fact, he realized, the general mood he was in almost welcomed the chance to offload some pent up aggression.

Snapping away his cigarette butt, he got himself set and moved to meet the advancing Fletch.

First, they traded a couple of feints, doing a little closer feeling-out of one another, then they suddenly clashed together in a flurry of hammering blows. Most of these were at least partially blocked and landed only glancingly. But then Braska got in a hard left hook to Fletch's ribs, knocking him sideways and pounding out a big gush of breath. He instantly followed with a right uppercut that streaked through the wrangler's guard and snapped his head back sharply when it landed. Fletch staggered away, spitting blood.

Braska lunged after him, but overestimated how telling the uppercut had been. This caused him to be left open for a right jab that snapped his own head sideways and jolted his forward momentum to a halt. The two men then stood toe-to-toe and traded another series of punches, mostly short, punishing body shots. Braska could sense that the layer of leaner, flatter muscles covering his torso was absorbing these better than Fletch, who packed plenty of beef in his shoulders and arms but also a bit too much around his middle. Each time Braska slammed a fist into his gut, it pounded out a loud grunt, and along with it, another gust of breath that was becoming harder and harder to suck back in.

Realizing the same thing, Fletch abruptly backpedaled away. He tried to hold Braska at bay with some straight jabs as he did so, at the same time gulping frantically to get some air back into his lungs.

The jabs worked for a little while, a couple of them even landing smartly, before Braska was able to bull through and go to work on Fletch's body again. He drove him back against the face of one of the large boulders heaped around the water pools, and that almost turned disastrous. Out of desperation, Fletch clawed into a crevice in the boulder and scooped out a handful of sand and gravel that he flung full into Braska's face. The result was twofold. First, it temporarily blinded Braska, then, when he inhaled sharply, it drew in a choking lungful of dust and grit.

Suddenly, Braska was little more than a coughing,

choking, half-blinded target for Fletch to begin punching at will. Now, he was the one being driven back, stumbling and flailing frantically in an attempt to block the blur of fists being driven relentlessly into him.

Twice he almost stumbled and fell, but Fletch grabbed him and held him so he could hit him some more. That was where the wrangler made his mistake. His greed to pile on punishment backfired when, in grabbing Braska the second time, he pressed too close and allowed Braska to grab back. Wrapping his fingers around what he recognized to be the bandanna hanging around Fletch's neck, Braska clutched it as tight as he could and used it to guide the head butt he rammed fiercely into Fletch's face. He heard the crunch of collapsing cartilage and felt the smear of hot blood and nose flesh flattening out. It felt so good he drew back his head and rammed it forward again.

Fletch howled in pain and tried to jerk away. But Braska wasn't ready for that quite yet. His vision partly returned, though still blurred and watery, he could make out things well enough to get in a couple additional blows aimed at bringing the battle to a close. What he landed was a left hook to the ribs that doubled Fletch forward—right into a waiting forearm uppercut.

The combination did the trick. Fletch fell straight back, like a falling tree, and when his shoulders hit the ground, it was clear they were going to stay there for a while. Clearing his throat, spitting the last of the grit out of his mouth, Braska took a lurching step forward.

Even with his vision not yet fully cleared, Braska was aware of any sudden movement by Burt. When he looked around, he saw that the man, though he remained in the saddle, had a six-gun drawn and aimed at him.

"That's close enough. You ain't gonna stomp him," Burt warned.

Braska scowled. "I never had any—"

His words were cut short by a strange whirring sound, turning instantly into a loud *thunk!* as an arrow streaked down and buried itself in Burt's saddle pommel. The wrangler was so startled by this that he recoiled to the point of nearly falling off his horse.

"Drop the gun or the next one pierces your heart!" This command was issued by Arrow, ringing down from where he stood on the crown of a high boulder, holding a drawn-back bow with a fresh shaft notched and aimed.

Burt let go of his gun like it was the working end of a hot branding iron, and without being told, thrust both hands above his shoulders.

But an infuriated Tayla Brighton was not so easily deterred. Shouting, "Oh no—to hell with that!" She dug her spurs savagely into the sleek black gelding she was astride and sent the beast hurtling straight toward Braska! At the same time, she raised the silver-knobbed quirt she'd been holding down along one thigh and cocked her arm back, ready to strike with it.

At the last possible instant, Braska spun away and managed to avoid being rammed by the black's shoulder. That wasn't enough, however, to save him from taking a stinging lash from the quirt, its leather tails slapping down hard across his shoulders.

Emitting a roar of pain and anger, Braska finished his spin and sprang immediately, desperately after his attacker before she had passed completely by. His right hand clamped on the arm still extended downward from swinging the quirt. Maintaining this grip, he started to pull Tayla backward out of her saddle as the black continued on. Lunging and reaching with his left, his fingers wrapped in her long hair and closed tight.

Screeching, "You dirty sonofabitch!" along with a string of other very unladylike words, Tayla was dragged, kicking and flailing from her horse.

Braska didn't let her hit the ground, though. Wrapping her in his strong arms, overpowering the ongoing attempts to kick and struggle loose and even bite the side of his face, he whirled her around and marched to the edge of the lower pool where he flung her out into the water, saying, "Your spoiled brat ass needs a good coolin' off, little girl!"

11

"THREE, FOUR MORNINGS A WEEK, ESPECIALLY since she broke in that black she calls *Thundercloud*," mustachioed Burt was explaining, "Miss Tayla likes to go on long rides, early-like, before it gets too hot. Her pa —that'd be Ranse Brighton, boss of the Slash B, the biggest spread hereabouts—worries about her running into trouble if she's too far out all on her own."

"From what I've seen," quipped Braska, "he oughta be more worried about anything or anybody she runs into."

Burt shrugged. "Since his wife, Tayla's ma, passed a couple years back and he has no other kids nor kin, I guess Ranse is, whatycall, overprotective. Anyway, unless she takes off without his knowing, whenever Tayla goes on one of her rides, he's taken to sending a couple of hands to follow along at a distance to make sure she's okay."

"Yeah, and that worked out real swell for me this morning, didn't it?" snapped a bedraggled-looking Tayla from where she sat on a nearby rock, wrapped in a bedroll blanket. "You two useless morons let me be nearly drowned by that big ape!"

Burt averted his eyes, unable to meet the fierce glare the girl was aiming his way. The other *useless moron*, Fletch, was sitting on another rock off to one side of Tayla, his head tipped back with a wadded bandanna held to his mashed nose, trying to get the bleeding stopped. Arrow was perched just above the pair, keeping a close eye on them.

Addressing the remark from Tayla, Braska said, "You had your chance to give an explanation of things, but all you wanted to do was cuss and call names. So I'll tell you just once more, like I told you then—less'n you want to be hogtied and have that blanket stuffed in your mouth to shut you up, best sit there and keep quiet while me and Burt finish our chin wag."

Now Tayla's glare turned to him, but unlike the old wrangler, Braska gave back as good as he got. Until, after several beats, it was Tayla who averted her eyes.

With that, Burt continued talking. "So anyway, as I guess you can see, this morning it was me and Fletch who drew the duty of tagging after Miss Tayla. Everything was going just fine, like it usually does, until we ran into Jeeter Dobbs riding hell-ablazin' on his way to the Slash B. He was coming from the Waldman place. That'd be Jim and Mary Waldman, who have a little spread up on Antelope Mesa. Jim used to work as a bronc buster for the Slash B. Still does, part-time, but nowadays is also trying to get his own horse breaking and training operation off the ground. Been doing okay, too, and Mary is about eight months along with their first child. That was why Jeeter was there—he was dropping off his ma, Mabel, who's a midwife from

Clavin's Crossing. She was gonna stay and see Mary through the final weeks 'til she gave birth.

"But when the Dobbses got there shortly after daybreak, they found things in a bad way with the Waldmans. Some horse thieves had hit their corral in the middle of the night, and when Jim tried to stop 'em he got shot up pretty bad. Mary dragged him in the house and was tending to his wounds the best she could, and that's how Jeeter and his ma found 'em." Burt's forehead puckered with concern. "Jim's still hanging on, but it's mighty touch and go. Mabel took over nursing him—and looking after Mary, too—and sent her son to get more help. That's when we ran into him."

"So, did you go to the Waldman place then?" Braska asked.

Burt nodded. "Sure. A-course. Straight off, after we let Jeeter continue on for more help. Wasn't a lot we could do once we got there, though. Not that Mabel wasn't already taking care of. So when Fletcher spotted sign—him a former Army man and still having a pretty good eye for that kind of thing—how it was only one rider who got away with three horses from the Waldman corral...well, that quick-like set a notion in Miss Tayla's mind that we oughta not waste no more time and should right away take after the thieving polecat."

Braska's eyebrows lifted. "And that struck you and Fletch, bein' assigned to look out for her safety, as a good idea?"

"Hell no, it didn't. We knew her pa would skin us alive for even *listening* to such a notion." Burt paused, the corners of his mouth pulling down hard. "But Miss

Tayla is a...a mighty strong-willed gal. After Fletch made the mistake of saying the tracks appeared to be headed in the direction of Jackrabbit Tanks, that was enough for her to be ready to strike out on her own. So, since there was no stopping her...well, we ended up here and I reckon you know the rest."

Once more, a blanket-wrapped, still-dripping Tayla Brighton could no longer hold her tongue. "Are you satisfied now, big man?" she demanded of Braska. "You not only interfered with the pursuit of a trigger-happy horse thief—maybe even a killer by now, if Jim Waldman isn't still clinging to life—but further, you incapacitated a man who was willing and able to stay tight on the trail before more precious time is lost!"

Braska turned his head and regarded her from under a cocked brow. "Do you hear yourself? You screech like a magpie, and make about as much sense."

"You go to hell."

"And, when you ain't usin' fancy words like *incapacitated*, you cuss like a muleskinner. Your old man must be proud of that."

Tayla's eyes flashed. "My father is very proud of me. And if you are anywhere in this territory when he finds out what you did to me—and to a pair of Slash B riders—you will damn well find out! He'll flay you to a pile of shredded meat and I will delight in providing the quirt to do it with."

"It's a damn shame something as pretty as you is so full of poison," Braska said, wagging his head in disgust. "But that's somebody else's worry, not mine."

"Don't count on that, big man. You've made an enemy of me. I don't forgive and I don't forget. Not ever."

Before Braska could reply to that, Arrow called down from his overlook. "Looks like we've got more company coming, Mr. Braska. Another bunch of riders approaching fast out of the east."

"Gee," said Tayla with a devilish smile. "I wonder who that could be."

Cutting his gaze to the east, Braska had no trouble spotting a new dust boil rolling toward them.

"Want me to disappear again?" asked Arrow.

Braska shook his head. "Do no good. Got three mouths here who'll be anxious to give you away. Keep in sight, but be ready to jump to cover if things take a wrong turn."

"Got it."

"And one more thing...if it's all the same to you, in case of such a turn, I'd feel better thinkin' you was reachin' for your Winchester this time instead of that bow."

Arrow responded in a way that was rare for him. He flashed a quick grin. "Whatever you say, Mr. Braska."

With that settled, Braska motioned Burt over to stand with Tayla and Fletch. He'd stripped them of their weapons earlier, leaving him now armed with his own Winchester plus Burt's six-shooter gripped in one hand and Fletch's Colt tucked in his belt. "Sit up straight and put on your best welcoming smiles for the company we got comin'," he advised the trio dryly.

"You go on feeling cocky and in control for the few moments you have left to do so," sneered Tayla. "But if our company turns out to be who I'm almost certain it is, your tune is going to change in a hurry."

It didn't take much longer to find out the identities

of the fast-approaching riders. They were three in number once again, and once again all cast from the wrangler mold, this time minus any females. The centermost rider, in this case, was a tall, beefy man with a square, ruddy face dominated by piercing eyes darting alertly from under a thick ledge of snow-white brows. He exuded power and leadership even from thirty yards out, and long before he and the others got close enough to draw rein, Braska knew he was looking at Ranse Brighton, boss of the Slash B.

"What in blazes is going on here?" came the expected demand.

And, equally expected, came the blurted response from Tayla before anybody else had the chance. "Be careful of these men, Father! They're ruthless villains who interfered with our pursuit of the horse thief who gunned down Jim Weldman. They may even be in cahoots with him! The big one beat Tom Fletcher senseless and tried to stomp him into the dirt. And then he tried to drown me in that pool of water!" Pausing for a quick gulp of air, she then concluded with, "And that savage up in the rocks threatened to kill Burt by putting an arrow through his heart!"

Brighton listened to all of this with no change in his stony expression. Only his eyes moved, flicking from one person to another as Tayla made reference to each. When she was done, his gaze returned to settle on Braska. "All that before breakfast," he said in a flat, unreadable tone. "You must be a real rip-roarer."

"If half of it was true," Braska drawled, "I'd plumb frighten myself."

"Now he's calling me a liar!" Tayla wailed.

Brighton heaved a weary sigh. "You had your say,

girl. Now pipe down your caterwauling and give me a chance to think and figure this the rest of the way out."

"What more is there to figure? I told you everything you need to know!"

"That's for me to decide. Like this, for instance: You two—Fletch and Burt—did you jackasses willingly go along with letting my daughter chase after a horse thief who'd plainly shown himself to be desperate and dangerous?"

Both men looked down at the ground and scuffed their feet like scolded schoolboys. "Jeez, Boss," muttered Fletch, his voice nasally and thick-sounding, "what was we supposed to do—hogtie her to keep her from takin' off on her own?"

"You goddamned right, if that's what it took to keep her from harm," Brighton barked in response. "Now, how about that busted beak of yours? True you got it from this stranger?"

"Yeah. But only because he got in a lucky—"

Brighton cut him off. "It don't matter! Saved me from doing it myself. Now the both of you saddle up and get out of my sight. Go back to the ranch and pack up your things. Then wait for me to return so's you can draw your pay, 'cause your incompetent asses are fired!"

"Father, that's not fair!" protested Tayla.

"If that's so, then give yourself a great big thanks," Brighton told her. "If you'd grow up and quit getting wild-ass notions that cause me to have to send men out with the impossible task of trying to hold you in check, then this kind of thing wouldn't be necessary at all."

"Maybe you could try *letting* me grow up and be a little bit wild instead of working so hard at keeping me smothered all the time! Did you ever think of that?"

For a long, tense moment father and daughter just stood glaring at one another. Until, abruptly, Tayla flung off her blanket and marched determinedly to her black gelding. As she slammed a foot into the stirrup and hoisted smoothly to the saddle, she said over her shoulder, "I'm going back to the ranch. With any luck, by the time you get there you'll be in a mood to fire me too!"

Wheeling the gelding, she put spurs to the sleek animal and went tearing away at a fierce gallop.

Brighton sat rigid astride his own horse, staring after her with his mouth pulled into a grimace. Then, with a choppy motion to the wrangler mounted next to him, a lean Mexican in a broad-brimmed sombrero, he said, "Go after her, Hermez. If she tries anything too crazy, you have my permission to throw a lasso on her and tie her to a corral post until I get there."

Hermez's expression became pinched with reluctance. "Senor Boss...given the state she is in, I do not want to be the next one put in a position to be fired if I am unable to—"

"I'll fire you right on the spot if you *don't* go after her!" Brighton bellowed. "You heard me give you permission to do whatever it takes. Now, damn it, get going!"

12

When it was down to only himself and one remaining wrangler facing Braska and Arrow, Ranse Brighton pinned Braska with a very direct stare from his piercing eyes and said, "I trust you aren't foolish enough to believe that any of what just happened leaves you two off the hook. I expect some straight answers out of you and will settle for nothing less."

The big rancher's awareness of the power he exuded—much like his daughter's awareness of the effect her beauty had—clearly made him used to getting his way when he spoke. Adding to this was how the tied-down double holsters and coiled spring readiness of the wrangler left saddled at his side painted the unmistakable picture of a skilled gunman ready to make sure his words were adhered to. So much for Simon Barkley's assessment, Braska recalled wryly, that no rancher anywhere in the vicinity had use for a hired gun. And yet, for all of that, there was somehow nothing annoyingly haughty or demanding in

Brighton's manner. It came across more like an *earned* expectation of respect.

To which Braska replied, "I got no problem with straight talk. As long as it cuts both ways, and questions ain't slammed down like high-handed demands."

This caused the gunny at Brighton's side to stiffen a little. But Brighton's expression didn't change. Until, after a beat, a corner of his mouth actually quirked up slightly. "High-handed and demanding...and certainly high-spirited, I might add. That is, if you're speaking in reference to my daughter?"

"Could be," Braska allowed.

"As you unfortunately witnessed, she's a handful even for me. Largely my own fault, I suppose, for spoiling her too much." Brighton heaved a sigh. "But she's mine and I love her, so I've got to deal with what I created."

Braska didn't know what to say to that so he stayed quiet.

Brighton cocked his head, and a kind of twinkle appeared in his eyes. "Did you really throw her in that pool of water?"

"Seemed like a good idea at the time. She was riled up mighty hot, I reckoned it a way to cool her down some."

"I'll have to remember that," Brighton said with a chuckle. "We've got plenty of water troughs around the ranch, it might be time to find a new use for some of them."

Braska cleared his throat. "If it's all the same to you, how about we get back around to that straight talk you wanted to have. You see, my friend and me are on the trail of some bad hombres and the longer we're delayed here the more ground they're gainin' on us."

"Bad hombres?" Brighton echoed.

"Matter of fact, I'm pretty sure the horse thief who shot your neighbor is likely tied to 'em," Braska told him.

"Well, good God, man, get on with it then. Tell me more!"

"Mr. Brighton—a minute?" spoke up the gunman at his side.

Brighton gave him a sharp look. "What is it, Reno?"

Reno pointed lazily. "That fella up there on the high rock is givin' me the willies. I don't cotton to him lookin' down on me like some hungry damn buzzard."

"That seems reasonable enough," said Brighton. Craning his neck to look up at Arrow, he called, "You up there! Get down here with the rest of us."

Arrow didn't move right away. Not until he called back, "That the way *you* want it, Mr. Braska?"

Braska suppressed a smile. Then he responded, "Sure, kid. It's okay. Come on down."

As Arrow descended, Brighton and Reno dismounted. Once all were gathered around the lower pool, Braska proceeded to relate how the stagecoach had been ambushed, the hostages taken, and the subsequent decision by him and Arrow to give pursuit. He pointed out the campfire ashes indicating where the gang had overnighted here at Jackrabbit Tanks, and with Arrow's aid, showed the sign of four horses arriving and seven continuing on—*after* gaining the three additional mounts stolen from Waldman. The tracks Arrow had discovered earlier, revealing one rider heading east out of camp and then returning with three new sets of tracks, had by now been obscured due to all of the recent arrivals coming in over the top of them. But Brighton had seen and heard enough.

"So the long and short of it," he summed up, "is that you're on the trail of five members of the Red Dog Blevins gang. That right?"

"What it boils down to," Braska allowed. Then he asked, "You familiar with Blevins's bunch?"

"I've heard some tales. That's as familiar as I ever wanted to be." Brighton looked grim. "If it's true they're up here in our neck of the woods, then it's a black day for the whole damn territory."

"I spent some time down in Texas awhile back," spoke up Reno. "I never ran directly afoul of Red Dog or any of his crew, but I once passed through a town shortly after they paid it a visit. They're a mighty rough pack."

Brighton eyed Braska and Arrow. "Which—if you don't mind my saying, and meaning no offense—makes setting out after 'em, just the two of you, a sign of being either a little touched in the head or possessing some powerful big sets of onions."

"Maybe a little of both," said Braska with a faint grin. "But don't misunderstand—we ain't goin' after the gang figurin' to take 'em on or try to apprehed 'em or nothing like that. That's the law's work. What we're lookin' to do is snatch those hostages free from them."

"Why? What makes the hostages important in the first place?" Brighton wanted to know.

Deciding not to get any more detailed than necessary, Braska answered, "Accordin' to what the coach driver and other passengers overheard after I got knocked out, the gang seems to think the man and girl they ended up haulin' off have some key information about a hidden gold mine or treasure of some kind off in the Sante Veyos Mountains."

"Oh, for Christ's sake," groaned Brighton. "Not the Diablo Gold again!"

Braska hid his surprise at the reference and waited for the rancher to say more.

"If it's what it sounds like—though it's hard to believe Red Dog would hear about it and take it serious enough after so long to come chasing it this far—then there's a legend about hidden treasure somewhere in the Sante Veyos that dates back to before the Civil War, back to right after the border conflict with Mexico." Brighton wagged in wonderment. "It supposedly was the plunder of another outlaw gang, damn near a small army, who raided far and wide and amassed, among other things, a collection of gold and silver artifacts. The gang called themselves the Diablo Lobos—the Devil Wolves—and were led by a half-breed Mexican named Wolfe. Story got built up that, before the Army cornered the Lobos and wiped 'em out, Wolfe hid a stash of this special treasure where only he and a select handful of his men knew. When all of them died fighting the Army, the legend got born that the treasure was still out there somewhere, waiting to be found."

"So there must have been others who came lookin' before this," said Braska.

Brighton chuffed disdainfully. "Oh, hell yes. Swarms of 'em over the years, crawling all over the Sante Veyos and surrounding hills like ants on a sugar cake. And everyone coming away as empty as a bald man's cap. Finally it tapered off, though, and I can't hardly remember the last time I heard anybody even mention the Diablo Gold."

Braska shrugged. "So *if* that's what this new trouble is centered around, then maybe some fresh interest was overdue. But, either way, it don't change what me and Arrow are set out to try and do."

"Which leads me to wonder, now that you've explained why the hostages are important to their captors—what makes them so important to you?"

"Speakin' for myself," Braska answered, "it goes partly to the man Tate being an old friend. Maybe not a real close one, but a friend all the same. The girl I know very little about, but she's with him. Moreover, she's in the hands of those animals and the thought of what they're bound to get around to doin' to her...well, you've got a daughter. I expect you understand plain enough."

Brighton gave no response, but the look that came over his face said he understood full well.

"Again speakin' for myself, and I guess overriding everything," Braska added, "is the fact I was ridin' shotgun on that stagecoach and it was my job to protect everybody. Failin' to do so don't set very well in my gut. Gettin' those hostages back would be a way to square things at least some amount."

Brighton regarded him closely once more. "Got to hand it to you, it's commendable to feel so dedicated about something. At the same time, however, it still doesn't make what you're attempting any less reckless or borderline crazy."

"Seems to me we already covered that."

"So we did." Brighton cut his gaze to Arrow. "So you're Arrow—both by name and deed, according to my daughter. It's taken me a while, but I recognize you now. You're Simon Barkley's son, aren't you? From the way station on the stage trail between Harrietville and Leaning Rock?"

Arrow acknowledged this with a silent nod.

"I make that run from time to time on business. I've met your folks, and by my personal experience and by reputation, they're fine people."

"Thank you for saying so. I feel the same."

Brighton frowned. "And your father has no problem with you participating in this dangerous venture with Braska?"

"My father understands that there are times when, to be a man, facing danger for the purpose of doing right is necessary," replied Arrow. "The captives deserve a chance. Mr. Braska represents that chance. Because I know the land and possess tracking skills, I was in a position to help. It is the right thing."

Brighton didn't say anything right away. Then: "Like I said, your father is a fine man. And it's clear he's raising a fine son."

"Again, thank you for saying so."

Turning to Braska, Brighton said, "I fear that me and mine have already delayed you too much. Was I twenty years younger without so much else to account for, I'd like to think I might be moved to ride with you." He sighed. "Wish I could help more, but it don't shake out that way. So the best I can do is get out of your way and wish you luck."

"Might be a smidge more," suggested Braska.

"Name it."

"When me and Arrow headed out—discountin' that bow he's packin'—we started a mite short on firepower due to Red Dog's bunch strippin' me and everybody else on the stage of all weapons. We only had a couple Winchesters and some spare cartridges that Simon Barkley luckily brung with him.

"But now, what with me relievin' Fletch and Burt of their hardware after buttin' heads with 'em, and then you runnin' 'em off as soon as you showed up...well, I still got their guns." Braska patted the six-shooters belonging to the two wranglers, where they remained tucked in his waistband. The empty holsters and gun belts that went with them, along with their rifles, lay on the ground nearby.

"So what are you getting at?" Brighton asked.

"I'm sayin'," Braska told him, "that even though our aim ain't to get in no gun battle with Red Dog's gang, I'd sure feel more comfortable hangin' on to these spare shooters and cartridges. Just in case." He paused, scrunching up his face. "But it plumb don't sit right with me to do what amounts to stealin' the gear of a couple hard-workin' punchers, even if they're numbskulls."

"I'm beginning to see. What I could do to help is cover the cost of those guns when I pay off Fletch and Burt, allowing you to keep 'em with a clear conscience. That it?"

"I'd be mighty obliged."

"You are one strange and crazy hombre, mister." Brighton huffed a short laugh. "But, for the sake of that young girl, if nothing else, I'll back your play as far as you keeping those guns. I'll square things with Fletch and Burt, you got my word. That'll leave you the guns *and* a clear conscience...I just hope that, if you have to use 'em, they help keep you alive."

13

"HEY, YOU TWO! HOLD UP, I WANT TO TALK WITH you!"

Although Fletcher and Burt had been dismissed from Jackrabbit Tanks well ahead of her own departure, the hard pace at which Tayla Brighton spurred her mount achieved catching up before they'd gone very far. When the pair drew rein and turned at her shout, however, the expressions they wore—especially that on the battered, black-eyed mug of Fletcher—were not very welcoming.

"I have a proposal that I think might appeal to you," she promptly announced upon reaching them.

"Don't count on it," responded a frowning Burt. "The last notion of yours we went along with got us fired. I for one don't want to get even more tangleways of your old man."

"Look, I'm sorry about that. I really am," Tayla assured him. "I had no idea the old rooster would react that way. If it's any consolation, he put me on the run, too. Which is all the more reason to listen to what I have in mind. It would spite my father and at the same time allow us to dish out a measure of well-deserved payback!"

"You sure you're talkin' to the right two hombres— you know, the ones you called *useless morons*?" Fletcher said tartly. "I'd think you would be lookin' for better stock than us to cast your loop at for an important new job."

Tayla scowled. "Okay, I guess I had that coming. But come on, you've been around me long enough to know I have a hot temper and a sharp tongue. It's hardly the first time I've snapped at you and plenty of other Slash B hands. You always seemed thick-skinned enough to take it before."

"We always before had jobs that made taking your sass part of keeping 'em," Burt reminded her.

"Very well. That's simple enough then," said Tayla. "All you have to do is view my proposal as a job—a far better-paying one, by the way, than you were getting from my father. Would that make my sass bearable once again?"

"Cut to it," growled Fletcher. "We're damn sure in the market for good payin' work. What is it you got in mind?"

"That mouthy so-and-so back there who humiliated the both of us—the one his half-breed pal called *Braska!*" Tayla's eyes flashed bright with anger. "That's *who* I've got in mind, and *what* I've got in mind, like I already said, is payback! I'll allow no man, especially no grubby saddle tramp, to treat me like that. When I said I meant for him to receive another taste of my quirt, I meant it and I'm talking a hell of a lot more than another mere strike across his shoulders. And I'd expect that you, Fletch, wouldn't mind another turn with him yourself—and you, Burt, maybe a chance to ram one of that half-breed's arrows back where the sun don't shine?"

By the time she was finished, Fletcher's mouth had pulled into a tight, grim line and his head was bobbing in agreement. When he spoke, his voice had an even harsher rasp than before. "You ain't necessarily wrong in what you're sayin'. Damn betcha I'd like another crack at that cocky bastard. But I ain't quite followin' where there's money to be made in it, and how do you figure to catch up with them two again?"

"The money is my department. I'll pay you and Burt to join me in this undertaking," Tayla told him. "Part of how you'll earn your portion is a further demonstration of your tracking skills. Following those tracks from the Waldman place to Jackrabbit Tanks was genuine, I trust—not some kind of fluke?"

"I can cut sign with the best of 'em," Fletcher said firmly.

Tayla started to say more, but Burt stopped her. "Hold on a minute. There's somebody coming."

They twisted in their saddles and looked back the way they had just come, back toward Jackrabbit Tanks. A lone rider in a wide-brimmed hat was approaching from there. It was Hermez, the sombreroed wrangler sent by Ranse Brighton as the latest shadow to keep an eye on his daughter. Hermez hesitated slightly at the sight of the three turning to look at him. But surely they recognized him, so what choice did he have but to continue on with his approach?

"Let me guess," Tayla snapped when he reached

them, "you're the latest bloodhound sicced on me by my father. Is that right?"

"He did not say it in such words, Senorita," Hermez answered, looking mournful. "He just wanted to make sure you remained safe."

"Same difference," Tayla stated sharply. "Well, as you can see, I *am* safe. And I have those previously assigned by him already looking after me. So go tell him that. Scat, get out of here!"

"Not so fast," objected Fletcher. "He goes back tellin' how you've hooked up with us again, it'll bring your old man a-whoopin'. What's more, he'll have Reno Coates with him. I ain't lookin' to tangle head-on with Ranse, and damn sure not if Reno's part of it. They catch even a whiff of this business you got in mind, they'll never give you a chance to get it off the ground."

"Not only that," Hermez was quick to add, "if I go back and tell your father I left you with those he now looks unfavorably upon, he will surely fire me too! I cannot afford that—I need this job."

Tayla's eyes narrowed shrewdly. "All right. What if I offered you a *better* job, Hermez?"

"I...I do not understand," stammered Hermez, looking confused and a little frightened.

"I don't have time to keep explaining and re-explaining," Tayla said through clenched teeth. "The bottom line is this: I'm prepared to pay each of you a hundred dollars—an extra twenty-five for you and your tracking skills, Fletch—to help me run down that impudent cur Braska and his half-breed sidekick! I have the money available at the ranch, where we'll have to return for weapons and provisions before heading out after them. You need to make up your minds, and do it quick. There's not a lot of time to waste or the whole opportunity will be lost."

Hermez's expression had turned from confusion to wide-eyed wonderment. "One hundred dollars, all at one time? Such a blessing! With that, I could return to my village in Chihuahua and be a very prominent man. I could make my sainted mother so proud in the final years before her passing."

"It'd make a helluva tidy road stake for strikin' out toward better things, that's for sure," allowed Fletcher. He eyed Tayla. "You hate mighty quick and mighty hard, don't you?"

"Don't ever forget it," she advised him icily.

Looking more thoughtful and notably less excited than the other two men, Burt said, "Take near an hour to make it back to the ranch, then however long to get outfitted, then another hour back to Jackrabbit Tanks as a starting point...leaves a mighty long, hard, hot day before we'd have any chance of catching up with those two."

"It can be done if we stay determined," Tayla insisted.

"And how many long, hard, hot days have we put in herdin' cows...for a lousy thirty a month and found?" asked Fletcher.

Burt sighed. "A lot. Too damn many, I reckon... okay. If we're gonna do this, then, like the lady said, we can't afford to waste any more time. Let's ride!"

———

"You wear that gun belt like you were born

to it," Braska observed, giving a head tip toward Arrow walking beside him.

The young man returned a somewhat sheepish look. "It is not the first time I have had one on," he said. "Though my father does not approve of handguns, I could not help but feel it would be worthwhile to learn how to use one. I seldom go against his wishes, but sometimes, one needs to proceed on his own when he feels strongly about something. So, about a year ago, a traveler on one of the stagecoaches showed great interest in a pair of moccasin boots I had made. When he offered to trade a spare gun belt and pistol for them, I accepted. Since then, unknown to anyone, I take them with me sometimes when I go hunting. Out where no one can see or hear, I practice."

THEY WERE MORE THAN TWO HOURS OUT FROM Jackrabbit Tanks, and the mid-morning heat was building fast and growing steadily more punishing. They had dismounted and were walking their horses for a ways, giving them a breather and letting them cool some before watering them and then returning to their saddles.

"So," Braska responded teasingly to what he'd just been told, "you're already a crack shot with a rifle and bow, but you're hankerin' to be a pistolero too, eh?"

"It is nothing like that," Arrow said. "But it seems there are some circumstances—like indoors, closer quarters, for instance—where a handgun is simply more practical. My grandfather, Strong Elk, my mother's father, believed a bow and a spear were adequate weapons for anything. My father, for years, thought the same of his Hawken rifle, and only recently has come to admit there are times when repeaters like a Winchester or a Henry are also worthy. I honor their beliefs, which is why I learned and continue to use both a bow and a rifle when they are suitable...but at the same time, I recognize they have limitations."

"I'd say that's pretty smart thinkin'," said Braska. "How are you doin' with that handgun when you take it out to practice?"

"Not as good as I do with my rifle or bow. But I'm improving. Mostly, when I take careful aim, I hit the targets I set up. The whole business about drawing and shooting fast, though...I don't seem to be having much luck with that."

"That's not all it's cracked up to be," Braska told him. "Nothing like the big talk you hear from some blowhards, or dang sure not like the stories in those pulp magazines. If you keep a steady hand and can hit what you mean to at a reasonable distance, that'll take you pretty far...providin' you ever *have* to use a hogleg, that is. And I hope you don't."

Arrow regarded him. "But you act and talk like a man who has...haven't you?"

Braska squinted out at the sun-blasted landscape ahead, having trouble meeting the kid's gaze. After a beat, he said, "Yeah. Unfortunately. But that don't make me no gun hand or nothing. Sometimes life takes a fella around some rough turns, and well, you have to act accordingly...ain't something I care to go into any more than that."

They walked a ways farther without talking.

Until Arrow said, "I have killed many animals on my hunts. But I have never faced a human enemy. My father—who, like you, has been put to that test and endured—assures me it is not a thing to hope for. Which I understand and believe. Yet there are times, such as now when we are about to confront some very evil men, when I can't help but wonder if I will measure up should the need arise."

"From everything I've seen and heard, you'll do fine if it comes to that," Braska told him. "You made a mighty strong showin' back at the Tanks when you sunk that arrow in the saddle of the one called Burt and scared the bejeebers out of him with the threat of sendin' the next one through his gizzard."

"Saying and doing are two different things. My hand was trembling all the while I held the second arrow drawn back, the one aimed at his chest."

"I'd still call that bein' ready and able—for doin' what you had to if it'd turned necessary."

"I just don't want to disappoint anyone. My father, you...or myself," Arrow said quietly.

Braska stopped walking and turned to regard the lad very directly. "You're about as far from bein' a disappointment as any young fella I ever came across. Comes to killin', just remember it's never wrong when survival is on the line. That means for food or other parts of an animal that can be put to use—and it means defendin' yourself or keepin' others from undeserved harm. You're smart enough to know the difference and strong enough to do what you have to if and when called upon. Don't doubt it."

With that, Braska turned to the horses. "Okay, let's us and our animals take on some water. After that we'll go back to ridin' and makin' up some ground."

They drank from their canteens and then watered

the horses from their hats. Before climbing back onto his Appaloosa, Arrow walked ahead to some previously deposited horse droppings. He squatted down, broke a stem off a scrubby bush and used it to poke at the droppings.

"What's it tell you?" Braska wanted to know.

"The hot sun dries such leavings very fast. This is clearly quite fresh, though. Three hours, maybe a little less."

"Good. We're gainin' on 'em. All the more reason to keep pushin'."

Arrow straightened up. "The want and need to keep pushing, as you say, is understandable. But at the same time, do you think there might be some benefit in not closing the gap on our quarry *too* fast?"

"You're gonna have to sift that a little finer. How might that be better?"

"Their pace and direction will have them reaching the next water hole, Bluecap Wells, at about dusk," Arrow explained. "They almost certainly will stop and make another night camp there. That will put them in a stationary position about the time we are closing in, leaving still plenty of light and an increased chance for them to spot us and be warned. But if we got near then held off closing the final gap until after dark, we could use the moonlight again, like we did last night, and have a chance of getting into the camp with the least risk of discovery or disturbance."

"By God, that's some slick thinkin'. I like the sound of it!" Braska declared.

"It will also help," Arrow added, "that the land as we travel farther south turns more broken, not nearly as flat. By the time we reach the Wells, there will be an increased number of rock outcrops and some small, twisty arroyos branching off to all sides. We will be able to use those to move in quite close before we hold up until the time is right. Then, if we can manage to scatter the outlaw horses after we retrieve the captives, those narrow canyons and arroyos will add to the difficulty of gathering them back up."

"Seems like that Army school your pa sent you to taught you more than just readin' and writin' and speakin' proper," Braska marveled. "If he'd left you there much longer, I wonder they wouldn't've made a general out of you by now!"

14

"I DON'T UNDERSTAND WHY YOU'RE BELLYACHING so much about the extra prints," Burt was saying. "Having 'em all jumbled together like they are just makes 'em easier to follow, don't it? Hell, this trail is marked so plain even I'd have no trouble sticking with it."

"I ain't complainin' about bein' able to make out the tracks so doggone easy," Fletcher snapped back. "What I'm findin' curious and wonderin' on so hard is where did they all came from, what do they mean?"

"How many horses altogether?"

"About seven, maybe eight. Hard to say more exact."

"Did they all get stamped down at the same time?"

"Pretty damn close. All sometime this mornin', that's for sure. If not all at the same time, then within just a few hours of each other."

"Are the two hombres we're after—" Burt started to ask.

But Fletcher cut him short. "What's with all the

questions? You tryin' to show I don't know what I'm lookin' at or something?"

The two were riding stirrup to stirrup a half dozen feet ahead of Tayla Brighton, with Hermez trailing just behind her. The four were barely out of sight from Jackrabbit Tanks, the spot where what Tayla viewed as her unforgivable humiliation had occurred, and subsequently the jumping-off point for their direct pursuit of those responsible in order to deliver payback. The interim spent going all the way back to the Slash B for a hurried bit of outfitting and then returning to the Tanks, circumventing wide to avoid encountering her father and Reno Coates, had already taken a toll of time and wear on the pursuers and their mounts, even as the meat of the rundown was just beginning. Adding to it was the weight of the steadily climbing temperature and the knowledge it would only prove more brutal before it eased at day's end.

And now, on top of all that, Fletcher was being slowed by his fretting over the discovery of so many more hoofprints leading away from the Tanks than just the pair they'd been expecting.

"Dad-blast it," Burt barked back at him now, "I wasn't meaning to call into question anything about your sign reading. What I was trying for was to figure out some explanation for those other prints so's you could concentrate on just doing the tracking we need you to do and keep us moving along. We got too much ground to make up to get bogged down by over-chewing something."

"You think I don't know that?" Fletcher growled. "But it's been my experience that it's never a bad thing to allow a little extra time for caution. What if those extra prints were made by a pack of hardcases passin' through here with reason to avoid folks? Matter of fact, it's kinda tough to think why *else* anybody' be on the move through this empty damn land. Case in point bein' the two we *do* know are out there ahead."

Burt frowned. "So, apart from them, the kind of welcome we might get was we to ride up unexpected-like on some different pack looking to keep clear of folks —that what's got your worry feathers so ruffled?"

"Uh-huh. Especially with Miss Tayla in our midst. That could bring on a situation to deal with that we ain't hardly—"

This time it was Tayla who did the interrupting, pulling up closer and wedging in between the pair. Back at the ranch she had changed to different attire, including trading her Levis for a split riding skirt. Even more notable than that, however, was the addition of an ivory-handled .38 caliber revolver pouched in a tooled leather holster belted around her trim waist. "Now hold on a minute. Remember me?" she said. "I'm hardly a delicate little flower who needs to be coddled and overly protected, no matter what my father thinks. I'm the reason we're even on this little trail ride, and I'm not about to let a handful of speculation over some odd development swerve us off course."

"Nobody said anything like that," Fletcher argued. "All I *did* say was—"

Tayla cut him short again. "Are the tracks of Braska and the half-breed in among these others? Answer me that."

"Even though I ain't sorted 'em out exact yet, they must be. Wasn't no other tracks leadin' away from the Tanks." Fletcher scowled. "The only print I can catch sight of for certain in this jumble is from one of the horses that got took from Waldman's place. It's got a crooked shoe on its right hind foot and that mark keeps showin' from time to time."

Tayla's eyebrows lifted. "Well, there you go. I'd say that right there explains everything we need to know about these tracks that have got, as Burt put it, your worry feathers so ruffled."

"It does? How?" said Burt.

"Don't you see?" Tayla replied impatiently. "This indicates that, even worse than what they did to me—to *us*—those two saddle tramps are horse thieves just like we suspected when we first rode up on them back at the Tanks. Hell, maybe by now they're even murderers too, if Jim Waldman didn't pull through."

The hang-jawed expressions on the faces of both Fletcher and Burt made it clear they weren't following her, not even a little bit. Sighing, Tayla proceeded to lay out more reasoning behind her claim. "One of the two must have done the horse stealing and shooting at Waldman's. While he was doing that, the second one must have hit some other outlying ranch—an act that didn't get reported right away, maybe because he left everybody dead in his wake. Anyway, the two scoundrels then re-joined at Jackrabbit Tanks with their stolen stock and were getting ready to ride off when we showed up. They would have had time to hide the animals farther back in the rocks when they saw us coming. Since we know there were three horses taken from Waldman's, if we figure the second man grabbed two or three more from another ranch, then that would add up to the seven or eight total sets of prints before us —*and* explain the why and how they got there."

Fletcher and Burt traded thoughtful looks.

"By God," said Burt. "You gotta admit that fits together with all the pieces we know. And it makes as much or more sense as, whatycall, the *co-incydance* of some hardcase pack just happening to roam through right about the same time."

Fletcher rubbed his jaw. "Yeah, I guess I gotta admit it does..."

"Good," declared Tayla. "So can we quit dragging our feet and get on with chasing down those two? If they're the horse thieves and possible killers we now believe them to be, we not only have to consider just settling our personal scores with them, but there'd also be the obligation of bringing them back to face legal charges." She paused, smiling smugly. "And don't think I wouldn't relish rubbing my father's nose in *that!*"

————

FRANK KETTLEMAN AND RED DOG BLEVINS RODE side by side at the head of a loosely spaced column. Behind them came Cotton Wilkes with Miriella Clemente following close to him, her wrists tied to her saddle horn and the reins of her mount tethered to Wilkes. Next came brooding Jeff Gint with Ira Tate attached to him in the same manner. Bringing up the rear was lean, lanky, hawk-faced McLaffert.

The pace they were maintaining was steady but moderate. The landscape stretching ahead and off to either side was a repeating pattern of low, lumpy hills and ragged rock outcrops cut randomly by sudden, sharp-edged arroyos and shallow wind blow-outs. The peak heat of the afternoon, hanging in the air as squirming, distorting vertical lines, turned the features of distant hills and outcrops into grotesque versions of their actual shape.

"At this rate," said Kettleman, mopping his narrow blade of a face with a bandanna, "we'll reach Bluecap Wells by dusk. No need to punish ourselves or our animals by pushing any harder. Once there, we will of course hold for the night. We'll sate ourselves on water and food and rest, then by tomorrow afternoon arrive at the Sante Veyos foothills."

"Arrivin' *any* damn place other than this gut-boilin' furnace floor we're ploddin' over right now sounds mighty good to me," growled Blevins.

Kettleman smiled thinly. "Have you so soon forgotten, Lieutenant, the numerous doorsteps to Hell that we stood at the foot of during the late war—and went charging through straight into the teeth of the Devil? We, though not without precious loss, survived those, didn't we?"

"Damn right we did," Blevins agreed.

"So, in this case, the Devil's fangs are rotted away. What we're charging into this time is the mere leavings —the *golden* leavings—of the Devil, now called Diablo. And while those previous charges and victories rang hollow, thanks to an overriding loss forced on us by the soul-wrenching surrender of others, *this* victory will turn that tide and be ours to claim and maintain solely for ourselves. Isn't a chance at the Diablo Gold worth enduring another breath of Hell?"

"Reckon that's what me and my boys came all the way from Texas to find out," replied Blevins. "Truth of the matter is, ever since the war, we ain't hardly done nothing *but* breath in whiffs of Hell and chase gold.

Unfortunately, what it got us ain't added up to nothing we can brag on. This here Diablo thing is a whole lot bigger than anything we ever went after before, though, so we'll have to see.

"But a big part of it, speakin' strictly for myself, is the chance to ride behind *you* again. That's what made those war years—even though we lost in the end, and the fightin' was bloody and awful at its thickest, and there was times we was cold and wet and half-starved— somehow seem to matter. So yeah, I'll follow you across this furnace floor and do my damnedest to help find that treasure. For you and for my men, for the poor scrapin's they've too often had to settle for. But I just want you to know that ridin' with you again, sir, is worth it no matter what else."

Kettleman regarded him. "I never doubted—then as now—that I could always count on you, Red. As for your words regarding me, they are very gratifying. I thank you."

The outlaw boss made a sour face. "I don't regret anything I said, but I'm glad the other fellas behind us didn't hear 'em. They think I'm an ornery, unfeelin' bastard who'd as soon chew off another man's ears as look at him. That's the best way to handle a bunch like them, so I can't let nothing different show."

Another thin smile from Kettleman. "I'll do my best not to let slip that you're anything less vicious than what you want them to believe."

They hadn't gone much farther before Jeff Gint called from back in the column, "Hey, Red! Ain't we ever gonna stop for some kind of breather?"

Blevins looked over at Kettleman. "Might not be a bad idea to walk the horses a spell, let 'em cool some then take on a little water before we finish the rest of the way to the Wells."

"Very well. Not unreasonable," Kettleman agreed. "But when it comes to any watering, hold off on our hostages." A sharp look from Blevins caused him to add, "I think it's time to give them a gentle reminder that our treatment of them could have been—and certainly *can be*—harsher than to date. They conferred during the night last night, as I expected. I further expect they will talk again tonight when they think it safe. If so, then having their food and water rations curbed, now as well as after we make camp, should start to inject in at least one of them some growing concern, perhaps a touch of desperation. That may help open the door to better cooperation once we get to the mountains."

"I get it. Reckon there are different ways of beatin' cooperation outta somebody, eh?" said Blevins with a sly grin.

"In a manner of speaking, yes."

Blevins wheeled his horse. "I'll spread word to walk the animals some—and hold off givin' any water to Tate or the girl."

15

WITH DUSK LESS THAN AN HOUR AWAY AND THE distinctly colored rocks that gave Bluecap Wells their name rising scarcely a quarter mile up ahead, Braska and Arrow were working their way closer, keeping unseen as they advanced through a series of deep gullies and twisty arroyos. The worst of the afternoon heat was abating and the shadows within the cuts eased it even a bit more.

Reaching a wide spot in a deep, particularly sheer-walled arroyo with some growth of coarse grass and bramble along its sides, Braska signaled a halt. "I'd say this looks like a pretty good spot to hold up until we're ready to make our move when the moon is right. What do you think?"

Arrow nodded. "I agree. It is well hidden, and close but not too close."

With that decided, they dismounted and saw to their horses—saddles stripped off, rubdowns and hatfuls of water, then staked to find what graze there was in the sparse patches of coarse, yellowish green grass. Only after the animals had been tended to did the men spread their gear and flop down to relax some themselves, leaning back against upturned saddles, mopping sweat and dust off their faces, sipping tepid water from their canteens.

At length, Braska said, "Strikes me there's no risk to buildin' a fire down in here. Neither the flames nor what little smoke these dry bramble stalks give off will be seen. And I sure could go for some hot coffee to wash down a bite of grub. How does that sound to you?"

Arrow flashed one of his rare smiles. "As you or my father would put it—I say that sounds mighty fine."

Braska sat up straighter. "In that case, maybe there's a way to make it even finer. As we were ridin' in, I noticed plenty of jackrabbit activity all around. Think there's enough light left for you to slip out with that bow of yours and silent-like bag a couple of those hoppers to cook over our fire? Fella can go a long way on jerky and hardtack if he has to, but a dose of hot coffee and fresh meat added in could give a real welcome boost."

Arrow was reaching for his bow and pack of feathered shafts before Braska was even done speaking. "You get a fire going," he said. "I'll return with some plump jacks by the time you have the coffee ready."

In a matter of seconds, the lithe young hunter had ghosted off into the shadows of descending evening. True to his word, he reappeared just as the pot of coffee Braska had set to brew over the fire he built was starting to bubble aromatically, from Arrow's belt hung three fat rabbits. These were promptly skinned and cut into meaty chunks spitted over the flames where they soon began to sizzle and drip fat, giving off their own aroma.

While he and Arrow sat back on their heels, sipping from cups of coffee and impatiently waiting for the pieces of meat to cook, Braska said, "Though we're confident they can't see the fire or any smoke, let's hope now that our neighbors don't catch a whiff of what we're cookin' and invite themselves over for supper. I'm too hungry to be in a sharin' mood—unless it was a chance to feed 'em some lead."

"Welcome as that last part might be, there's not much chance of any of it happening," Arrow replied. Then, sounding as if he'd taken Braska's remark more seriously than intended, he added, "For one thing, there is no breeze to carry any scent. For another, I'm not sure that bunch over there could follow it even if it reeked like a skunk."

"What makes you say that?" Braska asked from under a cocked brow.

Arrow chuffed disdainfully. "Those men. They may be dangerous and tough in many ways, but in the ways of open country and the desert, they are unwise, even foolish." He took a too-hurried sip of coffee and winced at the bite of its heat before continuing. "While I was out on my hunt, I found a high point that gave me good vantage for a look at their camp. As before, their horses are staked and their bedrolls are spread just a few yards away from the water pool— something no one with the most basic desert knowledge would ever do. You find the water, take what you need, then withdraw a safe distance to make your camp." Arrow paused again, wagging his head. "On top of that, the campfire they have burning, as you can see even from here, is large enough to be visible for miles. When you get a little closer, they are all gathered around it and exposed fully to its illumination."

"Did you see the captives?" Braska asked.

"Yes. They were bound and huddled together off to one side."

"Other than bein' tied, what was their condition?"

"They appeared to be unharmed," Arrow said in a tight voice. "But the look on the face of the girl—it was one of sheer terror." Again, he paused. This time, before continuing, he fixed Braska with a very direct look, and there was a somber, almost ominous glint in his dark eyes. "When I spoke before about being unsure if I had it in me to kill a man? I know now—having seen what I saw in the girl's eyes, watching the ruthless indifference of the men who put it there, sensing the deep evil they are soaked in...that, if the time came, I would have no compunction about killing such men."

Braska gave a faint nod. "Like I told you before, there are times when killin' ain't wrong. And to put a finer point on it, there are men who put themselves in the category of needin' it—men no better than rattlers or rabid dogs."

"If I'd had my rifle with me, maybe even with just my bow, I could have cut their number in half before they knew what hit them. Only that would have worked counter to our freeing the captives."

"That's right." Braska heaved a sigh. "And more's the damn shame that what we're after ain't so simple."

Deciding some of the meat must be done enough, Braska pulled one of the spit twigs away from the fire and began blowing on the impaled chunks to cool them sufficiently before taking a bite. Arrow followed suit.

After he'd enjoyed a couple mouthfuls of the jack,

his hunger making it delicious even though it was still a bit raw, Braska backhanded grease away from his mouth and spoke again. "The good news about the bad news is that those sloppy practices you're describin' can hopefully work to our advantage. If those varmints are spread out plain like you saw, then us goin' in by moonlight—maybe with that big campfire still throwin' some glow too—that oughta help bein' able to pick out the captives. That'll only leave spottin' where they might have a lookout posted."

"From what I saw, they didn't have any. I counted. All were gathered there around the fire."

"Yeah, but they were still gettin' settled, remember. Don't mean that, come full night when most are asleep, they won't want a set of eyes and ears left open." Braska rubbed his jaw. "On the other hand, them bein' as sloppy and arrogant as they're showin'...and who the hell do they have any reason to expect showin' up out here in the middle of nowhere anyway? Maybe they won't."

"We will watch and make certain, regardless," said Arrow.

Braska pulled another twig of meat off the fire, this one more thoroughly cooked and one he didn't tear into quite so ravenously. "Couple more things on my mind. If we succeed in snatchin' out the captives—whether we're able to scatter the gang's horses or not—from everything you've seen it seems a reasonable bet they don't have a top-notch tracker in their bunch. Agreed?"

Arrow just nodded.

"I'd further bet you're about as skilled at maskin' a trail as you are at trackin' one. So if we get Tate and the girl clear of that camp and make it out into this broken country, after that, we've got a pretty good chance of eludin' any chase from Red Dog and his boys."

Arrow nodded again and this time, said, "I believe that would be so, yes."

Braska tore off another bite of rabbit, finding this one tenderer and indeed more fully cooked. "So that leaves the question of water. We've already put a pretty good dent in the canteens we brought with us. Meanin' if we follow this plan the way we've built it so far, that won't leave no room for replenishin' our water supply at ol' Bluecap over yonder before we hightail it away with the captives. Plus we'll have their thirsts to also contend with from then on." Braska eyed his young companion. "But, the way you're always ponderin', I got a hunch you already have something in mind to address this. Care to share it?"

"Ten miles west of here," Arrow answered readily, "there is a small water seep. I was going to suggest we head there to refill our canteens. I cannot believe anyone in the gang would know of this place, and I would blur our tracks to make sure they could not follow. From there, I know other scattered small water holes across remote country. We could move in an irregular pattern, from one to the other, until we reached my father's place."

Braska grinned. "I knew you'd have something ready. And, until a few minutes ago, I would've followed that plan without question. But then you said that thing about when you were out on your rabbit hunt...how you could've started pickin' off Red Dog's men if that'd been your goal."

Arrow looked at him questioningly.

"Instead of just grabbin' the captives and goin' on

the run, turnin' ourselves into the hunted—what if we left room for a little huntin' of our own?" As he said this, Braska's expression took on a notable grimness. "Rather than grab Tate and the girl and head for that water seep, what if we only went as far as right back here? We could lay low again until the gang went off Hell a-whoopin' in search of us. That'd give us the chance to slip back to Bluecap in order to fill up on water. Then, with you readin' sign to keep us appraised of the search gang's movement out ahead of us, we'd still aim for your pa's place, but more directly. And if it happened any of those varmints got between us and where we want to go, this time, there'd be no reason to hold off thinnin' 'em out."

By the time he was finished, there was, in addition to the look on his face, a kind of wildness shining in Braska's eyes. The flickering campfire flames high-lighted this all the more.

Some of the same also glinted in Arrow's dark eyes. "No," he said in a somewhat hushed tone, "this time there would be none at all."

16

ONCE THE COFFEE AND MEAT WERE CONSUMED AND their plan was made and revised to as fine a point as they could make it, there was nothing left but to wait. That was often the hardest part.

On this occasion, however, for Braska, the chance at a respite was both welcome and much needed. He was operating in the neighborhood of fifty-plus hours without any sleep save for the brief nap he'd managed to grab last night at the site of the stagecoach ambush, before he and Arrow initially headed out on their track-down of the Blevins gang. The night before that had been spent with Maizie O'Dell in her room over the Whistle Wetter Saloon, and though certainly a pleasant dalliance, little in the way of sleep had been part of it. What was more, the time since then had not only demanded being awake but included two fistfights, getting a gun barrel bent over his head, countless hours under a brutal sun by turns on a stagecoach seat, on horseback, and even a self-imposed though still punishing stretch on shank's mare...all piling up to a grinding mound of exhaustion that Braska couldn't deny. His mind continued to churn restlessly, but his body had to shut down and recharge for a while, there was no two ways about it.

He addressed this now, grinding out a half-smoked cigarette and saying to Arrow, "I don't know about you, kid, but these old bones of mine are screamin' to have some sleep wrapped around 'em. We got about three hours before moon rise, and even after that, it wouldn't hurt to wait until a ways past midnight before makin' our move. That's when bodies, even ones belongin' to rats like them in the camp yonder, are deep in their slumber and tendin' toward bein' most vulnerable."

Arrow nodded. "Go ahead and rest. Sleep. I will wake you in five hours."

"What about you? You're comin' off a short night and a long day, too."

"I also will sleep. Then I will wake us both," Arrow assured him.

"Good enough," said Braska, smiling faintly in the gloom of the dying fire. In his time of being on the drift, he too, had developed a sort of inner alarm clock that he could set to roust himself on occasions when he desired to sleep for only a limited amount of time. He suspected his skill at this was probably not as finely honed as that of the Indian lad, though—especially not in his current state of exhaustion—so it was good to have Arrow on hand as a backup. Stretching out against his upturned saddle and shaking out a blanket he'd pulled from his bedroll, spreading it over his shoulders against the rapidly cooling air, he added, "Five hours then. I sure wouldn't want to sleep through the fun of yankin' Tate and the girl out to safety and leavin' Red

Dog's bunch to wake to nothing but empty tie ropes come mornin'."

Those might have been pleasant thoughts to doze off to. But Braska should have known better than to expect such things could truly play out so smoothly...

———

"Mr. Braska! Mr. Braska, wake up...something strange is happening!" These words came from Arrow, issued in a hushed but urgent tone.

Braska instantly jackknifed to a sitting position, flinging back the blanket and swinging up the already-drawn Colt he'd been holding down at his side. "What is it? What's wrong?"

His eyes swept the width of the arroyo. Arrow was standing at the south wall just a few feet away, poised in a half crouch with his rifle raised to chest level, peering intently over the rim of the cut. Overhead, the sky was awash with a spray of bright stars but the first pale glow of the moon was only just starting to show. No more than two hours had passed since Braska had gone to sleep.

He shoved to his feet and pressed in beside Arrow, asking in a hushed tone of his own, "What's goin' on?"

"A disturbance at the outlaw camp," Arrow answered, his gaze locked on the distant shadowy mounds that marked Bluecap Wells. "Four riders showed up a few minutes ago and approached the Wells in a very bold and reckless manner—calling ahead to the camp identifiable by its still burning camp-fire. They did not receive a welcome response."

Braska followed the line of his gaze and could

ake a slight
e west. That
ow shooting at

n the southwardly
ight on his heels, any
now completely gone,
renaline and a sense of
Miriella before they were

two men moved in a slightly
ture despite being deep in the cut
ere they'd likely go unnoticed, even
action of the gun battle that had
to the latter, after its initial frenzied
adence of the shooting had now changed,
ewhat more measured though still with
urries. It had broken down to—as Arrow put
des shooting at each other but with both accu-
nd advantage dulled by the murkiness and
ws of mere starlight. The outlaws had scrambled
over amid the rock formations around the water
ol, the new arrivals had done likewise behind
outlying boulders and in wind-scoured ground
depressions.

The crack and scream of lead fragments splattering
apart and ricocheting off into blackness followed the
majority of gunshots as rock surfaces were now taking
most of the bullet hits. That hadn't been the case
initially, though, as signaled by the cries and groans of
several men as a result of that first frantic volley. They'd
been joined by the scream of stricken horses too—for

place o...
argument...
flame licking...
fire. To the train...
able as the flash of a...
coming a split secon...
exploding bullet. Then, i...
more flashes and claps of gun...
front of the Bluecap mounds, ap...
vantage of Braska and Arrow—a gia...
dozen simultaneously erupting firecr...
scene.

"Jesus Christ!" Braska bit out through
teeth. "I don't know who those new riders are, bu...
just triggered a full-bore gun battle—and Tate and tr...
girl are right smack in the middle of it!"

"What do we do?" Arrow wanted to know.

Braska spun away from the arroyo wall and reached
for the Winchester booted to his saddle. Over his shoulder, he said, "We do what we came here to do, only
with all our careful plannin' shot to hell. But, more than
ever, we still gotta try to get 'em out of there!"

Stepping over next to him, Arrow said, "From my
hunt, I know the quickest way to reach the Wells. We

the most part, likely, the incoming mounts. Those not cut down could then be heard galloping away in terror, chased by curses and shouts of "Hold those horses!" While, in the outlaw camp, it was "Get the horses back —back farther in the rocks!". Yet even then, some of those animals had also emitted shrieks of pain and/or panic. And mingled in—sending an icy jolt through him —Braska thought he might have heard a brief, similar shriek coming from a female voice.

It was the command from somebody to "Kill that damn fire!" that plunged the scene into the deeper darkness that abruptly lessened the hits to flesh and bone for at least as long as it took night visions to become adjusted or the moon to fully rise. In the meantime, the assault on shadows and rocks continued.

Their own fire extinguished hours earlier and never being close enough to the one in the outlaw camp to have been affected by its glow, the sight of Braska and Arrow was already accustomed to what limited lighting was at hand. This, combined with Arrow's memory of the terrain from his earlier hunting foray, allowed them to progress rapidly toward the targeted western side of the Bluecap mound. Though they instinctively kept their movements as quiet as possible, the continuing exchanges of gunfire effectively countered any inadvertent sounds they did make.

Reaching the heap of blue-streaked rocks—many of the taller ones wind-rounded into massive egg shapes, others down at the base sharper-edged and weathered more raggedly—Braska and Arrow halted and appraised what now lay immediately before them. They were out of the arroyo, crossing a span of hard-packed ground with various-sized boulders scattered about. The moon

was rising steadily higher and brighter, casting everything in a blue-silver tint.

The water pool lay in a shallow, cavern-like recess
scooped into the north face of one of the largest egg-
shaped rocks. Centered in front of the recess was a
lumpy rock ridge about four feet high, tapering off at
the ends to leave a section of flat rock floor within the
side walls of the cavern. A pair of shooters were
currently throwing lead from this area—one flattened
out behind the ridge, one just around the corner of the
recess's near edge. Braska and Arrow could see the flash
of the latter's gun every time he fired, but the shooter
himself remained out of sight. Additional shots—
coming from somewhere past the ridge shooter—were
also popping periodically. All of this lay more or less in
front of where Braska and Arrow had halted.

Off to their left, out north of the water pool, only
two of the recently arrived riders seemed to be actively
firing from behind the cover of outlying boulders.
Incoming rounds from them continued regularly.

If their goal at that point had been merely to wipe
out or capture the Red Dog gang, Braska and Arrow
would have been well positioned to accomplish that by
boiling around the near edge of the recess in a surprise
attack with guns blazing. But, exactly as Arrow had
experienced earlier when he had the varmints in his
sights, it wasn't that simple. There was too much else to
consider—mainly, the safety of Tate and Miriella.
Where were they located? Somewhere farther back
within the recess, maybe? If so, charging blindly in with
blazing guns would damn near guarantee their harm,
not save them from it. What was more, openly exposing
themselves via their gun flashes—which, to the outlying

shooters, would look no different from those of the outlaws—Braska and Arrow would invite their own harm from incoming rounds before they could say or do anything to stop them.

Braska's mind churned, his thoughts bitter. *Damn it all, we didn't come this far, get this close, only to let it all turn to shit! There's got to be some way to—*

Arrow tugged at his sleeve. When Braska's gaze cut to him, the Indian lad pointed upward toward the higher rocks, then swung his finger up and over in a short arc before lowering it again to point at the opposite side of the cavern. Braska quickly saw what he was suggesting—that he climb up a ways and then work his way over to drop down on the far side. With him in position over there, they could call out and try to convince those in the recess—letting the outlying shooters also hear—that they were caught in a potential crossfire and would have no chance if they attempted to make a break or continue the fight. It was a crude and simple plan, but nothing better came to mind and there wasn't time to brain-wrack for options.

Braska gave a curt nod. Yeah, he was willing to give it a try. He waited for the bark of close gunfire to give his words extra cover, then leaned in and whispered tight to Arrow's ear, "I'll give you five minutes to get in place before I call out to 'em. Go!"

Arrow wheeled and began to climb, deftly balancing his rifle as his moccasin-clad feet seemed to find purchase like they had eyes. Braska stepped back and settled into a squat, watching, telling himself for the hundredth time how glad he was that he'd agreed to be sided by this young panther.

Scarcely had Arrow ascended half a dozen feet,

however, before everything took a sudden and unex-
pected turn. That was when the shooter who'd been
positioned just out of sight around the near edge of the
recess, decided to not only make himself seen but to do
so by hastily exiting the scooped-out area—and when he
did, practically bumping into Arrow's feet at eye level
on the rocks before him. The man—it was Jeff Gint,
though neither Braska nor Arrow had any way of
knowing his identity at that point—tilted back his head
and lifted wide eyes, blurting, "What the hell?"

Unfortunately, it wasn't just his eyes that he lifted.
The Colt .45 in his right fist also started to raise. Seeing
this, his presence going unnoticed by Gint, Braska
didn't take time to even straighten up. From his squat,
he triggered the already jacked and cocked Winchester
and sent a slug hammering into Gint's throat, just under
his Adam's apple. The big man flew backward as if
swatted by a giant invisible hand. But as he did so, a
dying spasm of his hand discharged the .45, and the
bullet it spewed screamed upward and splattered on the
rocky surface just a fraction of an inch from Arrow's
face. The Indian lad cried out, jerking away and losing
his grip, then toppled heavily to the hard, unforgiving
ground.

17

BRASKA SPRANG TO THE FALLEN ARROW AND dropped to one knee beside him. He set aside his Winchester, and his hands groped urgently, finding the lad's throat and feeling for a pulse. It was there, throbbing strong. But Braska also felt the sticky warmth of blood. Even as incoming rounds from the outlying boulders crashed and ricocheted off nearby rocks—drawn by his and Gint's gun flashes, exactly in keeping with Braska's earlier concerns—he hunkered low and searched for the source of Arrow's bleeding. Turning the unconscious lad's face up to a splash of moonlight, he saw it then. Just above his right eye, his forehead was torn by several short gashes from lead and rock shrapnel thrown by the near strike of Gint's bullet. Though freely dripping blood, none of this damage appeared especially deep or serious.

His own pulse hammering, Braska expelled a sigh of relief. He was hardly in a position to get too relaxed, though, not with bullets continuing to sizzle in and smack uncomfortably close. Twisting around, he shouted angrily, "Hold your goddamn fire, you idiots! We're on your side!"

That brought the incoming rounds to a stuttering pause. And, almost as quickly, it stirred another reaction. From inside the cavern, a panic-edged voice hollered, "They've circled 'round on us! We've got to get the hell out of here before we're trapped! Make for the horses—knock on it!" There followed the faintly echoing clatter of boots scrambling frantically on rocky flooring, accompanied by an equally frantic volley of outward-pouring gunfire.

Realizing whoever was left inside the recessed area was fleeing, escaping, Braska forced himself to hold in place. To stay hunkered low—partly for his own protection, partly to shield Arrow—until he felt certain they weren't at risk of drawing any more incoming fire. Bad as he wanted to take after the escapees, it wouldn't do much good if he rushed out and got inadvertently cut down after only a few steps.

No sooner had this thought crossed Braska's mind than the worry of more shots coming from the outlying boulders was suddenly reduced by half. As a result of that fleeing volley thrown by those within the cavern, one of the outside shooters stopped a bullet and cried out in mortal pain, "Aiieee, I am hit! Oh, God!"

Like a switch had been thrown, all shooting abruptly stopped.

There was a moment of heavy silence broken only by the painful groaning of the suffering man. Then it was joined, just briefly, by the muted stamping and shuffling of horses' hooves before this turned into the rumble of those same hooves galloping hard away and fading quickly.

Braska swore under his breath. The escape of the outlaws galled him, but he could accept it as a temporary setback in the hope that Tate and Miriella were with them and still safe—and as a trade-off for Arrow being hurt no worse than he appeared to be. As far as the latter, Braska's immediate intent was to lay out the lad as comfortably as he could make him while he went to fetch a hatful of water from the cavern pool and bring it back to clean his head wound and revive him.

Braska had started around into the cavern when the outlying victim voiced another long, ragged groan. It sounded like the poor devil was in a great deal of pain, and Braska felt for him, but Arrow remained his first and foremost priority. Until, that was, a voice spoke soothingly to the pain-racked man...a *female* voice, which was somewhat startling in and of itself, but making it even more so was the fact that Braska felt certain he recognized it. It seemed impossible, yet the certainty persisted.

"Try to hold still, Hermez...please...just lay back and let me keep this pressure applied to try and stop the—"

"It hurts so very bad, Senorita Tayla...I...I fear I will never again see my b-beloved Chihuahua nor my... my..."

"Hermez... Oh God no!... Not you too... Oh, God!"

Braska didn't know who Hermez was. But there wasn't a shred of doubt regarding the rest..."*Senorita Tayla*"...The female voice trying to comfort him belonged to none other than Tayla Brighton!

Realizing that his feet had dragged to a halt, Braska stood motionless and indecisive for a strained moment. Glancing back at Arrow, he could see his chest rising and falling with regular, even breaths. Out on the flat, cast in steadily brightening moonlight where she was on her knees beside the sprawled, bloody, totally still form of a man, Tayla was beginning to convulse with deep sobs—silent at first, but then gradually becoming loud, mournful wails.

Braska turned from the cavern and walked slowly out to her. As he drew nearer, he saw the bodies of two other men lying off to either side. One he recognized as Tom Fletcher, the other, though his face was lost in shadow, Braska had a pretty strong hunch was the wrangler called Burt. He then saw that the hombre Tayla was sobbing over was the Mexican who'd shown up back at Jackrabbit Tanks in the company of Ranse Brighton—only to be sent to follow and keep an eye on Tayla after she rode off in a snit. Braska recalled the fellow had balked some at the assignment. Considering how things had turned out for him and the other two Slash B men who'd pulled the same duty just prior to him, it looked like he should have balked harder.

Tayla's eyes lifted when Braska was standing over her. Her expression was one of torment, and her face was a smear of trail dust and tears. At the sight of him, she blurted between sobs, "You!"

"That's right. Me."

"B-but how...where...you weren't among the awful men in that camp...wh-where did you come from?"

"Me and my partner had our own camp, a cold one, a short ways to the north," Braska explained. "You rode past us in the dark. Reckon you aimed for the campfire you saw here at the Wells, figurin' it was us. That it?"

Tayla nodded distantly. "What reason to expect anybody else would be clear out this way?" Then, after having no choice but to use the back of her hand to make a very unladylike swipe at the tears and snot produced by her sobs, she spoke again in a low, sullen tone. "Who *were* those dreadful cretins, anyway?"

Braska pulled a wilted hanky from his pocket and held it out to her. "They're a ruthless outlaw gang up out of Texas. Lead by a hombre called Red Dog Blevins."

"Why in God's name didn't they stay in Texas?" Tayla wailed.

"Afraid God don't have much to do with the comin's and goin's of that crew."

Tayla blew her nose and then took to sobbing again. Braska left her alone for a minute or so. Then, gently, he said, "How about you come with me over to where the freshwater is? You can get cleaned up and try to settle down some. I've got to check on my partner over that way as well, he took a nasty spill. Then we can also work around to you tellin' me why you and yours had need to follow us all this way."

Tayla started to rise but then, after glancing down at the dead man practically in her lap, she sank back again and broke down anew. "This one, so gentle and kind...not at all coarse and rough, not even a little bit, not like Fletch and Burt and most of the others...a lost family man just wanting to scratch together enough money to make it back home to Mexico...and now I'm responsible for doing *this* to him!"

"I don't see no chains on him showin' he was dragged here by force," pointed out Braska. "He was a man growed who somewhere along the way made the decision to ride with you. Same for the other two. Ain't nothing can be done to go back and change that, or

nothing more to do for any of 'em right now. But what
you *can* do is come with me like I asked, start gettin'
yourself pulled together, and allow me the chance to see
to the needs of my partner."

This time, Tayla made it to her feet, though
unsteadily. Still shuddering with periodic sobs, she
pointedly did not look down again at Hermez or either
of the other two. She just jutted out her chin and looked
straight ahead, falling in behind Braska as he turned
and made for the cavern that contained the pool of fresh
water. Halfway there, Tayla stopped, doubled forward,
and heaved. When she was done, she straightened up
and continued on again without saying a word.

―――――

ONCE MORE, THE WALLS AND CURVED HALF DOME
of the cavern at the heart of Bluecap Wells pulsed and
writhed with the glow of a campfire. More than an hour
had passed since Braska coaxed Tayla here and then
also fetched a revived Arrow. Despite the latter's earlier
admonishment against making camp directly *at* a water
hole, Braska decided—for the sake of simplicity and
expediency—to remain and re-use what had already
been laid out before it was so hastily abandoned. This
allowed him to quickly re-stoke the fire from still smol-
dering coals and fuel already gathered, and then use
heated water and strips of cloth torn from strewn
bedroll blankets to cleanse and bind Arrow's wounds.
Tayla also used the hot water and blanket strips to clean
herself and begin re-building some composure.

As soon as the pair had been made relatively
comfortable, Braska went and retrieved his and Arrow's

horses from the arroyo. Leaving the Appaloosa for Arrow to tend to, he then mounted the bay and rode out in a wide sweep of the area to make sure that the driven-off gang wasn't perhaps still lurking close and getting ready to double back and retaliate. Turning up no sign of any such, he returned to the Bluecap mounds.

Arriving back at the cavern, Braska was surprised and pleased to find a pot of fresh coffee was waiting—brewed by none other than Tayla, he was informed. What was more, he discovered her and Arrow talking freely, almost cordially, in a manner that seemed to have carved away much of the tension to be expected for a situation like the one they were all caught up in.

Handing Braska a cup of coffee, Arrow said, "Here. You take care of putting away this, I'll take care of putting up your horse."

Braska cocked a brow. "Hadn't what you ought to be doin' is just sittin' back and takin' it a little easy?"

"That's what I've been trying to tell him," spoke up Tayla. "But he insists on prowling around like a restless colt."

Arrow frowned. "I fell down and took a bump to the head, that hardly makes me an invalid. Besides, I did not feel like sharing space with dead bodies any longer than necessary."

"He's talking about one of the outlaws we discovered after you rode off," Tayla explained. "He must have taken a bullet early on in the shooting, his body was lying farther back in this cave-like space. We spotted him in the campfire light. Arrow dragged him and the body of the other one, the one you shot, off into a jumble of boulders."

"They can stay there, undeserving of decent burials," Arrow said bitterly. "They can feed the coyotes and other scavengers after we are gone."

Saying this, he led the gelding off to where he'd earlier picketed his Appaloosa. Tayla's gaze followed him, then swung back to Braska. "I suppose I couldn't blame him or you if you felt the same about the men who rode with me, but I beg you not to. Their actions were the fault of me and what I acknowledge as my extreme and foolish pettiness. They already paid enough for that, they at least deserve better than to be left for scavenger meat. Give me something to dig with, I'll bury them myself if I have to!"

"I'm pretty sure we got it in us to do better than that," Braska told her. "For starters, I'll go out in a minute and bring their bodies up closer to the fire in order to keep the night critters away. Then, come mornin', we'll see what we can find to do some buryin' with."

"I'd be immensely grateful. Thank you."

Braska took a drink of his coffee, finding it considerably better than he would have expected from one so obviously pampered that she might not have developed anything in the way of kitchen skills. "You cook good coffee," he complicated her. "But now, since I don't know what you and Arrow may have already covered while I was gone, let's back up and start comparin' notes on what put each of us here. You can kick it off with the tellin' from your end..."

When all boiled down, it didn't take long.

A very contrite Tayla, speaking softly, huskily, choking back a few more sobs on occasion, related her side quick and straightforward. Other than explaining how she and her hirelings had come to believe Braska and Arrow truly were horse thieves and possibly murderers, she accepted full responsibility for the initial push to hunt them down out of her sheer obsession for personal payback. Upon hailing the camp of the Blevins gang in the mistaken belief of who it was they'd caught up with, the belligerence used to call them out was immediately met with counter-belligerence that quickly turned ugly. When one of the gang members spotted Tayla's undeniable female features and made a crude remark, Fletcher called him on it and put a hand threateningly to the gun on his hip. The response from the crude speaker had been to take it a step further—without hesitation, drawing his own gun and blowing Fletcher out of his saddle. "I guess you know how it went from there," Tayla said in weary summation.

After listening, minus any interruption, Braska poured himself some more coffee, lit a cigarette, and then proceeded to lay out the sequence of events that had brought him and Arrow to this point. The only thing he left out was his full back story with Ira Tate and the talk they'd had about the Diablo Gold. He mentioned hidden treasure only as far as what the stagecoach passengers had overheard when Tate and Miriella were being taken hostage.

That was enough, however, to get a reaction out of Tayla not too much different from the one displayed earlier by her father. "Good Lord!" she exclaimed. "It sounds like they're resurrecting that musty old legend about the Diablo Gold!"

"I don't know about that," Braska allowed. "But what I do know is that some very dangerous cutthroats have got a couple innocent people—one of them a young gal about your age—in their clutches. You heard just one crude remark that oughta give you a pretty good idea of how that bunch thinks when it comes to women. Gold or no gold...never mind what else...what do you think they got in mind for that gal, first chance they get, if we don't catch up and yank her away from 'em?"

Tayla gazed off to the south, the general direction of the Sante Veyos. "Oh, God...that poor girl," she whispered.

Her expression was deeply earnest, her tone sincere. To Braska, it looked and sounded genuine. At the same time, on reflection, it seemed so far removed from the brazen, mouthy, self-centered spoiled brat he had first encountered back at Jackrabbit Tanks that it was almost stunning. Braska couldn't help wondering how long it had been since Tayla Brighton had felt, let alone expressed out loud, so much compassion for someone else.

18

"I'M NOT EXACTLY SURE WHAT THIS IS...BUT I found it lurking in a dry wash about a quarter mile to the west of here."

So went the introduction given by Arrow upon his return to the commandeered camp, pushing ahead of him a bristly-bearded, sawed-off runt of a man clad in baggy, patched-over clothes and wearing the remnants of a black felt hat that looked like it had been chewed up and spat back out by a family of mountain goats.

The sun was barely an hour risen above the eastern horizon, having already burned all of the night's chill out of the air. A rekindled fire was once again crackling off to one side of the water pool, a fresh pot of coffee simmering on its edge coals. From where they'd been seated on low, flat boulders near the fire, Braska and Tayla now stood with cups of coffee in hand and came forward to greet Arrow and the guest he'd brought with him.

Before either of them could say anything, the guest beat them to it. And he had plenty to say. "What kind of scalawag outfit are you runnin' here—the two of you sittin' back all snug and peaceful-seemin' whilst you send yer pet hair lifter out sneakin' around to scare half to death a harmless old man who ain't got any years to spare!"

When he was finally able to get a word in, Braska responded, "Ease up, old timer, before you blow a gasket. You may not have many years left to spare, but it appears you got plenty of wind. How about you use some of it to tell us what's got you so worked up?"

"What's got me so..." The runt sputtered, his leathery, deeply tanned face taking on an exasperated purple tint. "You sufferin' heat stroke or some such? Don't you see the long, lanky, bow and arrow-packin' redskin standin' behind me, pushin' me around like a mongrel dog he's bringin' home for supper? And I'm sayin' *for* supper—as in, the main dish!"

Braska pooched his lips thoughtfully. "I see my partner standin' there, who is of Indian blood, true enough. I also see the string of jackrabbits hangin' on his belt that he went out to bag for our breakfast. Vittlewise, I don't see where a stringy, dried-up old cut of meat like you has any worry about bein' chose in place of them."

"Oh, that's cute. Real funny," barked the runt. "We'll see how funny you think it is when Geronimo Junior here gets you in closer to the mountains and then turns on you in the middle of the night so's he can serve up your scalp as a way to get in good with Sangriento!"

When Braska cut a questioning glance his way, Arrow merely spread his hands and said, "I cannot figure out his babbling. He has been spewing it since I came upon him. We should have brought along his burro that we left tied back in the wash—it might have made more sense."

"For crying out loud," said Tayla, setting aside her coffee and stepping forward. "Can't you see this poor old fellow is confused, and like he told you, scared half to death? My Spanish isn't the best, but I know enough to recognize that *Sangriento* means *blood*, or *bloody*—something like that. Just hearing it is enough to frighten me, too."

The old man shifted his gaze to Tayla, and his eyes brightened as if noticing her for the first time. "My apologies, ma'am. I didn't mean to scare you," he said in a much mellower tone than before. "But you should take heed. Whatever you're doin' here, wherever you're bound...please turn and head back north. Go back before Sangriento—and yes, that means *Bloody*, and yes that's the name he's hell-bent on livin' up to—raids back out of the Sante Veyos again and adds you to his list of victims."

"Who the hell is this Sangriento you keep yammerin' about?" demanded a scowling Braska. "And, come to think on it, who the hell are you? You got a name?"

"A-course, I got a name. It's Beedle, Alfred Beedle." The runt doffed his battered hat, unloosing a tangled swirl of snow-white hair, and bent at the waist, bowing smartly to Tayla. "At your service, ma'am."

"Judging by his burro and the equipment packed on it, he is a prospector," said Arrow. "Though apparently not a very successful one."

"Hah! Says you!" Beedle snorted in response. "Success can be measured in different ways, hair lifter. One, for me, is that I still got my scalp and all what's growin'

on. Two, in my time I have made and spent at least two
fortunes that would've satisfied most men for the rest of
their soft-handed lives. What's more, I was well on my
way to diggin' out a third when that Apache devil
Sangriento showed his red hide and caused me to pack
up my shovel and pull in my horns...for now. I allow as
to how I'll be back pickin' at that vein again as soon as
the Army comes 'round to put ol' Bloody in the ground
or back on the rez where he belongs."

"I thought all the Apaches hereabouts were already
penned up at San Carlos," said Braska.

"They are. 'Cept when they ain't. 'Cept every once
in a while when some young hotblood among 'em whips
up a handful of followers and leads 'em out on a tear to
re-live the old days. Reckon Ol' Bloody and his bunch is
the latest example. Way I heard, they've raised holy hell
out on the flats over the past week or so and now have
scrambled into the hills lookin' to shake the blue bellies
off their tails."

"And by *the hills*, you're meanin' the Sante Veyos
Mountains?"

"That's where they flushed me and Esmeralda—
that's my burro—out of, yeah. But if they're smart and
they really want to dodge gettin' caught up with, they'll
move on into the Spearpoints. Came down to it, that'd
be a good place to leave 'em rot."

"What are the Spearpoints?"

Beedle didn't answer right away. Passing the back of
one hand across his mouth, he looked past Braska and
Tayla and settled his gaze on the water pool. "Say, could
a fella get a drink of that water?" he asked. "Talkin's dry
work and I was kinda parched to start with."

"How about some coffee?" Tayla offered.

"That'd be swell. But just some water to start with, if you please. And Esmeralda could sure use some, too, if I can go fetch her before too long. The sight of Sangriento and his crew put us on the run unexpected-like with no chance to fill our water bags. By the time we made it here to the Wells last evenin', we was plenty dry —but it was too crowded to come on in. As I guess you know, it ain't hardly got no less so ever since. Plus, there was all that shootin' and hellfire in the dark last night."

Tayla handed him a cup of water. "Yes, we are unfortunately well aware of last night's shooting."

Saying this, she cast a brief, sad glance in the direction of a shallow gully some fifty yards off to the northeast where, while Arrow was out hunting, Braska had placed the bodies of the three Slash B wranglers. With Tayla's help he'd wrapped them in saddle blankets and covered them over with slabs of rock to shield them from scavengers. They'd marked the spot well in case Ranse Brighton wanted to send some men with a wagon at some later date to retrieve the bodies for a more proper burial on ranch property. Braska had also disposed of the two dead outlaws in a similar manner, though in a separate ditch and with less care.

Beedle drained the cup of water in two great gulps, emitting a satisfied sigh as he lowered it. "Boy, that hit the spot! Now, I'd be honored to have some of that coffee if the offer still stands."

As this further bit of hospitality was being extended, Arrow took the rabbits from his belt and laid them beside the fire. "I'll come back to skin these," he said. "But first, while he finishes talking—if he ever does —I will go get his burro so it can drink too." Then he glided away.

Looking after him, Beedle said, "Hair lifters are like that, ain't they? Never much on conversation."

Braska pinned him with a flinty look. "Quit callin' him *hair lifter*. His name is Arrow—use it, and use it respectfully. Him and his family are as fine a people as you'll ever meet. Now tell me more about these Spearpoints you mentioned..."

When all was said and done, Beedle's long-windedness provided some worthwhile information. That hardly meant it contained good news, not learning that a band of renegade Apaches was prowling somewhere smack in the path of where Blevins and his captives were headed. This also applied to Braska and Arrow following tight on their tails, of course, but at least they now had some warning there were renegades in the vicinity. Forewarned is forearmed, as the old saying went. To hell with Blevins and whatever was left of his crew if they walked into the teeth of the renegades—but as long as Tate and Miriella remained in their clutches, that meant the same risk for them. Making it all the more important and urgent for Braska and Arrow to catch up and yank them free.

In addition to just the raw information about Sangriento's presence, what else of value Beedle was able to provide were a couple of dirt-scratched trail maps and some verbal descriptions of key Sante Veyos features meant to help the hunters navigate once they got there. Among these, for whatever worth it might be, was the location of the old Diablo Lobos stronghold.

As for *the Spearpoints* that Beedle had spoken of, he explained that these were a small offshoot range of mountains stretching to the southeast. Though impressive neither in height nor span, they were known to contain viciously jagged peaks honeycombed by caves and sliced by pinched, sheer-walled canyons that meandered as aimlessly as fissures on a sheet of cracked ice.

"That's why some also call 'em the Hideaway Mountains," Beedle added. "But the trick has always been—and the reason I ain't ever ventured very far in myself, along with havin' no suspicion of any gold to be found there—findin' a way back *out* once a body has gone in too deep. Some claim that spikey ol' rock pile holds more picked-over bones of such lost souls than a hang rope ever would've claimed if those who got chased in had just gone ahead and put their fate in the hands of a judge and jury instead."

"Well, that makes for a real charmin' tale," Braska told him. "But luckily for us, our business—or, more to the point, the business of those we're after—seems targeted on the Sante Veyos."

Beedle chuckled dryly. "Yeah, the Sante Veyos and their legendary Diablo Gold." In explaining their reason for being in the area, Braska had once again given the vague explanation about the captive-taking outlaws they were pursuing having the end goal of *some kind of buried treasure,* and like practically everybody else, Beedle had immediately recognized what he was referring to. "It beats me how folks are so quick to look down their noses at ol' desert rats like me who dig for the kind of gold that God hisself put in the ground, but then some of those same ones'll backstab and throat-cut one another to scramble after a far-fetched tale about what got put there by some admitted scalawag."

"Ain't nothing far-fetched about the two captives our treasure-huntin' polecats have got with 'em," insisted Braska. "They're real and they're in danger.

Double danger now with renegade Apaches in the mix. That's why me and Arrow can't let up on tryin' to get to 'em in time."

"Nobody can call you short on nerve or stick-to-it-iveness, that's for sure. Good sense maybe, but not 'tother," Beedle declared. "So I'll wish you good luck and godspeed, but that don't mean me and Esmeralda ain't still gonna be headin' for Harrietville to lay low there until the Army gets those hair lift—er, I mean Apaches—put back where they belong. Until then, I got enough dust pouched up to keep us in grub and fresh straw in a livery stable stall we've shared before."

"That jibes with our plans just fine," said Braska. "Means you can escort Miss Tayla back that way as you go. Back as far as her pa's ranch where—"

"Whoa. Stop right there," Tayla cut him short. "No offense to Mr. Beedle's company, but I'm not going anywhere with anybody but you and Arrow."

"Oh no, you're not," Braska was quick to argue. "We've lost enough time already this mornin', we need to ride and ride hard in order to start gainin' some of it back."

"Thundercloud and I can keep up, as hard as you want to push," Tayla insisted. "Plus, if need be, I've already proven I can hold my own in a shootout."

While they'd been gleaning information out of Beedle, they'd finished a second pot of coffee and had cooked and eaten Arrow's rabbits. Now, they were all packed up and ready to move out. Both Fletcher's and Burt's horses had been shot dead during last night's gun battle. But Tayla's black gelding and Hermez's bay, after initially being frightened away by the gunfire, had come back around to the water before daybreak. Braska and Arrow had decided to utilize Hermez's former mount as a pack horse, loading it—after segregating sufficient supplies for Tayla and Beedle—with all the spare canteens, weapons, and other gear left behind by the fleeing outlaws.

The one thing they hadn't taken into account was how Tayla would feel about their plan.

Scowling fiercely, Braska said, "You can't be serious. You can't *want* to charge after those Texas varmints you almost lost your life to once already—not to mention runnin' the risk of tanglin' with a pack of renegade Injuns to boot. And even if I allowed it and we came through okay, what do you figure your old man would say to me for lettin' you take that risk? He'd have my onions danglin' off the flagpole in the front yard of his ranch house!"

"Who the hell are you—or my father either, for that matter—to think you have the right to *allow* me one way or another about anything!" Tayla bristled, planting her feet wide and thrusting out her chin defiantly. "You want to rescue those captives largely because, as the shotgun guard on that coach, you feel responsible for not keeping them from being taken in the first place. Right? How do you think I feel for leading Fletch, Burt, and Hermez to getting gunned down the way they did? What's more, if we hadn't come barging in and caused all of last night's chaos—again, thanks to me—then you and Arrow very likely would have been able to free those hostages during the wee hours and been done with it. There'd never have been the added risk of them or you needing to go anywhere near those renegades. Is it so hard to understand that I, too, feel an obligation to somehow try and offset all the wrong I've done? To not just turn and run away from it?"

Braska was caught flat-footed, rocked by this plea and the stated reasoning behind it. In a man, he would have immediately understood and admired such rationale...so why not the same for a woman? Did she deserve any less of a chance for atonement?

And then she drove in the final nail. "What about that girl captive? Who knows what those dreadful men might have put her through by the time you reach her? She could be in a state where you'd find it very useful having me, another woman, on hand to help comfort and console her."

Braska expelled an exasperated breath through his teeth. "I suppose if we tried to ride off and leave you, you'd follow anyway, wouldn't you?"

"You damn right I would. You'll have to finish drowning me to stop me."

"Don't tempt me. All right, saddle up then. I've already got outlaws and Injuns somewhere out ahead spoilin' for a fight, I'm too damn tired to pick another one with you too."

19

McLaffert caught up with the others as they were walking their horses, giving the animals a breather. He dismounted and fell in, walking beside Blevins. On the other side of the gang boss walked Ira Tate, his wrists bound in front of him and a tether strap running from around his neck to the grasp of Blevins's fist. Blevins also held the reins of his own mount, Tate's, and that of Miriella, who, due to her slight weight, was allowed to remain in the saddle with her wrists tied to the horn. Kettleman walked slightly ahead, leading his own horse.

"Well?" Blevins asked.

McLaffert mopped sweat from his face and spat dryly off to one side. "Nothing. Not a hint of anybody on our back trail."

Blevins nodded. "Good. Been long enough now that, if anybody was comin', you'd surely've seen a wisp of dust boil or something in all that flat empty behind us."

"Reckon so. But what does that leave then, as far as who it was who hit our camp last night?"

"Can't rightly say." Blevins frowned. "Couldn't've been law dogs—not that there's any way any law could know we're in these parts in the first place—or they'd be givin' chase. So the only thing that leaves, since we ain't all that far above the Rio, is plain old border-jumpin' bandits—out for any money they could've got off us along with our horses, saddles, guns, and any other gear they could turn around and sell."

"Well, they got some of that," McLaffert said bitterly. "But it cost 'em some, too."

"Yeah, it did. But I guess that's the risk scroungers like them are willn' to take."

McLaffert scowled fiercely. "I still think we should've circled back, waited 'til just before daybreak, then hit that camp—our *own* damn camp—and re-took it!"

"Yeah, we know that's what you think, Mac," Red Dog Blevins responded with a weary sigh. "We know it because we've heard you say it about a dozen goddamn times now. So that's enough, don't say it no more. We didn't circle back for the same reason we rattled our hocks gettin' clear of there to begin with—because some sonofabitch had got in position to put us in a crossfire, and I, for one, didn't feel like stickin' around and gettin' burned down by it!"

"But once they'd lost the edge of surprise, it would've been different," argued McLaffert. "There couldn't have been that many posin' such a threat. There was only four of 'em to start so—"

"There's where you're thinkin' falls short," Blevins cut him off. "True enough, we only saw four at the start, and I know damn well we cut down two of 'em right off the bat. So whoever came from the side and blew away Jeff wasn't part of that original four. Don't you get it? It had to've been somebody else entirely. Meanin' the first four was only part of a bigger bunch—or somebody altogether different showed up and decided to take sides."

McLaffert scrunched up his face. "Who'd do a thing like that? It wouldn't make sense."

"No, it wouldn't. So figurin' that side shooter was branched out from the four who let themselves be seen out front—likely him and even a couple more along with him—could've been a plan all along to catch us in a pincer in case trouble broke out. Only thing they didn't plan on was us bein' so quick-triggered when it came to dealin' with the first four."

"In other words," said Frank Kettleman over his shoulder, "your impulse to circle back for revenge and to reclaim some of the gear we were forced to leave behind—while certainly understandable, Mr. McLaffert—had the potential to encounter a larger awaiting force than we could afford to risk.

"So now we are left short on supplies and weapons and two close comrades have fallen. I deeply regret the loss. But with the mountains just hours ahead"—he swept his hand to indicate the reddish-brown sprawl of the Sante Veyos mounds and peaks rising in the near distance through the shimmering waves of midday heat —"the success of our undertaking is nearly at hand. We may be forced to endure one of the bitter truisms of the ages, that great achievement often only comes with great sacrifice, but we by-damn *will* achieve what we set out to do!"

Listening to this spiel and eyeing his former

commander as he marched—yes *marched*, as ramrod straight and chin-up, even out here in these baked-over damn barrens, as if he was crossing a parade ground before the high command—Blevins abruptly felt a twinge of something unimaginable. It was a feeling of uncertainty, maybe even doubt. Could it be that the major, one of the few men Blevins had ever looked up to, someone he'd followed unquestioningly into bloody battle, had gone a little mad with his obsession over this cursedly elusive treasure? God, Red Dog hoped not. It would be a final bitter blow to find out he'd let down Gint and Cotton Hawes—and maybe himself and McLaffert before it was done—over such a dismal turn.

Blevins jerked his thoughts back in line. No, the major was just *driven*, that was all, not mad. Driven the way a person had to be, exactly as he'd said, in order to achieve something big. After all, Tate and the girl were also after the same thing, and they had inside information handed down by one of the hombres who'd actually *been* a Diablo Lobo. You couldn't get much more real. All that was left was to get up into the mountains and then do whatever it took to force the captives to spill the individual pieces each was holding back so they could be fitted together for the final reveal.

In the meantime, the group continued wearily plodding—save for Kettleman and his disciplined posture—over the final stretch to those mountains.

"Once we're up into the foothills and I get my bearings," Kettleman spoke again, a continuation of seeking to provide reassurance and encouragement, "I know of several water sources complete with good graze for the animals and night shelter for ourselves. Wild game is plentiful in the lower reaches, too, so there's every reason to expect we can be dining on fresh meat for supper tonight."

"That's got a mighty nice sound to it," allowed Blevins. "Be a whole lot better to look forward to than just the jerky and hardtack we got in our saddlebags."

"Be better yet with some coffee to wash it down with," said McLaffert.

Blevins shot him an annoyed look. "Jesus Christ, Mac, do you have to take the most sour-assed outlook you possibly can at *everything*? I suppose if we find a bunch of gold and silver cups like is supposed to be among that treasure, the first thing you'll do is belly-ache. You ain't got no fancy wine or champagne to drink out of 'em?"

"So what if I do?" McLaffert snapped back. "A fella's got a right to have his own wishes and wants, don't he? Looks to me, the way this wild goose chase is goin', that's about all we're gonna—"

It was at that moment, while the two men were distracted by barking at one another, when Miriella chose to make a desperate attempt at breaking free. Shouting "Heeyah!" and digging her heels hard into the ribs of her mount, she caused the animal to bolt forward in a sudden leap, jerking its reins out of Blevins's grip. Then, leaning close over the saddle horn she was bound to, clutching as tight and best as she could to keep from getting pitched off, she shouted and clapped her heels all the more, urging a full-out gallop.

Blevins staggered, yanked off balance by the reins being ripped from his grasp. "Sonofabitch!" he bellowed, fighting to keep his grip on the reins of his horse and Tate's, as well as the tether to Tate's neck, all as both horses were rearing back and shying away from the commotion. "Get that damn girl before she breaks her neck!" he hollered to McLaffert, watching Miriella pick up speed while continuing to shout and dig with her heels, her uncontrolled mount veering wildly out toward the west with its reins streaming free and loose like wind-whipped ribbons.

As McLaffert struggled to get his horse turned so he'd be able to toe a stirrup and get mounted to give chase, Ira Tate suddenly dropped a shoulder and rammed it, backed by his full weight, hard into Red Dog's back. This knocked the gang boss off balance and sent him staggering into McLaffert, spoiling the latter's attempt to gain saddle and damn near toppling all three men. The air turned blue with an outburst of curses.

Blevins managed to stay upright by hanging on to the reins of the two horses he still had hold of. As soon as he had his footing more solidly under him, he lashed out viciously with the point of his elbow and drove it into the throat of the interfering Tate. "Goddamn you!" he snarled. Tate dropped to his knees, and the toe of Blevins's boot smashed into his ribs, knocking him flat. An instant later that same boot was raised over the prone man, this time its heel ready to slam down.

"Lieutenant! Red!" Kettleman's voice rang out sharply, halting the downward plunge of the boot heel. "He'll be of no use to us stomped to death."

Slowly, shakily, Blevins lowered his foot. He stood glaring down at Tate with fierce rage still burning in his eyes, his chest rising and falling in great, rapid breaths.

Kettleman spoke again, now in a strangely calm, almost gentle tone. "Mr. McLaffert, if you please...finish mounting your horse and go retrieve that foolishly troublesome girl."

It didn't take long for McLaffert's experienced horsemanship to catch up with a frantically, aimlessly fleeing Miriella. She glared at him with hate in her eyes and cursed him in Spanish all the way back to where the others waited. Once there, she turned sullenly silent. Though she had no way of knowing how close it had come to being worse, her forehead puckered with a mix of concern and sympathy at the sight of Tate sitting on his saddle, hunched in obvious pain from the blows he'd received trying to cover her attempted escape.

Wheeling his horse to face the captives, a flinty-eyed Kettleman declared, "Your treatment at our hands, up until now, has been far better than it had to be. This senseless episode has brought that to an end. You can look forward to a most unpleasant evening when we make camp, and that will be just a precursor to tomorrow. You have information I desire, and my patience is exhausted. Tomorrow, you will tell us everything we want to know. It will merely be a matter of how difficult you choose to make it on yourselves before doing so... now let's ride. We need to make up time and get up into those foothills before we lose the light."

Watching and listening to this, Blevins's earlier apprehension about the man he'd once followed into battle was effectively erased. Here was the same cold, commanding, no-nonsense leader he remembered. Not mad, just driven. And this time, after the battle had been engaged—and *won*—they would all come out draped not in medals or fleeting glory, but in the Devil's gold!

20

BRASKA, ARROW, AND TAYLA SET A STEADY, MILES-eating pace away from Bluecap Wells and through the heart of yet another punishingly hot day. Staying focused on the ever nearing outline of the Sante Veyos helped lure them on—that, along with the urgent, constant awareness of what their quarry was riding into unaware.

True to her word, Tayla kept up without lagging or uttering the slightest lament. This was helped considerably by a strong performance from the splendid black gelding that carried her. The same was, of course, true for Arrow's proud Appaloosa. More than once, Braska caught himself wishing he had Savvy, his own trusted buckskin who was stabled back in Leaning Rock, between his thighs, yet the steadfastness of the drab desert mare he'd bargained for after the stagecoach ambush really gave him nothing to complain about.

Inasmuch as Blevins's bunch stayed on a due south course, straight as a string, none of Arrow's tracking skills were put to the test. Once actually into the mountains, of course, it could become more challenging. The general information gotten from Beedle regarding certain trails and landmarks would be useful for general navigating, but that would be meaningless if those they were following veered off in different ways.

"Nevertheless," said Arrow with quiet confidence, though not being boastful, "the passage of any living thing leaves *some* sign if one is patient enough and careful enough to watch for it." He paused to show a rare, sly smile. "And the fact those we're after are on horses with iron shoes that scuff rocks and also have, er, requirements to frequently relieve themselves, will be helpful no matter how rugged the terrain."

"The horse apple trail," Tayla quipped. "There's one I bet they don't write about very often in those dime novels that seem all the rage."

Braska smiled wryly at the comment. He was still trying to get used to the transformed version of the petty, demanding spoiled brat they'd first encountered. Accepting this more likable side wasn't hurt by the fact she was so damned pretty. Hell, even Arrow, who held any outward display of his feelings so closely in check, was clearly a bit enchanted. Still, a cautionary voice kept whispering in Braska's ear. And then, overriding everything, was the circumstances they were caught up in. If he'd had any other choice, he wouldn't have been eager to drag even the bratty version of Tayla to within reach of what those mountains potentially held. He'd even toyed with the idea of chasing her and Arrow off to safety and leaving him to deal alone with this task he had initiated and set for himself. But, of course, neither would have ever gone along with that. Plus, Braska had to face another fact: Though it stung his pride some to admit, he was increasingly counting on Arrow's help to succeed. Moreover, Tate and Miiriella needed all the help they could get to have any chance at all.

With the long shadows and rose-gold hues of dusk settling over the terrain and the foothills of the mountains still more than two miles distant, Braska and Arrow once again decided to hold up and wait for moonrise before closing the rest of the way. Reckoning that Blevins's group had to be well up into the heights by then and assuming they might post a lookout, crossing that final stretch of relatively empty flat while it was still light would have exposed them like ants on a slice of bread. At best, it would have alerted their quarry they were in pursuit and near, at worst it might have set them up for an ambush as soon as they reached the high rocks.

To wait out the interim, they found a moderately deep ravine cut in behind a rectangular rock outcrop that hid them thoroughly from even an elevated vantage point up ahead. The floor of the ravine was dry and void of anything for the horses to graze on. They had plenty of water in their canteens, however, and they'd discovered a few pouches of grain in the confiscated outlaw gear that would suffice to tide the animals over. Confident there was no risk of a small, smokeless fire being spotted, especially with the murkiness of evening descending, Braska and Tayla gathered the fuel to get one going and brew a pot of coffee while Arrow went on another hunting excursion. He returned in short order, this time with a pair of plump sage hens.

As they waited for cuts of hen meat to cook on spits over the flames and with hot coffee warming themselves against the rapidly cooling air now that the sun was down, Tayla leaned back against her upturned saddle and said, "I grew up thinking that bows and arrows were awfully crude tools for making war or surviving. I see now, at least for the latter, they can be very useful."

"In the right hands, that is," Braska added. "You could send somebody like me out with the same rig, I'd likely lose all the arrows and come back empty-handed and starvin'."

Arrow smiled tolerently. "Not if, from the time you were no taller than an arrow, you were trained and had it drilled into you that a bow and a mere handful of strong shafts—silent, deadly, reusable, spent properly and wisely—were all one ever really needed to survive any situation."

"Havin' seen you in action, that ain't so hard to believe," said Braska. "Almost makes a body wonder how your side came up short in the Indian Wars."

This time, Arrow broke into the broadest grin, a full show of teeth, that Braska had ever seen him display. "Now you sound like my grandfather Strong Elk—that is a lament I have heard from him too many times to count!"

This got a good chuckle all the way around.

Until, his mouth pressing into a tight line, Braska muttered, "Let's just hope those Apaches up ahead, in case we're unlucky enough to run into 'em, ain't lookin' to try and make up the whole difference on this current tear of theirs."

———

WHILE BRASKA'S GROUP WAS BIDING THEIR TIME IN relative comfort within the outlying ravine, up in the lower reaches of the Sante Veyos, Ira Tate and Miriella Clemente were enduring their initial taste of Frank Kettleman's promised unpleasant treatment. First, they'd been stripped naked and shoved roughly together—chest to chest, stomach to stomach, thighs to thighs—then bound tightly in that manner, like a bundle of sticks. Next, they were tripped to the ground, hard and bare except for a gritty layer of dirt and bits of gravel that chewed their bared flesh between the strands of rope like broken glass. They were left like this with no cover or blanket against the cold bite of the night air.

That much alone would have made for many long hours of agony. Adding to it, however, was even more suffering bestowed on Tate as a result of the vicious kick he'd received earlier from Red Dog. It had broken two or three ribs, one of which was stabbing something inside that generated periodic bursts of painful coughing which each time brought a foam of blood to his lips.

"D-don't tell them," he urged Miriella through chattering teeth as the night grew colder. "It'll only m-make things worse."

"But it's my fault," she replied, stifling a sob. "If I hadn't tried to make my foolish break on that horse..."

"It d-don't matter...we have to stay strong...you know wh-what will happen as soon as we tell them what they want to know."

21

BRASKA, ARROW, AND TAYLA MADE THEIR moonlight move into the foothills without incident. They ascended as far as a grassy bowl scooped in under a cantilevered ridge and re-settled there for the balance of the night hours. All were exhausted and filled the time with another few winks of much-needed sleep. The last thing Braska remembered was the sound of the horses munching contentedly on the fresh grass.

Then, just after daybreak, he was awakened by the distant, though unmistakable, crack of a rifle shot. It brought him instantly out of his bedroll blankets and into a crouch, Colt in hand and traveling in a slow, flat arc under the matching sweep of his eyes. Six feet away, Arrow was also out of his blanket and going through duplicate motions though gripping a jacked and cocked Winchester rather than a handgun. In between them, Tayla was still in her blankets, propped up on elbows, wide eyes darting from one to the other.

After staying poised very still for a long beat, listening intently but hearing nothing more, Braska looked down at Tayla and motioned for her to stay right where she was. Gripping her pistol under her blankets, she nodded silently. Then, cutting his gaze to Arrow, Braska made a sign for him to circle out and around one end of the overhanging ridge while indicating he would do likewise at the opposite end. Arrow nodded and glided away. Taking time only to snatch up his own Winchester, Braska turned and threaded his way out through the picketed horses.

The morning was clear and crisp under a sky, still transitioning from pale gray to blue before another blazing afternoon would eventually turn it to burnished brass. Not a breath of air stirred and no sound carried on it.

Braska moved out the western end of the bowl, easing through some bramble and high weeds before ascending up onto bare, wind-scoured rock. He placed his feet carefully so as to keep his boot heels quieted and to not dislodge any loose stones. Twice, he paused and listened carefully. Nothing. Then he worked his way higher, angling slightly back toward the east, aiming for a notch in the rocks well above the ridge over the grassy bowl—a spot that looked like it would provide an elevated view without skylining himself. Plus, though sound traveled funny in this kind of broken terrain, he *thought* the rifle shot that wakened him seemed to have come from that general direction.

Halfway to the notch, he paused again. His ears had picked up a very faint sound from back down the way he'd come. The chuff of a horse? Possibly accompanied by the jingle of a bridle? Braska held fast and continued to listen. He was confident his group's horses were out of earshot, muted by the overhanging ridge. He heard nothing more. But then, when he'd just about decided the old mountain must have groaned somewhere down deep coming out of the night chill or his ears were just plain playing tricks on him, he heard a sound about which there could be no doubt.

It was Tayla's voice, calling out. "Braska! Arrow!"

It sent an instant jolt of alarm through him. And yet, even as he was wheeling about and starting back down toward it, he recognized that its tone did not seem to have a degree of urgency or fear to it. This was reinforced a moment later when she called additionally, "You need to come back to camp. Everything's okay, we have visitors!"

Braska slowed the pace of his downward plunge. *"Everything's okay...visitors..."* Those sounded like reassuring words, though at the same time, more than a little curious. His mind raced, part of him said to go ahead and let down his guard, but some intuitive suspicion warned him not to be too quick about it. Where would visitors come from, and what would make Tayla so sure they were *okay*? It couldn't be Apaches—they'd never give her the chance to call out at all. But somebody with a gun to her throat—somebody like Red Dog Blevins if he'd snuck up and got the drop on her—might force her into calling out whatever he wanted her to say.

Braska continued picking his way down slowly, quietly. Eyes sweeping, ears perked sharply. He wondered how Arrow was reacting. He had a pretty good hunch the Indian lad would be proceeding just as cautiously as he was.

And then Tayla called again. "There are soldiers here...a cavalry patrol out of Fort Driscoll!"

All of the tenseness left Braska in a great, gushing

sigh of relief. Soldiers! On the trail of Sangriento, of course. Something old Alfred Beedle had warned was in the offing. So, the events of the past few minutes all fit together. The faint bridle jingle and chuff of a horse —a cavalry trooper's horse—that Braska had overheard, followed shortly by the announcement of *visitors* that Tayla was so promptly willing to accept as being *okay*. The only part that remained uncertain was the origin and cause for the initial rifle shot. Had that come from the just-arriving troopers, or were they showing up in response to it?

The only way to find out, Braska told himself, was to get to where they were and ask. Which he proceeded to do, calling ahead to clearly identify himself and then crunching noisily through the high weeds and bramble that gave way to the western end of the grassy bowl. Threading his way back through his group's picketed horses was considerably more crowded this time with the added presence of a column of mounted troopers, sitting their saddles in await of word from their commanding officer.

The latter, dismounted and standing hat in hand over next to Tayla before the spread of saddles and bedroll blankets, was a tall, trim, ramrod-straight lieutenant, not too far into his twenties. Also dismounted and standing close by was a scowling, jut-jawed, towering human oak with sergeant's stripes on his sleeves. Next to him was a scruffy, bearded number wearing a buckskin shirt and cavalry trousers stuffed into high-topped moccasins, marking him as a civilian scout. The sergeant's hat was also removed and being held in his big paws, but the scout's remained perched atop his head with a long, bright-tipped feather sticking out of it.

"Braska," greeted a smiling Tayla as he strode up. "The lieutenant and his men are up here in the mountains pursuing the Apache renegades we heard about."

"I figured," said Braska.

The lieutenant introduced himself. "Lt. Micah Warren, C Company out of Fort Driscoll." He gave a curt nod, but did not offer to shake hands.

Braska nodded in return. "You can call me Braska."

Indicating the other two men, Warren said, "This is Sgt. O'Flynn and our scout Ebner Clapton."

Braska also traded nods with them.

The lieutenant continued brusquely, "Miss Brighton tells me your party is here in pursuit of some desperadoes?"

When Braska glanced Tayla's way she returned a quick, pinched-face look as if to indicate she'd been caught off guard as far as how else to explain their presence. Just as well, Braska decided. Might as well keep it simple and straightforward and not try beating around the bush too much. "That's right," he said. "I was riding shotgun guard for the Herbert & Haines stage run from Leaning Rock to Harrietville when we got ambushed by an outlaw gang. They took two of the passengers captive when they rode off. My partner and I set out after 'em. Miss Brighton and some wranglers from her ranch had the bad luck of runnin' into the bunch a ways back. Her wranglers didn't fare out too well, but she managed to get away and join us."

Warren arched a brow. "And you then brought her along to continue your pursuit of the outlaws?"

"Wasn't exactly a lot of other options."

"It didn't occur to you to take her somewhere to safety and *then* go back to your pursuit?"

Braska bristled, not at all liking the snotty, superior tone of this character. Before he could say anything more, though, Tayla quickly spoke up. "I *insisted* on remaining a part of pursuing of those villains, Lieutenant. To be clear, when Braska said my wranglers didn't fare out well in the encounter with them, what he meant was they were savagely gunned down. Three decent cowboys killed by a pack of human wolves. I may be a girl, but I'm no pampered princess—I was raised to stand up for those who ride for your brand, and that's what I mean to do."

Warren absorbed this response, regarding Tayla coolly throughout. When she was done, he said, "Under certain circumstances that may be a very bold, brave outlook, miss. But given all that we're dealing with here —since you've admitted your group is aware of the renegade break-out from the reservation—you'll have to pardon me for saying that I find it unwise at best, perhaps even a bit foolish."

"You are entitled to your opinion, Lieutenant," Tayla replied with ice dripping from each word.

But Braska wasn't feeling quite so tolerant. "Maybe, maybe not," he growled. "Callin' a gal *foolish* to her face, bub, don't hardly strike me as fittin' behavior from an officer and so-called gentleman."

"Here now! Watch yer mouth talkin' to the lieutenant," blurted Sgt. O'Flynn, taking a half step forward.

Warren held him in check with a hand placed against his chest. "At ease, O'Flynn." He then cut his eyes to Braska, meeting his glare. "I'd advise you the same, mister. Though I'll admit, I may have addressed Miss Brighton too bluntly. And for that, I sincerely apologize."

Shifting his gaze appealingly to Tayla, he added, "I can only say that my men and I just came from out on the flats, the basin, where Sangriento and his followers have been raiding for the past week. Some of what we saw there—what they left in their wake—makes it difficult to fully regain one's composure. Again, my apologies for my harshness."

Tayla met this with an impassive expression but no comment.

Turning back to Braska, Warren said, "You've mentioned a partner, another man. Where is he?"

"Reckon he'll be showin' up when he's ready. We heard a rifle shot a little bit ago," Braska explained, "so me and him spread out to investigate. Did that happen to come from one of your boys? Did you hear it as well?"

"No, it didn't come from us. But yes, we also heard it," Warren answered. "We arrived in these foothills late yesterday evening and made cold camp at a small stream a short distance west of here. We were just breaking camp this morning when some of the men heard that shot. We were on our way to check it out when Scout Clapton, in the lead, ran across your camp and Miss Brighton."

"And a pure-dee pleasure it was, too," spoke up Clapton. "A site better'n runnin' up on Ol' Bloody and his bunch, that's for sure."

"You really think that shot could've come from the Apaches?" Braska asked.

Rather stiffly, Warren replied, "At the time—though

Clapton expressed doubt they would be so careless, especially just one shot—we didn't realize there were so many other possible sources in the vicinity."

"Those red devils've picked up plenty of firearms durin' their raidin' out in the basin, that's no doubt," said Clapton. "But they've still got plenty of bows and arrers and such, too. If a buck was out huntin' that's what he would've used, keepin' his kill quiet-like. If he had to use a gun, it would've meant a fight and there would've been more than just one shot."

"Yes, Clapton. You've already made that assessment well known," Warren replied testily.

"Makes sense to me," allowed Braska. Then, addressing Clapton directly, he said, "That shot was some distance off. It sounded sorta to the south and east, but sound travels tricky through these hills and gaps. Was that the direction you figured it to come from?"

Clapton nodded. "Generally speakin', yeah. That's the way I was headin' us before—"

"And that's the way we'll continue to head," said Warren, cutting him short. "But first, there is the matter of..." Now he cut himself short, in a sense, letting his words trail off as his attention was drawn away by some commotion coming from the far end of the column of mounted men. He craned his neck, straining to look, before snapping, "Sgt. O'Flynn, what the devil is going on back there?"

O'Flynn wheeled and started in the direction of the commotion when one of the troopers from farther down the column came galloping wildly forward. He drew rein sharply, spraying dirt and dust. With wide eyes and a face twisted by anguish, he exclaimed, "Lieutenant!

Sergeant! You'd better come quick...Pvt. Mickles is gone!"

"Gone! Whatya mean *gone*?" boomed O'Flynn. "Ya mean the yellow rat deserted?"

"No...that is...well...I don't know! All of a sudden I looked around and him and his horse were just...just gone!"

"Uh-oh," Ebner Clapton muttered. "I think I've seen this before...and it ain't good. Not good at all."

22

"I TELL YOU IT AIN'T HALF BAD, MAJOR. ME AND the boys have got by on it before. Nice plump ones like this rascal that squirmed out practically under my nose, lookin' for a patch of warm mornin' sun, can be downright tasty."

"I'll take your word for it," Kettleman replied dryly. "When I said we could sustain ourselves on wild game once we got up into these mountains, I assure you I had in mind something considerably farther up nature's food chain than rattlesnake meat."

Red Dog Blevins chuckled. "Okay. I'm sure we'll soon run across something more to your likin'. In the meantime, this critter was too good to pass up shootin' to make breakfast for me and McLaffert."

"That better mean you saved some for me," came the voice of the latter as he strode into the camp.

"Sure did," said Blevins, pulling from the campfire a stick with a chunk of charred meat on it and holding it out. McLaffert took the offering as he sank down cross-legged.

"Did you see anything on your reconnoiter?" asked Kettleman.

"Nary a thing. Rocks and bushes and more rocks." McLaffert chewed a bite of meat. "Saw a whisker of movement down to the northwest, but it turned out to be just a skittish pronghorn."

"There's some wild game'd be more to your likin', Major," said Blevins.

"Perhaps. Except for the fact it's off in the wrong direction from where we'll be going."

Blevins lifted his brows. "Oh? What *is* our direction?"

"For starters, I had in mind to proceed to the old Diablo Lobo stronghold," Kettleman answered. "Maybe I'm just being sentimental, but it seems an appropriate place to begin what I intend to be the final—and finally *successful*—quest to retrieve the Diablo Gold. Maybe it will even help spur our two guests into being more cooperative toward accepting the inevitable."

"Speakin' of them," said Blevins, rising to his feet with a cup of coffee in hand, "we ain't heard from 'em yet this mornin' to see how they liked bein' cozied together all night long. I think it's time for the two lazy-boneses to be rousted up so's they can start enjoyin' a new day."

He walked over to where Tate and Miriella lay, still naked and bound together, on the bare, cold ground. They were positioned on their sides, her left, his right. Tate's face was turned down, his eyes closed, Miriella's eyes were open wide, glaring up at Blevins as he came to a halt, hovering above them.

He grinned nastily. "G'mornin' there, sunshine. I see you're awake but your friend is still snoozin', eh?"

"He is passed out," Miriella answered tersely. "He has been in great pain all night from the beating you gave him."

"Beatin'?" Blevins echoed. "I kicked him one time—you call that a beatin'? Hell, I been in brawls with fellas where we kicked and clubbed one another for a half hour or more before callin' it quits. Left both of us plenty bruised and limpin', but nobody curled up and whined about a beatin' afterward."

"Something is broken inside. He coughs and blood comes out his mouth."

"Is that so?" Blevins cocked an eyebrow. "You sure you and him, tied with your front parts all bare and jammed together like they are, didn't get to doin' a little ruttin' durin' the night and you ain't the one who tuckered him out so bad?"

"You are filth!" spat Miriella.

Blevins threw back his head and laughed. "Maybe so. But I ain't the one layin' in the dirt all trussed up like a hog ready to be dipped in the scaldin' pot, am I?"

"Is that supposed to frighten me—to think of it as a worse fate?"

Blevins laughed some more. "Oh, you're a spunky one, ain't you? That's good, that's just fine. Because before we're through with you, I *am* gonna treat you to some ruttin'—with a *real* man—and I like plenty of spunk!"

"I'd sooner lay with the scalding pot hog!"

"Since you put it that way," Blevins said, his mouth twisting into an evil smirk, "maybe we can fix you right up. You say you want to lay with somebody ready for scaldin'...how about this?"

Extending one arm out over the bound pair, he

rotated the hand holding the coffee cup and poured half its contents of steaming hot brew directly down on Tate's injured rib area. The man jerked back into consciousness with a scream of pain and was immediately sent into a spasm of coughing that spattered Miriella's cheek and bare shoulder with bright crimson blood.

As Tate struggled to get his coughing under control, Miriella threw back her head and wailed, "Enough! I will tell you everything I can—just don't torment him anymore!"

This brought Kettleman and McLaffert to their feet as if on springs, and then rushing in long strides to stand, bracketing a somewhat startled-looking Blevins.

Pinning Miriella with a stern, hard stare from his piercing blue eyes, Kettleman rumbled in a low voice, "If this is only more treachery, another foolish trick, girl, it will bring you agony you can't begin to imagine. Otherwise—"

"No! No, it is not a trick," she insisted, her eyes squeezed tightly shut, her face turned away from Tate's. "Cut us loose, cover us and do what you can to comfort him. Do that, I will reveal everything..."

———

THEY DIDN'T FIND MICKLES RIGHT AWAY. NOT ALL of him.

Lieutenant Warren, Sergeant O'Flynn, and Scout Clapton followed the agitated trooper who'd brought the matter to their attention—his name was Payton— back to the rear of the column. Along the way, the two officers gruffly ordered the other men in the line, mounted in standard side-by-side pairs, to remain in their saddles and hold in place.

Braska followed after them, urging Tayla to stay at the campsite and await the return of Arrow. She didn't like it, but she did as he asked.

At the far end of the column, where he and Mickles had been the last pair in line, Payton was now dismounted and talking, explaining excitedly. "When the man Braska showed up, returning to the lady's call, me and Mickles had to make room to let him by. As he made his way up the line, I—I sort of stayed shifted out some, I guess. Listening, and uh, concentrating to hear what was being said while—uh, while trying to get a better look at the lady. I swear it was for only a handful of seconds, not even a minute...but then, when I went to shift back straighter in line, Mickles wasn't there. He was gone!"

"Without a sound? Man and horse vaporized out of thin air from only a few feet away?" demanded Lieutenant Warren.

"Like a dog in heat!" spat O'Flynn. "So busy gawkin' to get a look at the woman ye wouldn't have noticed—"

"No! No, it wasn't like that, I tell you," protested Payton. "It was just a matter of a few seconds! I don't see how—"

"Back here," called Clapton's voice from a few yards away, back past some of the bramble and high weeds that choked one end of the grassy bowl.

The others trampled quickly to where he was and found him standing over a low spine of rock poking up out of the weeds. They followed his downward-cast eyes and had no trouble spotting the fresh smear of bright red that stained part of the rock's jagged crest.

"Aw, damn," groaned O'Flynn as they all stood momentarily frozen by the sight.

Then, breaking suddenly into motion and trying to push past Clapton, Payton blurted, "Well, come on! He can't be far and he may be only wounded! We've got to—"

The scout slammed a hand against his chest, halting him, and then shoved him roughly backward. "You ain't goin' no damn where! You're right about what's left of Mickles maybe not bein' far off—but he's past any help can be done for him, and any fool in too big a hurry to try would only be settin' hisself up to be the next one picked off!"

"What do you mean *picked off*?" demanded Warren. "By who?"

"The Apaches. Can't figure no other explanation."

"If they know we're here and mean to fight us, then why only pick off one man? Having caught us by surprise, why not a full attack?"

Clapton shook his head. "That's seldom the Apache way. They ain't like the Sioux or Cheyenne, or even the Comanche. They don't usually charge as a force very large in number. They hit fast—slash, kill, rob, burn— then move on equally fast. Didn't you see enough evidence of that out in the basin?"

"Then why bother with Mickles at all? Not to discount a man's life, but why bother to antagonize us for such minimal gain on their part?"

Clapton didn't answer right away, first taking time to drag a hand slowly down through his whiskers. Then: "You never can tell why or when any damn redskin will take a notion to do anything. In this case, though, they might not've seen it as bein' quite so minimal as you look at it. Thing is, they got themselves a nice solid horse for eatin'. An Apache's favorite meal, after mule, is horse meat. So what they did could have been as simple as that—grabbin' themselves some food." The scout shrugged fatalistically. "Could've also been some Apache sense of humor mixed in...toyin' with us. Lettin' us know that they know we're here, and showin' how they ain't all that scared by it. Up to and includin' makin' pretty easy work of claimin' a victim and helpin' themselves to some free grub all at the same time."

"Those savages damn well won't think it's easy work by the time we're through with them!" Warren exclaimed, his face flushed near purple with rage.

"We all feel the same way, Lieutenant. Now more than ever," Clapton allowed. "So I suggest a good first step toward gettin' that job done is to move this nice tidy line of targets the hell—er, that is, get this column relocated somewhere more in the open. Like that little meadow we passed through a little ways back, where they'll be able to see on all sides around 'em yet also have some brush and boulders for cover if need be."

"That ain't a half bad idea, sir," agreed O'Flynn. "I been feelin' a mite uneasy ever since we halted here, all bunched up under that high ridge like a thundercloud that could rain down arrows any second."

Warren scowled up at the cantilevered ridge, and then barked, "All right, prepare the men to move out. Tell them to look sharp and have their carbines at the ready."

"But what about Mickles? We can't just ride off and leave him!" wailed Payton.

"Let me worry about him," said Clapton. "I need to go check for sign on how many bushy-hairs was skimmin' on our heels and which way they went anyhow. I find Mickles, I'll take care of him for temporary, until we can come back and fetch him proper. Besides, boy, nobody ought to be in a hurry to see what I'm likely to find if I do come on what they left."

Despite the gruffness in his voice, O'Flynn put a big hand on Payton's shoulder with surprising gentleness. "Get back on your horse, trooper. Come ride beside me for a spell."

Warren turned to Braska. "You and your party have five minutes to gather your gear and saddle up. Obviously, in view of this new development, you will be accepting my offer for an escort away from here and not be continuing your—"

Braska held up a hand and stopped him. "No, that *ain't* altogether obvious, Lieutenant. I'm in hopes Miss Brighton may accept your offer, and will in fact encourage her to do so. But speakin' for myself, and I'm sure, my partner—the answer is still thanks but no thanks. We'll be stickin' around and keepin' after those stage robbers I told you about."

Warren went rigid in his stance. "Then I will say once again—and this time with no apologies—you, sir, are a damn fool!"

Braska's mouth spread in a thin, humorless grin. "That may be. But I wouldn't make a habit of sayin' it too many more times, buster. So let's just get out of each other's way and call it even."

23

"*THE THREE WIDOWS...IN THE CAVE OF THE ANCIENTS.*
That was the message Uncle Ignacio gave Ira Tate to
pass on to my father."

So reported Miriella to Frank Kettleman and Red
Dog Blevins after they had kept their word to untie her
and Tate and make them reasonably comfortable. This
included allowing them to once again get dressed—a
painful ordeal for Tate, given his battered ribs—and
then to each sit shrouded in a blanket beside the campfire with a cup of coffee in hand. Before Tate put on his
shirt, Kettleman, with the aid of McLaffert, sliced a
separate blanket into long, wide strips and secured
these snugly about Tate's middle to prevent sudden
deep breaths and thus help control his coughing fits.
The former major appeared to have some cursory
knowledge about such matters.

Now, having heard the girl's opening words when it
came time for her to *reveal everything*, the expression
Kettleman showed in response was one of quick, angry

dissatisfaction. "What the hell!" he snarled. "Riddles? *That* is supposed to mean something?"

"It would have to my father," Miriella was quick to explain. Then she added, "And though Uncle Igacio did not know he was dead, it happens those words also have meaning to me."

Kettleman's scowl relaxed some. "That sounds more promising. Go on with your telling."

"Yeah, cut through the bullshit about ancient widows with paintings!" Blevins advised harshly.

Sitting with his head hung low, taking occasional sips of his coffee, Tate murmured dully, "I'm begging you, Miriella...stop before it's too late."

"Any more noise like that outta the hole under your nose," Blevins warned, "the only thing it's gonna be too late for is you! It's becomin' pretty clear the girl is the one with the real goods, so it ain't gonna matter a hell of a lot if I go ahead and finish cavin' your ribs in the rest of the way."

"It will matter to me," Miriella protested. "If you attempt doing that to him, then my cooperation will end! And what I know of value to you cannot be told merely by words, cannot be achieved by trying to torture it out of me—I must be left in a condition where I am able to *show* you."

"Damn it, everybody calm down." Kettleman's voice was tight, barely controlled. "That includes you, Lieutenant. And as for your Mr. Tate, miss, we will refrain from further punishing him—as agreed—but that doesn't mean he can't be gagged and removed to where he won't be a distraction if he continues to interrupt. Understood?"

"Did you hear that?" Miriella said, glaring at Tate. "Stay quiet. I know what I am doing."

Tate once again hung his head, unable to meet her glare and saying nothing more.

Nobody spoke for a tense beat. Until, after taking a drink of her coffee, Miriella broke the silence. "The three widows are a term that my father and Uncle Ignacio came up with years ago regarding three gray, barren mountain peaks that stand in a row and are all tilted slightly at their tips. My father and uncle thought they resembled three widows with their heads bowed in mourning. This was from a time, after my mother passed away and I was a little girl living with my father as he prospected all through these mountains, when Uncle Ignacio came and stayed with us for a few months. The prospecting life was not for him, however, and he soon moved on.

"But during the time he was with us, though we found no gold of any significance, we did come upon a cave in among the three widows where there were carvings and crude paintings on its walls put there by people from some long ago time."

"The cave of the ancients," Kettleman repeated, his voice taking on a strangely hushed quality.

Miriella nodded. "Yes. So that is the place Uncle Ignacio was referring to in the message he sent with Tate."

"So what? What does some moldy old cave with pictures scratched on its walls have to do with the Diablo Gold?" grumbled Blevins.

"Don't you see?" said Kettleman, his mouth curved in a cunning smile. "If Ignacio Clemente was part of the select group of men Ed Wolfe chose to accompany him when he hid the artifacts they separated from the regular Lobo plunder, and Ignacio happened to know of this ancient cave from his past prospecting days..."

Blevins's eyebrows lifted. "So *that's* where the Diablo Gold is stashed?"

"It certainly sounds like that's what Ignacio was implying in his dying message sent to his brother." Kettleman cut his gaze sharply to Miriella. "And that's *all* there was to his message?"

"Si. That is all he told Senor Tate."

"And you obviously concluded the same—that your uncle was identifying the long-sought location of the treasure?"

"It was what Tate and I came to find out," Miriella confirmed.

Tate issued a muted, remorseful groan.

Kettleman leaned back, regarding the girl closely. "So you can't draw a map or provide adequate verbal directions, which is why Tate had to bring you along, but you can *lead* the way to the cave. Is that it? Even after all this time?"

"I was but a little girl and it has been many years, that is true. But yes, when I am closer, once again in the right area, I believe I will still be able to recognize features and landmarks well enough to guide me."

"To guide *us*," Blevins said pointedly.

"As long as I'm left in a condition where I am able to," Miriella replied just as pointedly.

"Touch`!" Kettleman issued a dry laugh. Then, his expression immediately turned flat and cold. "And if it comes to pass that you *do* successfully guide us— what do you expect then? Has Mr. Tate not convinced you that, once neither he nor you are of any further use, we will have no reason to keep you alive?"

"I have been well aware of that all along, and did not need Senor Tate to tell me," Miriella responded. "In fact, I wasn't without that same risk when it was just him and me. The chance at a fortune such as the Diablo Gold does not come without risk. I learned that early on when my father brought me here in the hope of digging gold out of the ground at a time when there was a threat from Indians."

Kettleman and Blevins exchanged looks. "You know, Major," said the gang boss, "I think this little tamale is turnin' out to be more of a cool cookie than we figured...and maybe more than even ol' Tate figured."

Ignoring him and directing her remarks more toward Kettleman, Miriella said, "Do not mistake this question for either foolishness or bravado, but tell me: If I succeed in leading you to the cave and the treasure is there, what is there for you to gain by killing us? As you once pointed out yourself, we would pose no threat to you after that. Not to take the treasure from you, not possessing any proof or right to a counterclaim, no recourse to go to the law. Nothing. Killing us would only serve a perverse satisfaction."

Blevins leered openly. "Comes to some overdue satisfyin', senorita, you and me already had that talk. Remember?"

"And after seein' her all stripped down good and proper, I'll damned well be wantin' some of that action too," spoke up McLaffert.

Kettleman frowned sternly. "Now just a minute. You'd better explain to your man—and remind yourself, too, Lieutenant—that I enforced strict rules against that sort of thing, even during the war."

"What the hell's he talkin' about, Red?" demanded McLaffert. "Who's he think he is to be layin' down rules for me? I ride behind you, not him!"

"We're all ridin' together, Kelce. Especially now that we've lost Cotton and Jeff," Blevins reminded him, "and especially since this has always been mostly the major's play that he invited us in on."

McLaffert shook his head. "That ain't how me and the others seen it. He was never *our* major. To us, that was only you."

"Well then now's the time to start lookin' at it different," Blevins told him. But the expression on his face seemed to lack the full conviction of his words. Turning to Kettleman, he said, "And it could be that now's also the time to remember the war is over, sir. Meanin' no matter my personal feelin's about the honor of followin' you, the times have changed and maybe some of the rules need to as well."

"I don't much care for the implication in those words, Red," Kettleman replied in a flinty tone. "At this point, getting our hands on the treasure—though sounding more and more promising—still has not been achieved. Until such time as it is, I suggest we consider it premature to fret over subsequent details."

Guardedly, Blevins allowed, "All right. We'll go with that for now."

"And I will remain caught in a desperate situation fighting to hold on to a shred of hope," Miriella said dejectedly.

"Your best chance to make the most of your situation," Kettleman advised, "is to get on with leading us to this cave of the ancients. How far is it?"

"You must remember that, when we first found it, we had not gone there in a direct way," Miriella explained. "We worked our way erratically, from dig to dig, over days and weeks."

"Where? How far from where we are now, damn it?" growled Blevins.

Miriella pointed. "It lies to the south and east. It is in a separate spur of mountains branching off from the Sante Veyos. The Dragon's Teeth, my father called them. I was sure to remember that since, as a little girl, it sounded so frightening...I heard my father tell Uncle Ignacio that some people also called them the Spearpoints."

"The Spearpoints! Yes, of course!" Kettleman smacked his right fist into his left palm. "I suspected all along that crafty Ed Wolfe would've stashed the Diablo Gold somewhere *out* of the Sante Veyos, but not too far out."

"I'm still waitin' to hear how far that is," said Blevins through clenched teeth.

Miriella momentarily chewed her bottom lip. "As a guess, I would say about two days. The last part of the way, when we get in among the widows, we will not be able to use the horses."

"Then the sooner we get started, the better," stated McLaffert.

Miriella looked appealingly at Kettleman. "What about your treatment of Senor Tate?"

"I've done all for him I can." Kettleman spread his hands. "We won't do anything to add to his misery, in accordance with my agreement. You can help him if you want, as long as it doesn't slow us down. But otherwise, he'll have to manage to keep up on his own. Now come on. Let's get moving."

24

THOUGH HE HIMSELF MADE A TOKEN GESTURE AND suggested she consider it, Braska wasn't at all surprised when Tayla once again turned down Warren's offer to have her safely escorted out of the mountains. "My reasons for coming here remain unchanged and strong as ever. So as long as Braska and Arrow are staying in pursuit of that outlaw pack, then I mean to stick with them," she told the lieutenant. "What's more, with my deepest sympathy for your recently lost trooper, it sounds like you can ill afford to spare any more men to nursemaid me."

Thus dismissed, Warren departed in a bit of a huff to rejoin his column as it swung away in keeping with the recommendations from Clapton and O'Flynn. As Braska and Tayla stood watching them leave, Arrow suddenly appeared from nowhere and moved up beside them.

"Was wonderin' when you'd show up," Braska said off-handedly.

"I have been near ever since you left to go investigate the disturbance down the line," Arrow replied. "I let Miss Tayla know this."

"That's right," Tayla confirmed. "He didn't abandon me like some people I could name."

Braska started to protest, but then realized she was only needling him, at least he thought that's all it was.

"But having so many anxious, Apache-hunting soldiers close at hand, and especially with you and their officers drawn away, I thought it best for me—an Indian, even though not an Apache—to remain unseen," Arrow further explained.

Braska nodded. "Probably the smartest thing."

"I had the chance to study the faces of some of those troopers. Most of them are so young it was heart-breaking," Tayla said. "You could tell they were scared half to death, yet at the same so determined to be brave and not show it."

"Yeah," Braska agreed, with a trace of sourness in his tone. "Trouble is, the determination to prove their bravery sometimes causes young fools like that, if given half a chance, to resort to behavior plumb foolhardy."

Tayla gave him a sidelong look. "Lucky we don't have anybody in our outfit who'd rate being called fool-hardy, eh?"

Braska grinned crookedly. "Yeah. Lucky." He then cut his gaze to Arrow. "Speakin' of luck—did you have any tryin' to pinpoint where that rifle shot we heard might've come from?"

"I couldn't be sure about placing the shot, other than having a general sense it came from the east," Arrow answered. "But then I did have some unex-pected luck. Just before Miss Tayla called out, I spotted

—ever so briefly—a thin wisp of smoke rising from a distinct point in that direction."

"Hey, now. That could definitely be a piece of luck," said Braska. "No Apache would be careless enough to let loose any telltale smoke. And we know there wasn't no soldiers in that direction. So that narrows it down pretty plain to one source."

"Those outlaw scum," hissed Tayla.

Braska asked Arrow, "You reckon you can locate where you saw that smoke rise up from?"

"I can," came the confident answer.

"Good. Then let's saddle up and go check it out."

———

EVEN WITH ARROW'S AIM AT ALL TIMES LOCKED firmly on where he'd seen the smoke wisp, it still took over two hours to negotiate the unfamiliar mountainous terrain before arriving there. The lower and middle reaches of the Sante Veyos were studded with sheer cliffs and cut by numerous bramble-choked gulches and twisty, ending up-nowhere canyons. The dirt-scratched *maps* and general directions that had been provided by Albert Beedle proved of little value because they'd been concentrated more to the middle of the mountain mass while Arrow's target lay in the tapering-off eastern reaches. Nor did it help that he was unable to cut even the slightest sign of the outlaw group moving anywhere ahead of them through the area. Not, that was, until they were almost on top of the spot he'd been working toward all along. There, at last, he spotted a horseshoe scuff on a rock and only a few yards away some droppings he judged to be only a dozen or so hours old.

When they, at last, reached the campsite where the Blevins bunch had built their morning fire, they found it in a clearing pocketed among some high rocks and low, thick brush, with a smattering of graze for the horses and a thin stream running along one side. The ashes of the fire retained only the faintest warmth, in keeping with the time elapsed between now and when Arrow had spotted its curl of smoke.

"So they nighted here but then didn't stick around long after their breakfast of cooked rattlesnake. Puttin' a bullet in the viper must account for the shot we heard," summed up Braska, using the toe of his boot to poke at the rattler remains beside the fire. "That puts 'em not more than a couple hours ahead of us."

"Not that I blame them for being in a hurry to get away from *that*," said Tayla, wrinkling her nose in disgust at the sight of the snake leavings. "But ahead of us headed where?"

As he continued circling the perimeter of the campsite, eyes constantly scouring the ground, Arrow said, "From the look of it, at least to start with, they headed east again—east and angled some south."

Tayla looked in that direction, frowning at the clumps of diminishing hills and mounds that tapered steadily away. "But wouldn't that basically amount to *leaving* the mountains? In that case, then why did they enter up into them to begin with?"

"That'd only make sense," said Braska, exhaling smoke from a freshly lit quirley, "if something turned up to make 'em change their minds about where they needed to point themselves."

Arrow had ceased his circling and now stood

closely studying a particular spot out on the edge of the campsite.

"What've you got?" asked Braska, going over to him. Tayla followed.

Arrow knelt down and plucked a couple of items off the ground—a short length of cut rope and a strip of cloth from a bedroll blanket. The ground where he'd knelt was a slab of flat rock with a layer of loose dirt and gravel spread across it. Holding the items he'd picked up in one hand, Arrow pointed with the other, saying, "Some kind of bundle seems to have been laid here for a period of time. See how the dirt is mashed flatter in the center area? Nothing especially odd about that, but look here, out on the edges." He stretched his arm, pointing closer. "Those are footprints—*bare* footprints."

"Okay. Yeah, I can make 'em out," said Braska.

"Mighty cold up here last night for anybody to be walking around barefoot," remarked Tayla. "Not to mention the discomfort of the dirt and gravel."

"Look closer. I make it *two* people with bared feet," said Arrow. He pointed again. "See? This print is notably larger than the one just a ways past it."

Braska spoke with a harder edge creeping into his voice. "Big feet, small feet. Like a man and a woman, maybe. In other words, Tate and the girl Mariella."

"What sense does that make?" asked Tayla.

"You said it yourself. Discomfort," Braska told her. "A little taste of torture, I'm bettin', to encourage the captives to spill what they're believed to know about findin' the Diablo Gold. And the piece of rope was almost certainly used to tie 'em somehow."

Tayla winced but made no reply.

"Here's something more to possibly fit with that,"

said Arrow. He'd shifted positions and was kneeling again and pointing again. This time to some reddish specks sprinkled across some of the gravel. "If I'm not mistaken, that's blood. Not a big enough spill to be from a cut or wound, though. Something more like..." His words trailed off for lack of an explanation.

"Like spittle from a cough or sneeze," Tayla suggested.

"Yes. Something like that," Arrow agreed.

"But blood all the same," Braska growled. "Ain't a good sign, no matter. And don't that strip of cloth look like it might've been torn to make a bandage?"

"But there's no blood on it. At least that's a good sign," said Tayla. Then, frowning, she amended, "Though strips of cloth can also used for other mending —like splints or slings."

"Yeah. Bust 'em up then patch 'em up. That still don't make it sound a helluva lot better, does it?" Braska made a sour face. "The thing is, though, whatever happened it left us with a fairly fresh trail to follow so we can't afford not to try and take advantage of that—no matter where it's switched to."

Straightening up, Arrow said, "That may not really be such a mystery." When the others pinned him with questioning looks, he added, "Remember how I said the trail appears to be heading east *and* some to the south? Forget how these Sante Veyos taper away due east and look farther out to the south. See that new stretch of mounds and peaks rising up in that direction?"

Braska quickly understood what he was driving at. "The spur range of mountains that old desert rat Beedle spoke of—the Spearpoints or Hideaways, he called 'em."

Tayla's eyebrows pinched together. "The ones he said the Apaches would be smart to use for evading the soldiers?"

"Exactly," Braska affirmed. "And why was that? Because, among other things, he claimed they were honeycombed with caves. Caves that could hide a pack of wild Injuns oughta also be suitable for hidin' a pile of treasure, don't you reckon?"

"It seems logical," said Arrow. "And, if it was something the captives only recently disclosed, it explains the gang's altered course after they were already up into the Sante Veyos."

Braska snapped away the remains of his cigarette and his mouth tightened grimly. "Let's not dwell too much on what it might've took for the captives to give cause for makin' that change. What we need to focus on is the same as it's always been—catchin' up and gettin' 'em out before they have to endure more."

25

THOUGH THE PEAKS WERE MORE BLUNTED AND decreased in height, and the gullies and canyons winding in and out lower down not quite so erratic, passage through the tapering eastern end of the Sante Veyos was still rugged going. Not even following the trail of the outlaw group having gone before made it any easier, inasmuch as it was obvious they were groping and struggling to make their way over unfamiliar ground as well.

What did help some was the fact that the day's temperature was less punishing, aided all the more by frequent stretches of shade thrown by high cliff walls.

Shortly past noon, Arrow used his bow to silently pick off a pronghorn they spotted up on a ledge of one such cliff. After climbing up and throwing the carcass down, he and Braska skinned it, then cut away choice slabs of meat that they wrapped in the hide and tied on their pack horse for later eating. Not long after, they heard another rifle shot ahead in the distance, signaling someone in Blevins's bunch also doing some hunting.

Eventually they came to the butchered remains of another pronghorn that proved their hunt had been equally successful.

"Looks like this time they'll be eatin' a little better than rattlesnake," remarked Braska.

"Unfortunately," said Arrow, eyeing the fly-infested pile of guts and gore, "the look of this doesn't indicate we've gained much time on them."

"That's all right," Braska allowed. "The fact they're still shootin' freely and makin' no attempt to hide their butcherin' shows they got no clue we're comin' up behind 'em—or that they think anybody's close, period. Just a matter of time before we narrow the gap and they find out different."

"If that means you're planning on making a move by moonlight again—like we've had luck with in the past," said Arrow, "then that wall of clouds building up off to the west could have something to say about it. At least for tonight."

Braska turned his head and glared over his shoulder at the distant ridge of dense, dark clouds. "Yeah, I've been noticin' that rascal too," he muttered. "It appears to be movin' mighty slow, though. Maybe it'll empty itself out over the desert before it ever gets here."

"Maybe," said Arrow. But his tone didn't convey much hope of that actually happening.

Braska shrugged. "If it don't, it don't. It might delay us but it ain't gonna stop us. Not like those clouds are carryin' enough rain to wash us all away or any such."

He had no way of knowing at the time, of course, how close to prophetic those words would turn out to be.

———

THE CLOUD COVER PICKED UP SPEED, KICKED ALONG by cold, gusting winds, and moved in, pulling with it a low, gloomy sky that hurried the descent of evening.

Braska, Arrow, and Tayla were fortunate to find a deep notch, shaped like an inverted V, cut low in the southeast face of a high, flat cliff. There was room for the three of them to fit in reasonable comfort, effectively blocked from the slashing wind. A few yards farther down the cliff face was a wide, shallow vertical seam where the horses could be tucked back in, also fairly well shielded. The spot lacked even the sparsest bit of graze, but there was still a few handfuls of grain left in the commandeered outlaw gear. Braska took care of feeding this to the animals, then hat-watered and securely hobbled them for the night.

While he was thus occupied, Arrow and Tayla gathered bramble stalks from outside the notch and got a fire going. They stoked the flames behind a large chunk of broken boulder, and any smoke that might have escaped would have been immediately seized by the wind and dispersed into the thickening darkness. These precautions were all taken in spite of every reason to believe the outlaw bunch was in no position to spot any sign of such activity, and in all likelihood, was putting every effort into finding their own place to hunker down.

At length, seated snugly between Braska and Arrow, with a cup of coffee between her palms and chunks of spitted meat sizzling over the fire, Tayla said, "I feel awfully torn in this moment. On one hand, I'm very grateful for being in the competent hands of you two and being as comfortable as we are. On the other hand, I *want* to hope with every fiber of my being that those outlaw bastards are miserable to the opposite extreme. Only that means the captives would be too. And that makes me feel not only sad but guilty and undeserving, due to some of what I caused, for any comfort I'm experiencing."

Braska took a sip of his coffee. "Such a thing as frettin' too deep, too much. Seems to me it boils down to doin' the best you can *when* you can, then movin' on and livin' with it. Even when you step wrong and stumble, you still got to live with it. But, if you got the right stuff in you, then you aim not to step wrong again and go from there."

"What if you *don't* have the right stuff?" Tayla asked quietly.

"Then you become like Red Dog and the other curs out ahead of us. You keep steppin' wrong until somebody comes along and stops you from continuin' on."

Nobody spoke more for a time. There was only the faint howl of the wind outside and the crackle of the meat over the fire.

Until Tayla said, "I've taken plenty of wrong steps. I've been nasty and petty and selfish, and have stepped *on* other people. Walked all over them. People I saw as being lesser than me, so I didn't figure it mattered. Three of them were the Slash B wranglers we buried back at Bluecap Wells." She looked over at Braska, then at Arrow, then turned her gaze out at the campfire flames. "When is it going to be time for somebody to stop me from continuing on?"

"Appears to me," drawled Braska, "somebody already has."

Tayla cut him a sharp look. "What do you mean?"

"Just what I said. Yeah, you was on a course of wrong steps all right. I saw some pretty clear signs of it the first time I laid eyes on you and you tried to take a quirt to me." Braska let his eyes bore into her for a long beat. "But I don't see those signs no more.

"What I see is somebody who put a stop to steppin' wrong her own self. I see somebody who set out to right the wrongs done to fellow riders of her brand. I see somebody who's been showin' compassion for a young girl she never even met. I see somebody who turned down—not just once, but twice—the chance to ride off to safety with the soldiers because she was hell-bent on finishin' a job she'd started instead...the only thing I ain't seen—not yet, and I'm willin' to bet I won't—is somebody who's gonna go back to walkin' over *lesser* folks with a quirt in her fist."

Tayla smiled guardedly, a bit devilishly. "Not even to use it on Red Dog if I get the chance?"

"Reckon an exception could be made just once."

"Good," declared Arrow. "If we've got that settled, I think the meat is done. So can we eat now?"

———

BUFFERED BY DISTANCE AND MINGLED WITH THE howl of the wind outside, the sound at first seemed strange and somewhat puzzling. But to the battle-experienced ears of Braska, it didn't stay puzzling for very long. He recognized it as the crash and rumble of gunfire. A *lot* of gunfire, coming first in a heavy exchange and then fading into smaller, sporadic bursts until it sputtered and ceased almost completely.

This came right after he and the others had finished eating and were in the process of spreading their bedroll blankets with the goal of catching a few hours sleep. All stopped what they were doing, and three faces snapped around to stare out the notch opening.

"Was that thunder?" Tayla said in a half-whisper.

"There is no storm within the clouds outside. Not yet," Arrow responded.

"But it was thunder all the same. The thunder of guns," said a grim-faced Braska. "Sounds like the Apaches and Warren's cavalry boys bumped against one another pretty hard."

Tayla's eyebrows pinched. "But I always heard that Indians wouldn't fight at night. And I thought Apaches only engaged in quick hit-and-run strikes, not pitched battles."

Braska smiled thinly. "Don't know if you could call what we just heard exactly a *pitched battle*. But I expect it was plenty bloody for everybody involved. And as far as when and how men in a conflict will fight, I reckon the decisions on that can only be made by those caught in the teeth of it at a given point."

Arrow walked closer to the notch opening and stood listening. The sound of the distant gunfire had by now sputtered out almost completely.

With the heat from the dying campfire now fading fast, Tayla wrapped a blanket more tightly about her shoulders and asked, "So do you think that clash could have been enough to resolve anything—that Sangriento's renegades might have been sufficiently subdued? The soldiers will keep coming, one way or the other."

"My gut feel," Braska said, twisting his mouth wryly, "is that it probably wasn't enough to settle the whole shebang. My sense of this Sangriento is that, even if he suffered a serious loss of men, he ain't gonna quit easy. Comes down to it, it don't take a lot of men to keep raisin' hell with those quick hit-and-run strikes."

"Only if Sangriento fell in the fight tonight would it matter," Arrow spoke solemnly. "The other Apaches might think their medicine had turned bad, and would possibly give up. Otherwise, it is not over."

"And whatever the fate of Warren's green troopers..." Here Braska's tone and weathered face seemed to take on a trace of sadness. "Well, like you said, Tayla, the soldiers will keep coming one way or the other."

"Those poor boys!"

Abruptly, Braska shook off his brief display of sentiment. "Hey, let's not be too quick to write off those young fellas. No reason to believe they didn't give a good account of themselves." He scowled. "But how it scalds out for us, cold as it might sound, is that we got to keep on with what we're doin' regardless. I make the sound of that gunfire as havin' come from someplace not too far from where we left the soldiers earlier—what say you, Arrow?"

The Ute lad nodded in agreement.

"Meanin' there's no reason to think the Apaches are anywhere close or even know we exist. Same for 'em knowin' anything about Red Dog's bunch movin' ahead of us. So let the renegades and the soldiers stay busy conductin' their business, we'll keep on with ours... startin' with gettin' back to grabbin' some much-needed sleep while we can."

———

In the camp of Kettleman and Blevins, a far less effective shelter hacked out of thick underbrush and pine growth tucked under a low rock shelf, the sound of the distant shooting was also plainly heard. The big difference, since no one in this group had any awareness of all the other activity taking place in these mountains, was the heightened bafflement and concern stirred as a result.

"What in blazes would bring on such a hellacious round of lead tradin' as that?" growled a tousle-haired Blevins, pushed up on one elbow in his bedroll.

"Not only what—but who?" questioned McLaffert from the shadows close by. "That sounded like a considerable bunch of shooters goin' at it."

Stern-faced and maintaining his composure as usual, Kettleman said, "An unexpected and unusual occurrence, to be sure. But let's stop and consider a moment, weigh some possibilities, before we get too wrought up over it."

"What possibilities have we got to weigh, and how can a body not get a little worked up at the notion of a bunch of unknown shooters crawlin' all over this same mountain we're on?" McLaffert wanted to know.

"You very nearly answered part of your own question," Kettleman replied. "If the shooters blazing away at one another are unknown to us, doesn't it stand to reason that we—both our presence and location—are unknown to them? The parties involved seem plenty busy with each other. Further, that gunfire came from quite a ways off so those triggering it are hardly crawling around just down the slope from us. Plus, we're on our way *out* of these Sante Veyos while they seem quite engaged right where they are."

"When you put it that way, yeah," said Blevins, "then whoever's out there and whatever they're up to don't necessarily have to crowd us none at all, does it?"

"Not necessarily, no," affirmed Kettleman. "Unfortunately, that fails to provide an answer as to who they are or what their conflict with one another is. But as long as it stays removed from us and our business, it doesn't really matter."

"You know, we never did fully figure out who-all was involved in that shootout back at Bluecap Wells," McLaffert said thoughtfully. "I still think there was two different groups. And even though I checked our back trail regular and am confident nobody followed us from there, this new shootin' tonight might still have a tie-in back to there."

Kettleman smiled, though no one could see him in the dark. "There's some of that weighing of possibilities I mentioned. But, in view of everything else that's been said, I don't think we need or can afford to spend further time on it. If you reconnoiter first thing in the morning, McLaffert, and don't see signs of any nearby activity, then I think we'll be clear to proceed on into the Spearpoints."

"Though we'll have to take the precaution now," Blevins added, "of no more shooting to bag fresh meat. No need to advertise what whoever else is out there don't yet know."

"Precisely. Good thinking, Lieutenant," said Kettleman.

Lying silently in the shadows, listening to this, Miriella had quite a different reaction. She had no way of knowing who the mysterious shooters out there in the night might be, but she couldn't imagine how they could pose any worse fate for her than those she and Tate were already in the hands of. So now, in addition to the still-harbored notion of throwing herself off a high cliff if given an opportunity, she would also be looking for the chance to make a loud enough noise— something more significant than merely crying out—to draw attention to the presence of this group she was so miserably a part of.

26

THE MORNING STARTED OUT PRETTY GOOD. BRASKA woke to the first whitish-gray streaks of dawn showing outside the notch opening, having gotten his first decent sleep in days. The silence accompanying the dawn indicated the howling, gusting wind had abated sometime during the night, but the slice of sky Braska could see still appeared overcast with sooty clouds.

He sat up in his bedroll blankets, pushed the hair back out of his eyes, built his first cigarette of the day and smoked it unhurriedly. Arrow and Tayla continued to sleep. After he'd burned through the quirley, Braska pulled on his boots and went to work piling some previously gathered bramble stalks over the cold coals and then stoking up a fresh fire. Arrow and Tayla woke while he was doing this. Tayla came over and began preparing a pot of coffee, and Arrow announced he'd go check on the horses and water them.

Right after that was when things went sideways.

Arrow was gone barely a minute before he reappeared to say, "Mr. Braska, you had better come have a look at this." His tone signaled plainly enough that something was wrong.

Yeah, it turned out there was plenty wrong. When they got outside and walked over to the vertical seam in the cliff face where Braska had left their horses hobbled, the area was empty. The animals were long gone.

Braska spat out a curse. "What the hell! No way they could've broke free from the hobbles I put on 'em."

"They didn't. They were *cut* free," Arrow told him, gesturing to indicate pieces of sliced hobble rope lying about the area.

Braska's mouth pulled into a grimace. "Apaches?"

Arrow shook his head. "No. Not Apaches, nor any doubling back by the men we are in pursuit of. But I know who it was. Step over here, let me show you."

He walked a few feet farther down in front of the cliff face, then stopped. Gesturing out away from the cliff, he said, "Our horses were scattered, chased off in that direction. But look closer in along here—see those prints?" He leaned over and pointed to a stretch of bare, hard-packed ground.

It took Braska a minute before he responded, "Okay, yeah. I make out some hoofprints and a boot mark or two."

"Notice how those hoofprints are smaller than would be left by a horse? And the boot mark...these are all familiar to me." Arrow lifted his gaze to hold Braska's eyes and said flatly, "They belong to the old prospector Beedle and his burro Esmeralda!"

Braska's mouth sagged. "That sun-shriveled runt we left behind back at Bluecap Wells? You sayin' he followed us, somehow made it all the way here last night and cut loose our horses?"

"I know it is hard to believe," admitted Arrow. "But the signs are there. I am confident in my reading of them."

"I have no doubt about that," Braska said. "But... damn."

Tayla came out and walked over to them. "What's going on? What happened to the horses?"

Braska gave her a quick rundown and a look of astonishment was gripping her face by the time he was done. "That's incredible! He doesn't ride that burro, does he? So you mean that ancient little leprechaun followed us on foot and caught up to where he was able to do this?"

"Thinkin' back on it," Braska growled, "I'm figurin' now that sawed-off little bastard must be bred and born to the desert—him and that burro both—like a couple of lizards or something. Can probably go all day, even under the hottest conditions, on a teaspoon of water. And once in the mountains, where they been searchin' and diggin' for years and likely know every damn crack and rock hump there is, they can scamper around as easy as monkeys in a tree."

Picking up on the picture Braska was painting, Arrow said, "And while we were struggling practically every inch through this unfamiliar terrain—having to back out of dead-ended canyons and start over, reaching impassable drop-offs we had to turn away from—Beedle and his keenly honed knowledge of the area was able to keep closing on us the whole time, swiftly and with relative ease." You could tell it galled him to admit another's mastery of negotiating a landscape he, too, was traversing.

"But why? What made Beedle come after us at all—

and then chase away our horses like this?" Tayla questioned. "He seemed so anxious to get clear of the Apaches and make it to safety in Harrietville."

"I can answer that in two words: Gold Fever," Braska told her. "Don't you get it? Despite his claim to view Diablo Gold chasers as nothing but hopeless fools while his way of diggin' ore out of the ground was the only noble method, something I said about the outlaw captives maybe havin' a worthwhile clue to the treasure must've swerved his way of thinkin' and brought out a dose of plain old nasty greed in him."

Tayla's eyes flashed. "So running off our horses effectively knocks us out of the chase and only leaves Red Dog's bunch for him to deal with if they actually do succeed in finding the treasure."

"I don't see no other way to look at it."

"Why, that conniving old bastard!" Tayla seethed.

"You'll get no argument on that out of me."

Tayla swung her gaze appealingly to Arrow. "But you'll be able to find our horses again and bring them back, won't you?"

"Given enough time," Arrow replied solemnly. "They'll instinctively seek out water and graze. But there are dozens of streams and meadows in these mountains, and there's no guarantee the horses will stick together. Rounding up our mounts isn't likely to be a quick, easy task."

"And time is something we're already runnin' thin on," grated Braska. Now, he and Arrow locked eyes. After a beat, Braska said, "You thinkin' what I'm thinkin'?"

"A horse in mountainous terrain is useful for packing gear and making it easier on your feet though harder on your behind. But for speed and ease of travel, they add little—plus can be noisy and tend to leave easier sign to follow." A wistful smile briefly touched Arrow's lips. "I've heard that speech from my father too many times to count. In his years as a mountain man in the high Rockies, he claims to have kept a horse with him only a small percent of the time."

Listening to this, a frown suddenly tugged at Tayla's expression. "Wait a minute. You two wild men aren't suggesting we commence *walking* from here, are you?"

"Matter of fact," drawled Braska, "we are. If that human prune Beedle can hoof around on shank's mare, why can't we? Besides, it's all there is that still leaves a chance of reachin' those polecats in time to do their captives any good. Stalled here for who knows how long, hopin' to gather up those horses, amounts to certain failure after all we've already put into this. Keepin' on the move, keepin' after our quarry by the only means left is what we *got* to try."

"But I'm the daughter of a rancher. You know the saying every true wrangler lives and dies by: Any job can't be done from the back of a horse, ain't worth doing."

Braska looked at her. "Ain't keepin' after tryin' to save Miriella Clemente still a job worth doin'—horse or not?"

Tayla glared back. "Damn you...all right, what do we have to do to prepare for this hike we're about to embark on?"

"Strip down as light as possible for traipsin' over rugged ground. Only essentials. A bedroll, canteen, weapons and cartridges. Maybe a small sack of possibles."

"Can I bring my quirt—or would that be considered too nonessential?" Tayla said sarcastically.

"For you it's probably essential. Nobody'd recognize you without it," Braska told her. Then, a corner of his mouth quirking up, he added, "Long as you don't try to use it on me again out of blame for the sore feet and weariness we've got ahead of us."

27

THE SOUTHEAST SIDE OF THE SANTE VEYOS dropped away quickly over considerably gentler slopes and with fewer jagged rock outcrops to maneuver through or around. This was the welcome discovery of those in the Kettleman/Blevins group as they made their descent on the morning following the windy, blustery night. McLaffert's reconnoiter at first light had revealed no sign of anything in the near vicinity that might be a deterrence or concern associated with the sound of gunfire that had also been part of the previous night. Thus encouraged, his group had wasted no time striking out toward their their goal of transitioning into the Spearpoint range that rose up ahead.

The speed and ease with which they were now proceeding was both surprising and dismaying to Miriella. Her childhood recollection of the passage through this area had seemed much slower, more challenging. At this rate, they would reach the three widows far sooner than she'd been expecting and she would be forced to make some fateful decisions also sooner than she'd been counting on—for herself and also for Tate.

So far, in spite of considerable suffering, he'd been enduring and keeping up better than most had figured. Guiltily, Miriella had come to realize that a deep, dark part of her had been hoping Tate might falter and fail so that he would be left behind—either to fend for himself, or be put out of his misery with a quick bullet. That would at least save him the possibility of prolonged torture and would free her to make a final desperate decision—whatever she had the opportunity and courage to actually do—with only her own fate resting on it. *God forgive me for such selfish thoughts*, her mind wailed. *And if you're up there looking down now, God, All Mighty and All Knowing, why oh why couldn't you have produced a real storm in all of last night's fury to strike me down with a lightning bolt to spare me this ongoing agony!*

But God did not answer. And, even though this new day's sky continued to be bloated with dark clouds, once again, no lightning bolts came to save her either. Miriella sat her saddle in silence, head hung dejectedly, staring down at the ground in front of her plodding horse. Staring down...*maybe*, she thought, *my prayers and pleas have been aimed in the wrong direction...*

———

Now set afoot, Braska, Arrow, and Tayla caught a somewhat bitter break when they, too, found that descent down the back side of the Sante Veyos was aided by less challenging terrain than any encountered prior. That didn't make it easy by any means, but nevertheless better than it might have been.

Also of benefit was having the sign left by Albert Beedle to guide them. True, his course was mirroring the trail of Red Dog's bunch—but where they still trudged unnecessarily through rugged patches here and there, Beedle's sharper sense of the area guided him on detours over far easier ground before re-converging with the way his quarry had gone. Sticking with the old mountain rat's choices made consistently easier going for Braska and company—Arrow being able to easily cut his sign, partly due to the Ute lad's skill and partly due to Beedle making no attempt to blur his trail because he held no belief anyone would be coming along behind.

Another break of sorts came in the form of the heavy cloud cover that continued to hang low in the sky well after the wind that brought it had dissipated. The day was still quite hot, but the clouds at least blocked a direct hammering from the sun. As the hours wore on, however, though the air stirred not in the least, it seemed to gradually fill and thicken with humidity such as was very rare to this arid region. It pressed down with a near-smothering intensity that left the three walkers soaked and pouring sweat as they trudged on.

"Good Lord," gasped Tayla. "If I stopped and stood still for very long, I think I could sweat out my very own lake—Lake Tayla."

"Ain't there an old saying," Braska drawled, walking beside her, "that goes something about how men perspire, horses sweat, but ladies only glow?"

Tayla aimed an arched brow at him. "Are you saying I'm not a lady?"

"Not at all. I'm questionin', since you are one, how you're gonna *glow* out that lake of yours?"

Tayla gave a little laugh. "First off, no matter where that lady business may or may not fit, I'm a ranch gal. And on a ranch, anybody worth their salt—man, woman, or critter—had better figure on doing some sweating."

"I wouldn't've thought it at first," said Braska, "but you set quite a store by bein' part of a ranch, bein' a ranch gal. Don't you?"

Tayla kept walking, kept staring straight ahead. Her face took on a stony expression. "Yes, I do. Now. For too long, though, after my mother died, I lost sight of that. Getting as far away from the Slash B and everything else remotely related to ranching and horses and cows and cow shit was what I thought I wanted the most in the world.

"But standing on the brink of maybe never seeing any of it again, hell maybe never making it out of these lousy mountains to ever see anything else again...due largely to my own wrong-headedness yes, but also helped along by other factors...makes me want to fight hard *not* to let it go. And included is the realization that if I succeed, it'll be due in no small part to the strength found at my ranch gal core...oh yeah, and also with a smidgen of help from some stubborn-ass shotgun guard and his Indian sidekick."

Braska grinned. "Well, let me say that me and my sidekick appreciate you lettin' us string along so's you can keep pullin' our fat outta the fire along with your own."

"Think nothing of it. Just don't press your luck by making too many more missteps like losing our horses and then coming up with the alternative notion to haul ourselves around in their place."

———

ONCE AGAIN, THE DENSE CLOUD COVER HURRIED the onset of evening. Nevertheless, Frank Kettleman was more than satisfied with the progress his group had made this day. Faced almost all the way by a less arduous landscape, they'd completed the descent out of the Sante Veyos, crossed a narrow basin of baked, mostly flat ground cut by a handful of jagged-edged arroyos, and then actually ascended some distance up into the foothills of the Spearpoint range.

But having accomplished all this, which was considerably more than anticipated, the most exciting part came at the very close after they halted and were getting ready to make night camp. It was Kettleman himself who spotted it. While McLaffert was seeing to the horses and Blevins was securing the captives against the inner wall of the shallow, cavern-like rocky recess they'd selected in which to settle, the former captain had climbed a few yards up an incline that ran along one side of the cavern. This gave him a more wide open view of the Spearpoints' higher peaks looming ahead. And that's when he saw them, presented to him from just the right angle. Perfectly aligned, gray and barren-looking, unmistakably tilted at their tips exactly as the girl had described—the *Three Widows*!

Kettleman's excited shout brought Blevins and McLaffert scrambling up to where he stood and they instantly saw the same as him, the distinct mounds that held so much promise.

"I'll be damned!" said Blevins. "There they really are—and not too far off. We can be in among 'em by the middle of the day tomorrow."

"*The cave of the ancients*," McLaffert echoed in an awed tone. "Up until now, I been thinkin' that has an awful corny sound to it. But now it sounds sweeter and more invitin' than the come-on of a beautiful woman!"

Blevins guffawed lewdly. "Your share of what we take out of that cave will buy you the come-on from more beautiful women than you can ever begin to handle."

Down in the rock-walled recess, Miriella overheard this exchange, and her heart sank. She cursed herself. Why had she been so foolish as to not only reveal what Uncle Ignacio's message had been but then to also give such accurate details about the three widows. In the moment, she'd only been able to think about buying time and stopping further torment of Tate. She should have lied, been more creative. But somehow, in some hopelessly naive way, she had believed it would never come this far, get this close.

Sprawled on the ground next to her, Tate had once again lapsed into unconsciousness. Miriella strained against the ropes that bound her ankles and her wrists at the small of her back. She gazed longingly at the ledge just beyond the cavern opening and wished the drop-off from it was higher. If it was, she told herself, she would this very minute be struggling fiercely to get to her feet or roll or crawl—whatever it took to make it out there and throw herself over.

Only it wasn't to be.

Not yet.

But there was still tomorrow. That was all Miriella

had left to believe in. There would be no calling out for rescue by last night's mysterious shooters, no hope for a last-minute burst of heroics from Tate...nothing she could count on from the God who'd obviously abandoned her. It was strictly up to her. They would reach a point where they'd have to leave the horses and proceed on foot. They'd have to pass along some high ledges. As their guide, she would make sure of that. And then, at the right spot, she would make her move and assure her escape. She would take Tate with her if possible. But no matter what, she would save herself from the unspeakable...

28

IN THE STRETCH OF CHOPPY FLATS BETWEEN THE trailing off of the Sante Veyos and the rise of the Spearpoints, Braska, Tayla, and Arrow were also overtaken by the early dusk. Their level of exhaustion after trudging all day without mounts made a halt most welcome, and the significant distance they'd managed to cover under those circumstances made a rest damn well earned.

As a spot to spread their blankets, they chose a bed of drifted sand that had accumulated in the bend of some low, spiny rocks poking up above the rim of one the numerous arroyos that cut gashes in the surrounding expanse of dry, crusted earth. A campfire was out of the question so they dined on jerky and hard-tack they'd scrounged from the saddlebags they were forced to leave behind, washed down by water from the canteens they'd filled in the last stream they came across in the Sante Veyos.

Small talk while they ate was minimal, and the meal of stringy meat and rock-hard *teeth dullers* was soon followed by dropping quietly, wearily back onto their bedroll blankets. Even Arrow, whose youthfulness and pantherlike way of moving had previously seemed indefatigable, this evening showed signs of being worn thin.

Braska rolled a quirley in the dark and lay flat on his back, smoking, staring up at the blank sky. He felt physically drained yet restless, not ready for sleep. In his time on the drift, during his prison stretch, even during the closing months of the war often with guns and cannons rumbling in the near distance, he had trained himself to grab precious sleep whenever possible. But tonight, with plenty of quiet and no sense of immediate danger, it was proving elusive.

What he did sense was that tomorrow would be a key day. Maybe the make or break point for this whole endeavor. Maybe that was it, what was churning in him. But all the more reason he should be sleeping, recharging his mind and body, getting himself as ready as he could.

Maybe it was Tayla's talk about ranching, being a *ranch gal* at her core, stirring old, unresolved feelings in him. Braska's late father and brother had had that same kind of drive and devotion toward ranching. He, however, had known from a very early age that he wanted something different, even though he didn't know what. He stayed as an obligation to his father's dream, though, until the war—and prison—knocked everything to hell in a basket. Now his father and brother were both dead, the ranch was long gone, and Braska had his wish of living life on the drift...along with occasional pangs of guilt over wondering if things might have gone differently had he possessed that same ranch-loving core.

His cigarette burned down to nothing, and he flipped away the butt.

The weather, too, was nagging at him. The strange stillness contrasting so sharply with last night's howl and bluster, and the even stranger—for this arid region—blanket of humidity that continued to linger so thick and muggy. It made Braska think again of his youth back in Nebraska when such ominous stillness often preceded a fierce summer thunderstorm or sometimes even a tornado. Yet tonight's sky showed no hint of a storm, not even out on the farthest horizon.

He closed his eyes and willed sleep to come, trying to let the rhythmic breathing of Tayla and Arrow lull him.

But it didn't work. The restlessness wouldn't let up. His hands felt fidgety and the muscles in his tired, aching legs fluttered and jumped under the skin. Finally, ironically, tired as he was, he knew he had to get up and move around some. If for no other reason than to avoid disturbing the rest being enjoyed by his companions.

Braska pushed off his blanket and slipped quietly down to the floor of the shallow arroyo. Sliding one hand along the rim, using it as a sort of railing to guide and balance himself, he began easing slowly away from the camp. He was somewhat surprised to find that, despite the absence of any illumination from the hidden moon and stars, his night vision had adjusted to a point that he could still make out many things with reasonable clarity. The sprawl of empty, sun-bleached land on all sides made a pale backdrop against which features stood out.

He moved leisurely along, following the twisty

course of the cut. He extended his legs fully, purpose-fully with each step, aiming to work out the pesky kinks that had nagged him when he'd been lying down. After a hundred yards or so, he paused and leaned back against the arroyo wall, resting his elbows on the rim. He hung there in a comfortable slouch, slowly sweeping his gaze across the vast, murky, silent emptiness that surrounded him like an impervious moonscape.

After a while, he dug the makings from his pocket and idly fashioned another cigarette. Fishing out a match, he was just about to strike the lucifer on his belt buckle when he froze. A dozen feet ahead, right where the arroyo made another abrupt twist, something—nothing more than a shadow within a shadow—moved. Braska held motionless and kept his eyes locked on where the vague, phantom-like movement had occurred. Or did it? Maybe it had only been—

And then, while his own hand remained stayed from striking a match, that wasn't the case for somebody else's. As Braska watched, a lucifer suddenly flared, and in its brief, limited glow could be seen the face of a man lighting a cigarette thrust out from pooched, whisker-surrounded lips. The match flame died quickly, and in its place, bobbed the tiny red glow of the quirley's burning tip.

All at once the tense restlessness was gone from Braska. Here, finally, was something solid and real to get his hands on. A piece of unexpected good luck. For, as his mind rapidly sorted through a flood of possibili-ties, he came to the conclusion that the smoker squatted down in the arroyo twist up ahead could only be one person. The soldiers were somewhere behind, the Blevins bunch was somewhere farther ahead, and any lone Apache who might be on the prowl wouldn't be stopping to have a smoke...so that shadowy lump piled around the glowing red dot had to be none other than the sly, horse-rousting little runt Alfred Beedle!

Braska set aside his match and unlit cigarette. He slowly eased out of his slouch and turned full in Beedle's direction. He dropped into a half crouch, getting ready to move forward, reaching down to flick the keeper thong off his holstered Colt. He didn't want to let loose a shot into the still night unless absolutely necessary, nor did he want to kill the little bastard. But he wasn't about to let him get away either.

"Yiieee!" The guttural screech split the night just as Braska was taking his first step. Up ahead, from the rim of the arroyo opposite where Beedle was squatted, leaped the shadowy form issuing this war cry. Across the gap and down, this form streaked—landing heavily on the shadowy lump that was Beedle, landing with outflung arms aiming a flurry of menacing strikes. "Sonofabitch!" Beedle roared in response, struggling violently against the attack. Braska saw—for just a fraction of a second, in stark relief against the pale backdrop —an arm raised, gripping a vicious tomahawk in its fist. The arm swooped down and he heard a loud, solid thud but couldn't tell if it came from striking flesh and bone or the hard-packed arroyo wall.

In the next instant, his ears were filled with only the sounds of the curses he was growling and the pounding of his feet as he raced toward the struggle taking place between Beedle and the Apache warrior who'd come out of nowhere to attack him. In the long run, Braska didn't give a damn if they hacked each other to pieces. He certainly had no love for the Apache, other than wanting to know if he was the only one lurking close. Nor did he give a rip about the fate of the back-stabbing old desert rat—but not until after some more information could be gleaned from him.

Braska reached the combatants with his Colt drawn. It was difficult to determine which was which in the shadowy tangle of flailing arms and kicking feet and roiling dust. But then a bushy head clearly discernible as belonging to the Apache separated itself for a moment and Braska immediately smashed his gun barrel down onto it.

The warrior grunted with pain and surprise, his head and shoulders jerking back. As part of this movement, his right arm—the one wielding the tomahawk – swung out wide and poised to instinctively strike back. Braska's free hand shot out, clamping this arm at the wrist and twisting savagely, forcing it down. The warrior howled with more pain, but it wasn't enough to slow him from whipping around with his other arm, this one fisting a knife aimed at Braska's throat. Braska yanked his head back barely in time, but not without still receiving a skimming slice to the point of his chin.

With the warrior stretched out crossways directly before him, both arms extended away to the side, Braska again swung his gun barrel down at the shaggy head and upturned blur of a face. It smashed solidly. Enraged, feeling hot blood running down his throat from the chin slice, he smashed down again and was drawing back for another when the Apache's body suddenly convulsed in a manner that had nothing to do with the blows to his head. Along with that came an agonized gurgle from somewhere deep within, and then the warrior's entire body went limp.

Braska was caught like a statue, with his Colt raised above his shoulder. Before he could break from that pose, a man's voice, strained from the attack and from the weight of the dead man on top of him, said, "You can go ahead and hit him again if you want, all you care to, but he ain't gonna feel it—I just carved his heathen gizzard out of him."

Now, Braska lowered his gun. And promptly aimed it at the shadowy mass where the voice had come from. "Before you think about tryin' to do any more carvin', Beedle—like maybe on me, for instance—I wouldn't advise it. I don't want to raise a shot if I don't have to, but for you I wouldn't hesitate too damn much."

There was a slight pause before the response came. "Why in blazes are you threatenin' to shoot me after you just got done savin' my hide? And who the hell is *Beedle*? Ain't that you pokin' a hogleg in my face, shotgun guard?"

Braska scowled fiercely. Something was even more out of kilter here than it had first seemed. Among other things, he realized belatedly, the voice now barking questions at him. "Who the hell are *you*?" he barked back.

"It's me, Ebner Clapton," came the answer. "The scout for Lt. Warren's cavalry patrol."

29

AFTER ARROW AND TAYLA WERE ALERTED, consensus was quickly reached that the risk of a small, brief fire was warranted in order to provide illumination for addressing wounds received from the skirmish with the Apache. Namely, these were the slice to Braska's chin and two more serious lacerations suffered by Clapton—a tomahawk chop to his left shoulder, and not far below, a knife slash across his ribs.

Arrow located a crumbled-away spot low along the base of the arroyo wall that made a partial dome in which the flames would be effectively hidden from most any angle. Using a needle and some gut thread Braska had included in his possibles sack, Tayla did the necessary stitching and also furnished bandaging material torn from the thin camisole worn under her blouse. She did Braska first and then, while she worked on Clapton, Braska and Arrow put in the effort to collapse dirt and rocks from the arroyo's rim down over the carcass of the Apache brave. This was not done as an act of decency or compassion but rather for the practical purpose of discouraging buzzards from appearing and circling in the sky overhead next morning, drawing unwanted attention.

Once the fire was built, also putting it to use for making a pot of coffee only seemed natural. Then, after the mending and burying were done, they sat back with cups of steaming brew in hand and fitted together the different pieces of what had occurred to form the fullest picture they could of where things stood since they'd last seen one another.

For Braska and his companions, it was pretty straightforward, and that's how he laid it out.

Clapton's tale was a little more complicated, but he did his best to deliver it equally as tight and straight.

"After you folks parted off yesterday—while I was gone checkin' on those what ambushed our column— Capt. Angus Meams and some more C Company boys showed up to join with Lt. Warren. Meams is the officer in charge of clappin' a lid on the whole renegade outbreak. He stayed in the basin a while longer, over-seein' that the survivin' ranchers and settlers got took to safety, and sent our outfit to give chase when Sangri-ento broke for the mountains. With the basin cleaned up, he then followed. Meanin' when he showed up he took over the soldierifyin' command. And his chief scout he brung with him, a windbag name of Taber who by his own lights is a sign-sniffer the likes of Boone, Crockett, and Carson combined, but in truth couldn't make out a mule turd from a...ah, never mind. I'm gettin' off on a personal track, and apologies for my coarseness, ma'am."

"Never mind that. No apology necessary," Tayla

assured him. "But did you have any luck finding that young trooper?"

Clapton made a sour face. "Yeah. Sad to say, only what was left of him. I buried him temporary, like I promised I would. Then I tracked those what picked him off—three hunters, like I figured, takin' his horse for food—far enough to get a good idea where they was headed. Havin' that figured, I returned to report to the lieutenant and then's when I found how Meams and the others had showed up."

Clapton drank some coffee and continued. "The captain was decent enough to right away assign me to show a couple troopers where I'd buried Mickles so's they could take his remains back to the fort for a proper service. After that, I returned again to the now rein-forced outfit what was already gone in pursuit of Sangriento and his butchers. Based on the information I'd given 'em, they were headed on the course taken by the hunter-ambushers. Taber was gone ahead, markin' the trail farther."

Mere mention of the other scout's name caused Clapton to pause momentarily and grimace with distaste before going on. "Toward dusk, Taber dropped back to report he had the Apache camp located and they was ripe for bein' struck and their whole outbreak brought to a close. Without hearin' or seein' no more, I had a feelin' right off that something was fishy, that it sounded too easy. And when I slunk ahead with him and the officers to have a closer look-see, it didn't take but a minute to see it was nothing but a trap!

"The camp was back deep in a pinched-off little canyon with trees and even a stream tricklin' through. Looked real nice. Too nice. Apaches plain don't seek comfort like that, and ain't no way in hell any renegade chief on a tear would tuck hisself into a corner that way!" Clapton's eyes blazed with anger. "I tried to tell 'em, but that damn fool Meams wouldn't listen. His lame-brained head scout had him too snowed. O'Flynn could see, same as me, it was a lousy setup. I think even Warren knew, but there was nothing he could do to buck a higher command. And Meams, as much or maybe even more than on Taber's advice, was out for the glory.

"So we went in under Meams's *Hand-Clap* plan of attack. A third of the men slipped up through the trees on either side of the canyon until they had the camp between 'em. Meams and the final third of the outfit moved up in the mouth, effectively shuttin' the door on escape. Then, at Meams's command, the two sides would close suddenly on the camp—like hands clappin' together—and catch the Injuns by surprise. Any who tried to run out on the fight that followed would be caught by Meams sweepin' in at the mouth."

At that point, Braska said dryly, "Not to spoil your big finish, but let me take a stab at guessin' how it really went instead—the camp was a dummy setup. Nobody in it except maybe a couple sacrificial lambs, braves who'd been previously wounded and weren't gonna make it anyway. The rest just fluffed-up empty blankets. And after the two hands came clappin' in on all that big nothing, then the true trap got sprung... Apaches firin' down from the rim of the canyon."

Clapton groaned. "You nailed it. A hunnert percent. It was worse'n awful. Some of our boys scrambled to cover back in the trees, but the losses was heavy before they got in thick enough. O'Flynn didn't make it, and Warren is hit pretty bad, may or not pull through. The only thing that goddamn stupid Meams had to shut the door on was our own survivors stragglin' out."

Tayla gasped, her face looking anguished in the flickering firelight.

"Though I'm sure it seemed otherwise to those of you caught in it," said Braska, "the shootin' we overheard from a distance didn't last an overly long time. Not that it ain't something to be thankful for, but I'm surprised the Apaches didn't give more pursuit to your withdrawal."

Arrow spoke, saying simply, "Ammunition."

Braska looked at him. "How's that?"

"Lad's right," said Clapton. "The only reason we didn't get riddled more has got to be 'cause the renegades ain't overly blessed with bullets. They gathered a bunch durin' their raids in the basin, but they also have been usin' 'em mighty freely and that business last night caused 'em to spend plenty more. The one thing Meams was smart enough to do was right away send a team to gather up the guns and cartridges of the fallen so's they didn't fall into the hands of the redskins to help strengthen their arsenal."

"God, what ghastly business," remarked Tayla. "Giving priority to securing guns and bullets ahead of the dead bodies."

"War ain't pretty, ma'am," Clapton told her. "Especially not fightin' redskins." No sooner were the words out than he cut his eyes to Arrow and added, "There I go needin' to apologize again. Sorry for blurtin' it out that way, lad. War is ugly business that drags out ugly behavior, skin color be damned."

Arrow smiled thinly. "No need to apologize, Mr.

Clapton. I know what you meant. My own father has killed evil men of red, white, and brown races because they were a threat giving him no choice. The men our group is after happen to be white and evil and may need killing as much or more than any Apaches we also encounter. Like you said, skin color be damned."

They let the fire die down as they continued talking.

It didn't take long for Clapton to finish telling the rest of his story. After getting caught in the Apache trap, the surviving troopers now under the exclusive command of Captain Meams had seen for their dead and wounded as best they could in the dark and howling banshee wind, then endured a very edgy, guarded night at the mouth of the canyon. At first light this morning, the captain had gathered all—living, dead, and in between—for a return to Fort Driscoll in order to regroup and re-supply before coming back to again take up pursuit of the hostiles. At his request, Clapton had stayed behind to track the movement of the renegades for the sake of being able to guide such pursuit when the time came.

"Havin' determined the scoundrels were headed into the Spearpoints," the old scout summed up, "I was on my way back to report that much. Goin' after 'em into that scarred, barren corner of Hell with the fire burned out is gonna take a whole different mindset and chase plan. The Sante Veyos are challengin'—the Spearpoints are downright mean and frightenin'.

"But earlier this afternoon, with dusk closin' fast, I was pushin' my horse to make it off these flats and he stepped wrong, busted his leg. I had to cut the poor critter's throat, put him out of his misery. I was left to shoulder my canteen and some gear and set off on foot. Made it as far as this gully and decided to hole up for the night. The red devil that came in after me must've been checkin' back trail for Sangriento and found my dead horse. Followed me from there and waited until he thunk I was relaxed and totally off guard...I was, too. He was all over me like a hungry brother-in-law with a passel of starvin' kids. Reckon I'd've been dead meat if ol' shotgunner Braska hadn't been out for a stroll."

"So what will you do now?" Tayla asked.

"Come mornin', I'll continue on like I was."

"With those fresh wounds?"

"I've suffered through worse. You did a good job stitchin' me," Clapton told her. "I'll take it slow and steady, be back in the Sante Veyos by evenin' tomorrow. I got gear, my gun and cartridges. There's plenty of shelter, water, and game to be found there. I'll heal, pick my way along, and be ready when some soldiers eventually come back around."

"Sounds like you got it all figured out," said Braska. "I'd invite you to stick with us but I expect that wouldn't hold much temptation."

Clapton grunted. "More like it'd be smarter for you to accept an invitation to join me. Let the Apaches and those owlhoots you're chasin' have at each other—and the cold, ragged peaks of the Spearpoints chew up anything that's left."

"Don't sound half bad," Braska allowed with a crooked grin. "Except for the fact there's a couple of innocent folks in the mix that we've all along been tryin' our damnedest to keep from gettin' chewed up."

30

CORNER OF HELL WITH THE FIRE BURNED OUT WAS how Ebner Clapton had described the Spearpoint Mountains. Those might not be the exact words of everyone, but as an accurate description after venturing very far in, they could hardly be disputed. An elongated sprawl of dirty gray rock, stippled by minimal amounts of vegetation or contrasting color, heaped high and then tumbled away to leave a staggered line of tall, jagged peaks, sheer cliffs and steep slopes, spiderweb patterns of pinched, boulder-cluttered canyons and gullies snarling the lower reaches—that was the Spearpoints.

Yet to the eyes of Frank Kettleman, as he urged his group higher and deeper on a new morning under a relentlessly cloudy sky that seemed to press down ever heavier, more humid air without a hint of breeze, it was a fine, invigorating setting filled with nothing but the promise of fulfilling half a lifetime's dream. They'd started out at first light, and in the beginning, both Blevins and McLaffert, excited the same as him after having laid eyes on the Three Widows the previous evening, pushed with equal eagerness. But as the morning wore on and the going got harder while the heat and humidity worsened, their inclination to ease up a bit, take a breather now and then, came to the fore. At the same time, Kettleman's sense of getting ever closer to the treasure was driving him all the harder. Almost maniacally so, Blevins sometimes thought with a touch of alarm when he looked too tight into the eyes of his former commander.

Building tensions finally eased somewhat when they reached a point where the narrow, sharply inclined ledge they'd been traversing flattened out and came to a wall of rubble and large boulders at the base of a high cliff from which they'd fallen. They were three-quarters of the way around the girth of the first of the Three Widow peaks.

After Kettleman paused to take a breath after turning the air blue with a string of curses, Miriella said quietly, "We have nearly reached where it would have been necessary to abandon the horses anyway. So we will need to do so now, a little earlier, then can make our way around the boulders on foot and proceed from there."

"How much farther to the cave?" Kettleman demanded.

"We should reach it by early or mid-afternoon. It is near the base of the middle Widow."

Kettleman's shoulders sagged with relief. "Thank God!" He swept his gaze over the dust- and sweat-streaked faces of the others. "We'll take a break here then. Drink, cool down, rest. Not too long, though. Then we'll hobble the horses securely, leave them and move out again." Here he paused, eyes widening and glistening bright, before he added, "And when we stop next, it will be in the cave of the ancients surrounded by the treasure of the Diablo Lobos!"

Everybody quit their saddles and sprawled wearily against the cliff face on the inner side of the ledge. Though the wrists of Miriella and Tate remained bound together, they were freed from the additional ties to their saddle horns. The tethers running from around their necks to the grips of their individual handlers—Blevins for Miriella, McLaffert for Tate—were left to trail free at this juncture, they had no place to run and the horses remained under the control of their handlers.

Miriella helped Tate down off his horse. His face was ghastly white, he was pouring sweat, and he grunted with pain at every movement. As Miriella turned him toward the cliff, she whispered close in his ear, "This is my chance. I'm going off the ledge. Do you want to go with me?"

Tate groaned. "Oh, God. I don't have the guts...d-don't leave me."

"I must. It is my only chance."

"Oh God," Tate groaned again.

Miriella kissed him quickly on the cheek and issued a final desperate whisper, "May He be with you—Goodbye!"

Then she spun and broke for the rim of the ledge. She'd been watching and calculating all during the ascent. This spot suited her needs perfectly. The height was sufficient, there was nothing but jagged rocks at the bottom. All she had to do was leap out into space, and it would be over in a matter of seconds...she would be saved from the unspeakable.

Miriella's front foot lifted, and her back leg thrust to

full extension, sending her in a final surge that would take her past the rim of the ledge. But then—sharply, painfully—the tether around her neck jerked tight, and her forward momentum was halted, chopped short, and her back and shoulders were brought crashing back onto the solid surface of the ledge. The breath was knocked out of her, gushing from between gritted teeth. She heard heavy feet pounding and men running and cursing. She rolled onto her side and looked back through watery eyes. And that's when she saw Tate hanging fiercely onto the free end of her tether. His face was racked with pain, and his mouth was moving. Miriella couldn't hear him, but she could read his lips plainly: "I'm sorry...I couldn't let you."

———

BRASKA, TAYLA, AND ARROW WERE ALSO ON THE move at first light. Along with Ebner Clapton, they had slept through the remaining dark hours, each—including Tayla, at her insistence—taking turns at standing watch. There were no further incidents, and this time, when Braska had the chance to stretch out on his blankets, slumber wrapped around him immediately.

After exchanging goodbyes and good wishes with Clapton, they once more set their aim for the dark, ominous swell of the Spearpoints. Some concern was harbored about the possibility of being spotted from the heights ahead while making a daylight approach across open ground, but there was little could be done about it. The gloomy cloud cover helped, as did continuing to stick with the trail of Alfred Beedle, who'd made the same approach with the same concerns and therefore, used the depths of gullies and arroyos whenever possible.

Still, it was a relief to get up into the craggy foothills, where the sense of standing out too openly was thankfully diminished. The ugly dark mountains now looming over them certainly carried their own threatening aura, but no more for them than for those they were stalking. The intermittent patches of shade thrown by the higher rocks now thrusting up about them offered little relief from the hot, muggy air that pressed down with or without direct sunlight. There was, however—felt ever so slightly—a very subtle shift taking place in the air. Not quite a breeze, not yet, and seeming to come more from the south than the weather fronts that more commonly rolled out of the west-northwest.

Arrow sensed it first and more keenly than the others. "A storm comes," he said quietly. "An unusual one, brewed by this very still, strangely damp air. I have heard my father and grandfather talk about such, after conditions like these, from their time on the plains of Colorado. Storms containing the dreaded black wind, my grandfather called them."

"Tornadoes," Braska muttered. "I've had a taste of a couple of those from my days growin' up in Nebraska."

"I've heard the term, heard some stories of how fierce they can be," said Tayla. "It sounded almost unbelievable."

"Whatever you heard, you can probably believe. They can be mighty powerful," Braska told her.

"Oh, great. So now, in addition to these big, ugly damn mountains standing in front of us with owlhoots and Apaches crawling all over them, we're also going to have to worry about being blown away by some rip-roaring *black wind*?"

Braska grinned. "Take it easy. Ain't nothing even happenin' yet. It could turn out to be just a big thunder-storm. Or, it might even blow itself out comin' up over these tall ol' ugly mountains."

Tayla gave him a sidelong look. "You said that about these clouds rolling in, and we haven't seen a clear sky since."

"Reckon that makes it a pretty clear sign the weath-er's gonna do what it takes a notion to do, no matter what," said Braska. "So me makin' guesses about it or you frettin' about it is just burnin' up time better spent continuin' after the trail left by that weasel Beedle and seein' what it gains us."

Two hours later, what it gained them was the discovery that Beedle—for all his mountain savvy and the greedy shrewdness he'd displayed in masking his true intentions from them—over-reached too far for that one more vein of gold when it brought him face-to-face with Sangriento and his renegade Apaches. The tortured, mutilated remains they left behind were barely recognizable as anything that had once been human. The burro carcass that lay close by, merely split open for choice cuts of meat to be removed, appeared more kindly treated by comparison.

When Tayla, after she finished several bouts of throwing up, protested against not taking time for a burial of the man, and Braska and Arrow had to get it through her head that to do so would only put them-selves at greater risk by leaving indication of their pres-ence should any of the renegades return. As it was,

Arrow was able to determine that Beedle's slayers had left in a direction different from the trail of Blevins's bunch that the old prospector had been following. Whatever this meant, whether it was some kind of ruse or the slayers simply had other interests, could not be known. In any event, Arrow now taking up where Beedle had left off—and doing so with an even greater sense of urgency—was what they were left with.

As they moved away from the carnage, low growls of thunder could start to be heard from somewhere not far beyond the high mountain peaks.

31

MIRIELLA GLARED AT FRANK KETTLEMAN WITH defiance and anger burning in her narrowed eyes. "Why should I care anymore now what happens to him—after he betrayed me?"

"Because," Kettleman sneered, "you have the virtue of empathy. A weakness, as far as I'm concerned. But a virtue I very much do care about, in regard to you, is honesty. Is the cave of the ancients as near as you have previously claimed, or has the whole thing been a deception?"

Miriella's eyes dropped, and in a voice barely above a whisper, she said, "No. Stupidly, foolishly, I have been telling the truth...always hoping, praying, a chance to escape would present itself."

"Praying!" Kettleman spat. "Did you think that leaping from that ledge was going to deliver you into the arms of God?"

"It would have taken me away from you—that's all I cared about!"

"Treacherous little brat!" Kettleman backhanded her across the mouth.

From where he still lay sprawled against the cliff face, Ira Tate reacted with a curse and tried to push himself up. Standing over him, McLaffert lifted a foot and stomped him back down. Tate fell back and rolled onto his good side with an agonized whimper.

"Leave him alone!" Miriella cried, wheeling back around from the slap.

Kettleman laughed tauntingly. "I thought you didn't care any more what happened to your betrayer?"

Miriella's gaze swung back to him, filled with hate. Her emotions swelled in her throat and she couldn't get out any words.

Kettleman's expression went blank, cold. "All right. No more stinking games. To spare that wretch terrible torture, I ask you once and for all: Is the cave of the ancients truly near?"

"Yes. Only a couple of hours away," Miriella answered woodenly.

"Very well. We will proceed then. And just to keep you from trying any more tricks, my comrades and I are going to put in place a little insurance policy. It's based on a practice I saw used once during the late war." Kettleman then motioned to Blevins and McLaffert, saying, "Bring him over here beneath this outcrop."

Tate was hoisted none too gently and walked over to the indicated spot. Ten feet above, a flat slab of bluntly pointed rock poked out independently, solidly from the rest of the cliff face. As Miriella watched, Tate was positioned to stand upright directly underneath this. His wrists were re-tied behind his back rather than in front. The free end of the tether around his neck was then tossed up over the jutting slab above him. By pulling down on the tether's dangling end, the slab was proven to be securely embedded. Finally, the tether was pulled tight enough so that the tug on Tate's throat pulled his entire body fully upright, stretching his damaged ribs painfully and lifting him almost onto his tiptoes. The tail end of the tether was then tied into the loop knot already at the back of his neck.

All of this was done according to instructions calmly issued by Kettleman. And the end result, assessed in horror by Miriella, was clear and simply, brutally effective. As long as Tate stood upright he would be uncomfortable but okay. If he grew weary and his knees buckled, he would choke himself. If enough time passed so that he simply could no longer stand, he would strangle to death.

When his *insurance policy* was suitably in place, Kettleman turned to Miriella and said with no emotion on his face or in his tone, "I trust the picture paints itself without need for further embellishment. If the cave is as near as you say, then we should be able to reach it and return before your man's strength fails him. If you bring forth any more trickery or deceit, he will die slowly and rather unpleasantly. Now, I suggest you lead the way that will determine his fate."

As they moved away from the area, the clouds above the peaks to the south were growing steadily darker. Rumbles of thunder came more frequently, and a few dim lightning flashes could be seen in conjunction. A widely scattered handful of fat, cold raindrops tapped down on the dusty surface of the ledge...

———

FARTHER DOWN THE MOUNTAIN, BRASKA AND Tayla, with Arrow in the lead, forged grim-forced onward and upward. Eyeing the high, darkening clouds, Braska grated. "Look at it this way: We only got one storm to face down—the one bein' sent by Mother Nature. Red Dog and his bunch have got two—Mother Nature's, and the one *we're* bringin'!"

"What about the Apaches?" Tayla asked.

Braska kept looking straight ahead and straight up, saying out the corner of his mouth, "Reckon I can't hear you over the sound of that approachin' thunder."

32

As before, passage through the dour gray Spearpoints seemed to somehow go faster and easier than Miriella remembered from her childhood time spent within them. Once past the boulder wall that had briefly halted them—and provided her unfortunately failed escape attempt—rounding the rest of the first Widow and starting up the base of the middle one, familiar features started to fall into place, and she realized with a quickened pulse that they were getting very near the cave opening! Was her excitement strictly because things going so quickly and smoothly increased the chances of getting back to Tate in time—or, she wondered with a pang of guilt, was a part of her unexpectedly getting caught up in the lust for uncovering the treasure? And what if they found the cave, but in spite of Uncle Ignacio's clue and his history with the Diablo Lobos, there was no treasure there? The thought of this possibility, of how the treasure-obsessed Kettleman might react in that case, sent a literal shudder through Miriella.

A moment after this dreadful thought gripped her, Kettleman suddenly shouted, "Look here!" He dropped to one knee beside two small rocks arranged in an unnatural way, standing on edge and tipped against each other to form an inverted V. On the edge of one of the rocks, in some pale, faded stain, could be made out: *oro*.

"Oro! Spanish for *gold*!" Kettleman crowed excitedly. "We must be very near the treasure!"

"Actually, we are there," Miriella said with quiet, contrasting calm. Then she pointed. "That slanted crack in the rocks—it is the entrance to the cave of the ancients."

Kettleman barged forward, digging frantically inside his jacket for the long-stemmed candles he'd brought specifically for this moment. The opening was not overly large, but by ducking and twisting one's torso only slightly, a grown man could fit okay. Once through, the cave itself was a spacious area about a dozen feet in depth and width, a ceiling half again that high. But it wasn't necessary to go very far. The bags of treasure— five of them—were right there, arranged neatly to one side. The bags were tightly sewn leather pouches about five feet in length and as big around as a portly man. There were thongs to tie them shut, but as they stood lined up along the cave wall, their mouths were open, and their contents of golden cups and bowls, necklaces and bracelets, religious symbols and family crests, and more...all a gleamingly wondrous sight in the glow of Kettleman's candles.

What was more, off to the opposite side of the entrance, the Lobos had left some coal oil lanterns and cans of fuel. In short order these were lighted and the cave was awash in illumination that presented the array of riches even more grandly. The wall paintings left by the ancient ones were visible now, too, but no one noticed or cared.

"There it is, men. The dream of many who came before, but the prize of only we who stand here now," Kettleman proclaimed, his tone slightly awestruck even after all the years and effort he'd put into being able to drink in the sight. "I have buyers and collectors lined up for much of it already. Some will take a little longer to make the right deal. But in the end, I assure you, we are looking at a fortune to last our lifetimes and beyond."

"We just have to find a way to get it all out of here," said McLaffert.

Kettleman gave him a sharp look. "What do you mean *find* a way? We have one—we're standing right here right now, are we not?"

Even Blevins frowned a bit dubiously. "You sayin' you figure to take it all with us right away?"

"You damn right that's what I'm saying!" Kettleman declared in a loud voice. "I don't intend to leave here without every cup and bauble."

Blevins's forehead puckered. "But them're bags full of gold bits and pieces, Major. Bound to be mighty heavy."

Kettleman marched to one of the bags, seized it and lifted it. It clearly tested him some, but he raised it full off the ground before letting it thump back down. Turning to Blevins and McLaffert, he said, "Yes, it's heavy as hell. But how much straining have you put into your lives so far—menial tasks growing up, riding hard and long and constantly on the dodge from the law in your current state of outlawry? And what better lies ahead? What if you get caught and not hanged but instead sent to a prison stone-busting crew? Does not a couple hours of strain to drag some heavy bags for the guarantee of living in ease and luxury the rest of your days sound like a better option? And what do you propose instead? Bring in some hired help, cut down on our profits, run the risk of getting double-crossed or turned over to the authorities who might claim sovereign rights to some of these artifacts?"

Blevins and McLaffert frowned, averted their eyes and scuffed their feet like chewed-out green recruits. Blevins said, "What you're sayin' all makes sense, Major. I guess we didn't think it all the way through like we should've."

"Well, it's not going to be easy. I certainly can't claim that," Kettleman replied in a partially relented tone. "But luckily, it's downhill much of the way and we only have to make it as far as the horses. Luckily also, those bags are tough leather and can be dragged. I figure we can tie two of them together and take turns dragging that tandem. The lightest one we'll give to the girl—it'll keep her busy and help weigh her down in case she's of a mind to try taking flight again."

Outside the cave entrance, there was the rushing sound of wind picking up, and also the splatter of rain starting to fall.

"Sounds like that storm we saw buildin' up in the peaks is startin' to make its way down. That oughta make things more interesting," McLaffert muttered sourly.

"If nothing else, it surely will make our footing slippier on the rocks. So we'll have to take added care about that," Kettleman allowed, displaying a measure of concern. "But it also might aid in pulling the bags along. At any rate, let's get started before it turns any worse."

———

"NOT MUCH HOPE OF FOLLOWING SIGN ANY LONGER in this," said Arrow, pushing rain off his face as he squinted up at the lumpy, rising ground before them. "What tracks I *could* make out, which were scarce, will be hopelessly washed away. The storm has already been strong for a while up in the peaks, now it is working its way down. It will come harder before it lets up any."

As if to accentuate his prediction, a howling gust of wind came whistling between two nearby rock outcrops, thrusting up like a pair of tall, ragged-topped pillars, and brought with it a lashing tongue of rain.

"Jesus!" exclaimed Tayla, pulling her soggy hat brim down lower over her face. "Do we keep trying to slug through this, or find some place to hole up until it blows over? We passed some openings in the rocks off to either side back a ways that looked like they might be caves."

"Yeah, I saw 'em too," Braska replied through gritted teeth. "Beedle mentioned that when he first spoke of the Spearpoint Mountains—how they was riddled with caves. Appears the old bastard was tellin' the truth about at least that much."

"Then don't you suppose Red Dog's bunch has seen them too, and is smart enough to be looking for—or maybe has already taken—shelter in one of them? So shouldn't we," Tayla said, scowling and spitting rain along with her words, "show we're at least as smart as them and be considering the same?"

"That's just the thing. If they're stopped somewhere and we keep pushin'," Braska insisted stubbornly, "then that's a chance for us to gain ground on 'em. If we stop and hole up too, we gain nothing."

"And if we drown or get washed off the side of this mountain, we gain even less," snapped Tayla.

"Not to take sides," Arrow said with obvious reluctance, "but if the outlaws do take shelter in a cave and we keep going, there would be a chance we might pass them by without ever knowing."

Braska ground his teeth. "All right, you've ganged up and whipped me with logic. I guess we need to start lookin' for a cave. There's an incline up ahead, that's the way the polecats seem to've been headed. Let's continue that way, there ought to be a cave somewhere in that cliff face. We'll grab the first one we come to. Hell, maybe it'll be the one they already picked and we can drop in for supper."

They pushed off into the blowing rain. They passed between the two rocky pillars and picked their way across a slippery, flat-slabbed surface with water swirling ankle-high over their booted feet. They approached the ledge-like incline running up the face of a high cliff, the way it appeared to Braska the Blevins group had been headed before the rain came and washed away their tracks.

Then, faintly at first, as if from a distance but rapidly coming closer, a new sound reached their ears. Cutting into the stuttering claps of thunder and wind-driven hiss of rain. A sharper-edged rumble, a clatter. Something out of place yet somehow familiar. Braska stopped and put an arm out to also halt Tayla and Arrow coming up behind him. And then, abruptly, he knew. Incongruous as it seemed, he recognized the sound as that of horses being pushed to a hard gallop, hooves clattering on rocky ground. And then he saw them—five saddled horses pounding down the cliffside ledge, panicked, bumping and slamming together, each desperate to break free and get clear of the others.

What was more, if that surprising sight wasn't enough, an even more startling one was the handful of yipping Apache braves to be seen among these steeds, obviously the cause for their reckless descent. Two were mounted and hanging on precariously, and three or four crazy, fleet-footed others were running and managing to keep up in the thick of grinding bodies and flying hooves.

But while that potential exposure to being trampled appeared to be willingly participated in by those braves, the same potential Braska and party suddenly found themselves in by virtue of being directly in the path of this stampede was *not* something they cared to stick around for. To exclude them from it, Braska wheeled around with a shouted curse and spread his arms wide, sweeping Tayla and Arrow with him as he made a twisting dive that carried them back between the upthrusting rock pillars. They landed hard in a tangled heap, with Braska on top and driving out loud grunts and expulsions of breath from those underneath him. But just mere feet away, the horses and Apaches went pounding over and past the very spot where—if not for his quick action—they would all have been ground under in a far worse manner.

33

AT THE FLAT AREA ATOP THE INCLINED LEDGE, Kettleman and the others came around the boulder wall, dragging the bags of treasure through wind-whipped sheets of rain and ear-splitting roars of thunder, wearily dragging their feet as well as the heavy bags. Yet, at this stage of the endeavor, each was feeling a surge of relief knowing their burdens would soon be out of their aching hands and onto the backs of the horses.

In the lead, taking his turn at bringing along the doubled bags, Kettleman was the first to see the changes from how they'd left this place. Part of the change was what no longer was there, the other part was what very horribly remained. He stopped short, stunned by the rain-swept scene before him. He let go his grip on the treasure bags, allowing them to settle rattlingly to the soaked ground.

Blevins moved up from behind him. "What is it, Major? What's wrong?" Then, looking over and out past his old commander's shoulder, the hardened outlaw's eyes bugged wide, and he let out a groan as if in pain.

This was enough to alarm Miriella, who wasn't all the way around the piled rocks yet. "Is it Senor Tate? Is he not okay?" she wanted to know.

"Keep her back—don't let her see!" Kettleman barked.

"See what?" McLaffert bawled from the rear, where he could hardly see anything. "Did that sonofabitch get away somehow?"

Miriella released her bag and rushed forward, pushing past Blevins before he could stop her. Then, moving up beside Kettleman, she too jerked to a sudden, stunned halt as her eyes fell on what he'd tried to protect her from seeing.

No, Ira Tate hadn't escaped. He was right where he was supposed to be...at least a grotesque, barely recognizable version of him was still there. The visitors who'd shown up in the meantime had left him hanging, left him tied as they found him. Six arrows—three running up each side, thigh to shoulder—remained in him. Target practice no doubt taken while he was still alive. Ragged cuts of varying depths, too numerous to count, covered his body and face, and at some point while suffering these, he no doubt died. Then, for good measure, they'd disemboweled and castrated him and left his testicles and penis stuffed in his mouth.

Horrified by what she was seeing but unable to look away, Miriella's knees started to buckle. Blevins stepped forward and wrapped his arms around her, keeping her upright.

"Hang on to her tight," Kettleman said tersely. "If the fate of being in our hands was enough to make her want to leap before, not hard to imagine what the thought of falling to Apaches might do."

"Apaches?" echoed McLaffert, barging forward. "Where the hell did they come from? And hey—where the hell are our horses?"

"Can't you figure it out, for Christ's sake?" growled Blevins. "Our horses were stolen by the same red devils who mutilated Tate that way. As far as where the hell they came from—"

"Renegades who jumped the reservation. It's the only explanation that fits," cut in Kettleman. "It happens every so often, but I wasn't aware of any recent incidents in this area. Damn the wretched timing!"

"So what do we do now? What if they come back?" wailed McLaffert.

Kettleman frowned, sweeping his gaze to all sides through the sluicing rain. "They took our horses for food. Right now, those animals are more important to them than we are—especially since they've already had themselves some fun with Tate."

"What an awful thing to say!" cried Miriella.

"I'm just relating it from the Apache point of view," Kettleman responded. "Had any more of us been present, you can be assured...well, never mind. Thank God we weren't."

"Ask me," Blevins said bitterly, "God lit a shuck far away from this place."

A stern, thoughtful expression gripped Kettleman's face. "Which, it seems to me, is an action it would be wise for us to follow. I suspect that, wherever the Apaches have taken the horses, they will be busy butchering at least some of them for meat. That will keep them busy for a while. Yet knowing that the animals had to belong to somebody and being on a rampage off the reservation for one main purpose—to kill and raise havoc with Whites—there's every reason to suspect they might come back around. Were they to catch us on this open ledge, we would be hard put to mount a defense."

"So what then? Shift back around this boulder pile?" asked McLaffert.

"And trap ourselves higher *up* the mountain?" Kettleman scoffed. "Don't be ridiculous. We need to get back down, find a way back out—to escape!"

"In the rocks back down at the bottom of this ledge," said Blevins, "I saw a number of openings that looked like they could be caves. If we made our way into one of them, we could ride out this damn storm and have a chance to think and plan. Plus, it'd give us some defensive cover in case we had to face those stinkin' redskins."

"I'd say that's not just our best, but our *only* option," agreed Kettleman.

Blevins eyed him. "And we take the treasure with us?"

Kettleman's return look was as flat and hard as the cliff face rising off to the side. "Do you really have to ask? We're damn sure not leaving it here." Then, abruptly, his face took on an uncharacteristic plaintiveness. "Look, I know we've already been through a hell of a tough slog and everybody is worn gauze thin. But we can't let up now. It's downhill the whole way, I'll take the doubled bags by myself...and consider this: If the Apaches should return before we reach the bottom, we could drop behind the bags and use them for emergency cover."

Blevins was visibly taken aback. After a minute, he barked out a harsh laugh. "By God, Major, that's the damnedest thing I ever heard!" Then he laughed again before adding, "But I reckon gold with a few bullet or even arrow holes in it would still have its value, wouldn't it?"

"Maybe more!"

"All right then, let's get it down this damn slope!"

Miriella jerked in his grip. "What about Senor Tate?"

"There's nothing we can do for him. Even if we had time, we have no means to bury him in this granite hard ground," Kettleman told her.

Then he stepped forward and took her by the wrist. Gently, he drew her to him. "Look at me, child. And listen." Miriella tipped her face up and gazed into eyes that had turned surprisingly and incredibly, soft and caring. "You have been through a most punishing ordeal, especially for a young woman. Yet you have endured admirably," she was told in a low, soothing voice. "For that, when this is all over, you will receive not only your release but a portion of these riches. You have my word as an officer and a gentleman on that.

"In return, I ask that you promise no further attempts to end your life prematurely. You see, I have some appreciation for what goes through a young woman's mind when it comes to the terrible possibilities of falling into the hands of savages such as those responsible for what we see clearly before us. Some years back, I lost a very dear and special niece—so grand and exquisite in every way—to the Comanche. Her loss has haunted me ever since." Kettleman's hand squeezed just a bit tighter around Miriella's wrist. "So in her name I make these two promises to you: One, I will do everything in my power to see you are protected from these current savages. Two, should it reach a point where it looks hopeless, I will save a bullet for you. Do you understand and believe?"

"Y-yes. I do," Miriella answered in a weak, trembling voice.

Kettleman nodded. "Good. Then we need to get away from here."

34

WHEN THE FRANTICALLY STAMPEDING HORSES came barreling down the inclined ledge and reached the flat, rainslick rock footing at the bottom, they'd been thrown into skidding, slipping, crunching chaos. Their screeches of heightened panic cut through even the near-constant booms of thunder. Some of them fell and struggled back up. Two weren't able to manage that, their legs breaking with loud pops of bone and gristle accompanying squeals of pain.

Three of the Apaches swarmed all over these unfortunate beasts and quickly ended their misery with flashing, throat-cutting sweeps of their knives. Then they kept at it with the keen blades, immediately beginning to cut open the fallen animals so they could slice off choice chunks of meat. A large sheet of hide was peeled from one horse and laid out to use as a wrapper for carrying away the pieces of meat that then got tossed onto it. Each of the impromptu butchers worked rapidly, skillfully, seeming to take no heed whatsoever of the raging storm pouring down on them. The other braves had gone off with the remaining horses, leading them into and out the opposite side of a deep gully that ran parallel to the high cliff face they'd recently descended—leading them, most likely, to also be butchered at wherever the rest of the renegades had their camp.

Braska, Tayla, and Arrow watched all of this from where they lay, gazing out between the upthrust pair of rocks where Braska had swept them to escape the stampede. They were bruised and slightly worse for wear, but now that all had regained the breath knocked out of them, a hell of a lot better off than being carpets for five sets of horses' hooves would have otherwise left them.

Not that this made the situation they *were* left in an exactly enviable one. Apart from lying in an increasingly deepening puddle of water on a hard, lumpy slab of rock getting lashed relentlessly by wind-driven sheets of rain, they were arguably trapped by a handful of knife-wielding Apaches. But at least the noise of the storm gave them the sound cover for some low, close-in conversation to discuss the degree of that entrapment and how best to handle it.

They all still had their handguns and cartridge belts, and even with the drenching rain, most bullets could probably be counted on to still fire. That made the notion of rushing out and blasting away the crew of meat cutters a mighty tempting one. But countering that was the question of how many more renegades would that leave and might they be close enough to hear the shooting and come boiling in response.

"Clapton said he tracked an even dozen away from

the dummy camp where they ambushed the soldiers," whispered Braska with rivulets of rain pouring down his face. "We killed one—the one that doubled back on him—out on the flats last night. So that leaves eleven as the full bunch when they're all together."

"We've got three in front of us," said Tayla, "and three or four more—I couldn't tell exactly—went with the rest of the horses."

"There were three of them," Arrow said confidently.

"So that leaves five more somewhere, either in a bunch or also split up and maybe on the prowl."

"Yeah, it's the goddamn *somewhere* part that's like a club hangin' over our heads," muttered Braska.

Tayla made an anguished face. "Good God! In a storm like this, wouldn't it be only reasonable to think they'd all hunker together in a cave or camp of some kind to wait it out?"

"You cannot apply reason to the Apache," Arrow said in a flat tone. "They will never do what you expect, and will never do what another might calculate as the unexpected. The Apache is born to pain and discomfort and lives to inflict worse on his enemies—and all are enemies to the Apache."

"There's a rosy outlook if I ever heard one." Tayla pushed a long, dripping tail of hair away from her eyes. "Their birthday parties must be a real hoot."

Braska waited for the reverberation from a particularly loud thunderclap to let up, then said with his mouth pulled into a grimace, "The thing we ain't talked about yet is what might be up at the top of the slope where those horses came down from."

"They obviously must be the mounts of Red Dog's

crew. Right?" said Tayla. "So that can only mean the Apaches beat us to the quarry we've been chasing so hard."

"Yeah, that's the first thing comes to mind—that the outlaws and their captives are likely layin' up there, all massacred," admitted Braska. "But it ain't the *only* possibility. There's the chance *some* might still be alive. Or, hell, maybe all of 'em—maybe they were off on foot, huntin' for the treasure, and left the horses behind in a camp where the Injuns found 'em and snatched 'em."

Tayla regarded him, brows pinched together. "I know how hard you've fought to save those captives. But you can't torment yourself by reaching too far when—"

"Mr. Braska," Arrow interrupted with a touch of urgency in his tone. "Look there, across that gully."

The faces of Braska and Tayla swung in the direction he'd indicated.

Murkily, through the hammering downpour, they could see shapes approaching on the opposite side of the rain-frothed gully, coming from where the other horses had been driven away. As the shapes took clearer definition, Braska counted. There were eight of them, all of Sangriento's remaining renegades. One of the eight, broader through the shoulders than most Apaches, shirtless, the rich copper of his bare chest water-beaded and slick-looking, sat astride saddled horse. His broad, scarred face stared straight ahead, and not even the whipping rain made his black eyes blink.

"Holy cow," Tayla said in a hushed whisper. "That must be—"

"Sangriento. The he-goose himself," Braska finished for her. "Something big must be brewin'."

One of the warriors standing beside the renegade chieftian's horse pointed across the gully and up the inclined ledge. A warrior on the other side began bobbing his head excitedly. And the meat cutters paused to also point and bob their heads.

"It appears like they're getting worked up for a return to that slope," said Arrow. "I'd say those first six braves may have stolen the horses from up there without ever encountering the outlaws. And now Sangriento is looking to lead a charge to find and wipe out whoever the horses belonged to. I think you might be right, Mr. Braska, about Red Dog and the others still being up there and—"

"No," Tayla stopped him. "No, they're not up there. Not all the way." She thrust a finger angled upward against the slanting rain. "Look!"

"Jesus God," Braska ground out through clenched teeth as he, along with Arrow, saw what she was calling attention to—the five heavily burdened shapes making their way down the steep ledge. "They're slippin' and slidin' straight into the teeth of Hell...and ain't got a clue."

"What are those bulky blobs they're pulling with them?" said Tayla.

Braska strained harder to see against the slicing rain. Then a brilliant bolt of lightning slashed across the sky and from the tops of some of the *blobs* he saw a glittery reflection. His mouth twisted wryly. "I'll be a sonofabitch. They found it. They found the Diablo Gold and they're draggin' bagfuls of it down with 'em."

"It's not going to do them much good where they're headed," Arrow remarked.

"But we've got to do something to help them!" exclaimed Tayla.

"Exactly how gets a mite tricky," Braska said, eyes darting back and forth. "We've got three guns with wet ammunition to go against eleven Apaches primed for a fight. And if we do open up on 'em, that crew comin' down the slope ain't gonna know who's who or what the hell's even goin' on—they're as apt to start shootin' back at us as the Apaches."

"Well, we still have to do something!" Tayla insisted.

"It looks like Sangriento is going to help us decide," said Arrow. "He also has spotted those coming down the slope and appears eager to go meet them."

Sure enough, that's what was happening. Sangriento had gone rigid in his saddle and his fierce black eyes were fixed on the five bulky shapes slipping and sliding rapidly down the steep incline, already nearly to within a third of the way from the bottom. Hoisting a carbine rifle high above his head, he thrust its snout in the direction of the five and let out a loud whoop. The warriors on either side of him unleashed a chorus of their own whoops and yips and charged forward. With Sangriento spurring his horse in their midst, they plunged into the swirling, frothy gully and then surged up and over the near bank before veering toward the base of the slope. The meat cutters abandoned their task and ran to join with them.

"There it is," Braska declared, his jaw set tight. "Another couple seconds and Red Dog's crew can't have no doubt what's comin'at 'em. Then we open up from here and catch the Apaches in a crossfire!"

"When?" Tayla wanted to know.

"Right about...now!"

Rising up, stepping out from between the rock upthrusts that had been shielding them, Braska, Tayla, and Arrow opened fire. A few of their cartridges failed to discharge, but the majority did their job, and they poured an effective volley of lead into the attacking Apaches. The latter, with carbines and bows, released their own initial volley up the slope.

———

ONCE AGAIN AT THE HEAD OF HIS GROUP, FRANK Kettleman was fighting to maintain his footing and keep control of the twin bags of treasure that—instead of any longer being a burden he had to drag—were sliding so easily on the drenched, soggy incline they threatened to overtake him. In addition to the constant battering of the storm. So intent was he on all of this, as were the others behind him, that none of them had taken any notice of what was taking place at the bottom of the slope.

Not until the hail of bullets and arrows came streaking up at them.

It was the possibility he'd dreaded the most, yet he'd allowed himself to become so preoccupied he was caught totally off guard. The saving grace came from the poor vision imposed by the howling storm and the general difficulty of shooting accurately uphill. For these reasons, nobody was hit even in the slightest by the first wave of this surprise attack.

"What the hell is going on?" hollered Blevins amid the swarm of incoming slugs and arrows whistling through the air and ricocheting off the cliff face.

"Apaches attacking from down below," Kettleman called back over his shoulder. "Take cover behind the treasure bags like I said—return fire!"

He sensed a flurry of frenzied activity and cursing behind him, even as he maneuvered himself frantically, trying to get his gun drawn and get flattened down behind his pair of shifting, slipping bags. Bullets and arrows kept pouring up yet somehow, if his ears weren't deceiving him, it sounded like there was a volume of shooting down below greater than the amount of lead reaching this far. In the damnable pouring rain, Kettleman could make out the clot of Apaches directly below, but so much else was but a watery blur.

And then, just as he was getting set, ready to draw a bead on what he *could* see, Miriella and her bag came skidding down from behind and rammed hard against him. "I couldn't control it, couldn't stop it from sliding!" she wailed.

From further up, from just past her, Blevins hollered again. "McLaffert just got hit! We're slippin' and slidin' all over hell, Major—we can't fight like this!"

Kettleman looked around desperately. An arrow thudded into one of the bags he lay behind, clanking dully against the contents inside. He peered over the rim of the ledge at the gully running parallel below. It looked to be about an eight foot drop, the depth of the torrent of water in it unknown. It was an option—one that could hardly be worse than the fix they were in where they were at.

"Over the side!" Kettleman ordered. "Pull the bags with us, we'll fight from there!"

"We'll be fish in a barrel!" Blevins protested.

"At least we'll be able to hold still enough to shoot

back!" Kettleman turned to Miriella and said with a rueful smile, "You wanted to go over the edge, here's your chance. I'm again asking you to trust me, child—or do you want that bullet now?"

For an answer, Miriella pushed her bag over the rim and followed after.

35

THE OPENING SALVO FROM BRASKA, TAYLA, AND Arrow had cut down nearly half of the Apaches they fired on—some fatally, some only wounded. But now, aware of the attack from their rear and facing no effective return fire from those on the ledge they'd initially been sighted on, the Indians were wheeling about and re-focusing their attention with a vengeance. Making this all the more menacing to their new targets was the timing of it coming when they'd mostly emptied their cylinders and were fumbling to reload, a task made slower and more difficult than usual due to the cold, soaking rain that had their fingers numbed and caused the cartridges to seem as greased.

"Scatter and go back to cover!" Braska shouted to his comrades. "All the heat's commin' our way and it looks like Red Dog's crew ain't in no shape to pitch in and help!"

He'd seen Kettleman and the rest drop off into the gully, placing them in a possibly better defensive position but for all intent and purpose, nullifying any offense because of having to shoot up and over the edge of the cut, with the Apaches now dropping back out of sight.

And then Braska's sweeping gaze fell on something else—a sudden change that might provide a much-needed break. Sangriento's horse had stumbled and fallen to its knees as a result of him jerking it around too suddenly. This pitched the renegade chieftan from his saddle and sent him skimming across the slick, rain-sopped slab of hard ground like a flat stone sent skipping across a pond—and it brought him sliding to within a half dozen yards of where Braska crouched watching.

The thought raced through Braska's mind about what Arrow had said when relating how the death of a war chief in battle was often seen by his followers as a sign their medicine had turned bad and thus might cause them to withdraw from further fighting. Arrow had also said how the behavior of Apaches was the least known and most unpredictable. But regardless, having Sangriento right there in front of him was something Braska wasn't about to pass up. No matter what else, the bloodthirsty red bastard just plain needed killing.

With no time to complete a fumbling reload, Braska shoved his Colt in its holster and turned to Arrow. Holding out his hand, he said, "Your knife."

Half a second later, Arrow's Bowie was in his fist, and he was spinning back to face Sangriento. He covered the distance, separating them in a great leap and rushed the renegade leader sweeping the knife out ahead, held low, blade up, gut-slasher style. Braska was no knife fighter but he knew Sangriento doubtlessly was, since boyhood. So he was going to have to make this quick and merciless, no feinting or parrying or locking of blades.

Sangriento saw him coming, and his eyes immediately dropped to the way Braska held his knife, gauging how experienced he might be. His cruel slash of a mouth curved into a satisfied smile as he reached to draw his own knife. This was going to be easy. Only the Bloody One shouldn't have been watching *just* Braska's knife hand. But because he was, he didn't see the vicious left hook that whipped around and landed square on the hinge of his jaw. Bone and cartilage popped loudly and Sangriento's head snapped away, flinging a spray of rainwater from his long hair. He staggered and his knees buckled much like his horse's had when he jerked it around too roughly.

Braska immediately followed up, leaning close and plunging his Bowie deep in under the Apache's rib cage. He twisted and ripped upward until he couldn't tear any higher through the rib bone. Then he withdrew the blade and swung it around fast in a flat, choppy arc, slamming it to the hilt through corded stomach muscle. Sangriento groaned but did not cry out. His head lolled to one side and wide, wild, unbelieving eyes stared into Braska's from just inches away. The hand that had closed on the handle of the renegade's never-drawn knife unclenched and dropped limply to his side. Then the rest of him sank down and away, slowly sliding off Braska's blade and crumpling to the puddled ground.

Braska looked around. Now came the moment of truth. How were the other warriors going to react?

They all had turned motionless, just stood staring at him.

But no...it was something more than that. They weren't frozen in place because of him. Their faces were clouded by puzzlement, concern, and their ears were cocked. Listening intently to something.

Then Braska heard it, too. A deep, ominous rumbling. Not thunder—something more constant, unending. Getting louder. Coming closer.

All heads seemed to turn as one and everybody saw it at the same time. Coming down the deep gully that ran parallel to the inclined ledge and the high cliff face it angled across. A huge, roaring, foaming, tumbling wall of water pouring in a destructive rush. A monstrous flash flood, fed by scores of individual channels in the higher peaks where it had been raining the longest. All converging, accumulating more and more water as the mass grew and worked its way down until it found a singular outlet in this long, deep, accommodating lower cut now serving as a release, a demolishing threat to everything in its path.

That meant all currently bunched in this flat sprawl at the base of the slope and to either side of the soon-to-be-overflowing gully! Most of all, it meant the treasure hunters who'd placed themselves down *in* the gully.

Braska saw what was coming and saw what precious little time there was to react. The Apaches scattered wildly on their own, it never to be known whether or not they would have considered their medicine gone bad due to the slaying of Sangriento. But they were now the least concern to Braska.

Foremost, of course, were Tayla and Arrow. He turned and waved his arms wildly, signaling and shouting to them, "Up! Climb up on those pillars! As high as you can, and hang on—I don't think the water will reach you there!"

"But what about you?" Tayla called back.

"I've got a job to finish!" he hollered over his shoulder as he was wheeling about and breaking into a run in the direction of the inclined ledge. Sheets of rain sliced down to meet him, and farther up the gully but churning down fast, the menacing wall of water seemed to increase the volume of its roar—as if affronted and angered by the sight of this puny human racing *toward* it.

When Braska reached a point on the incline directly above Kettleman and Miriella, he dropped flat onto his stomach and leaned over the rim. They were the only two still alive. The bullet- and arrow-riddled bodies of two men were bobbing face down in the swirling water behind them, jammed and held in place by heavy bags of treasure. Neither were recognizable as Ira Tate.

"You've got to get the hell out of there—don't you see what's comin'!" Braska hollered down.

"We can't. The sides are too slippery!" Miriella called back.

Braska extended his arm down as far as he could. "Grab hold!"

Kettleman gripped Miriella by the waist and shoved her up. "Take her."

Braska pulled her up over the rim and pushed her back tight against the cliff face. Then he reached down for Kettleman. "Come on, you can make it. Stand on that bag and grab my hand. Hurry!"

The roar of the approaching water wall was deafening.

"I'm staying!" Kettleman shouted. "I won't leave my treasure! I'm a strong swimmer and the weight of the bag will keep me anchored!"

"Not that against *that*, you fool!" Braska tried to tell him. "You'll be crushed to hell and—"

But it was too late. The foaming, smashing, grinding giant fist of water hit and went churning past! Braska rolled away from the rim of the ledge, wrapped himself over Miriella, and pressed them both hard against the cliff face. He hoped to hell he was correct in his calculation that they were high enough up out of the gully to be safe from getting washed away.

It turned out he was. They got some overflow, some battering, but nothing that threatened to tug them into danger. And when Braska raised his head and craned his neck to look down the incline he spotted Tayla and Arrow safely atop the ragged peak of one of the tall pillars. He lay his head back and breathed a sigh of relief.

After several minutes, Miriella spoke softly. "Senor?"

"Yes?"

"Aren't you the shotgun guard from the stagecoach? Ira Tate's friend?"

"That's right, I am. I take it Ira didn't make it?"

"The Apaches killed him. It was horrible."

"I'm real sorry I wasn't able to get here in time for him."

"Is...is that why you are here? Why you went through everything you must have to reach us?"

"It is," Braska affirmed.

The roar of the storm and the rushing flood water

had combined into a dull, otherworldly blur of sound that somehow seemed inconsequential to the moment.

"And what of the Diablo Gold?" Miriello asked.

After a pause, Braska said, "I figure the mountain has claimed it for its own. This time forever. A thousand scattered pieces now ground deep and absorbed into its very skin. The legend of it will probably continue on, and every once in a while scroungers will come diggin' and lookin' without ever realizin' that bits of it may be under their feet with every step."

"And the loss of it does not sadden you?"

"For me, it was never about the Diablo Gold," Braska explained. "I came to finish a job. I was supposed to protect the folks on that stage, and I failed when it came to you and Ira. I had to try and set things right, that's all. That's the long and the short of it."

A LOOK AT BOOK THREE
GUN RIVER

Wayne D. Dundee returns with *Gun River*, a gritty tale of cross-border violence, shifting loyalties, and one man caught in the deadly current of history.

In the hard years after the Civil War, the Texas borderlands simmer with unrest. Ranchers struggle to sell their beef, out-of-work cowboys drift with little to lose, and bitter ex-soldiers return to shattered lives. Across the Rio Grande, revolution brews—along with a high-priced demand for guns and men willing to use them.

Braska rides into the town of Pordito on personal business, unaware he's entering the heart of a smuggling route for mercenaries and weapons—a volatile trail known as the Gun River. Trouble finds him fast. So do those looking to hire a steady gun, or silence one.

Surrounded by suspicion, greed, and growing violence, Braska must choose sides—or carve his own path through the chaos. Because once the bullets start flying, survival depends on more than just aim. It takes resolve, grit... and a Colt that never misses.

Saddle up for a high-stakes Western adventure where every step could be your last, and justice rides on a hair trigger.

COMING SOON

ABOUT THE AUTHOR

Wayne D. Dundee is an American author of popular genre fiction. His writing has primarily been detective mysteries—such as the Joe Hannibal PI series—and Western adventures. To date, he has written several dozen novels and forty-plus short stories, ranging from horror, fantasy, erotica, and several "house name" books under bylines other than his own.

Dundee was born March 24, 1948, in Freeport, Illinois. He graduated from high school in Clinton, Wisconsin, in 1966. Later that same year, he married Pamela Daum and they had one daughter, Michelle. For the first fifty years of his life, Dundee worked his way up from factory laborer to various managerial positions. In his spare time, he was always writing. He sold his first short story in 1982.

In 1998, Dundee relocated to Ogallala, Nebraska, where he assumed the general manager position for a small Arnold facility there. The setting and rich history of the area inspired him to turn his efforts more toward the Western genre. In 2009, following the passing of his wife one year prior, he retired from Arnold and began to concentrate on his writing full time.

The founder and original editor of Hardboiled Magazine, Dundee's work in the mystery field has been nominated for an Edgar, an Anthony, and six Shamus Awards from the Private Eye Writers of America.